The Bad Detective

'Caught. Jack knew he had been caught. Like a fish jerked all in a second out of the water where it had been contentedly swimming. Just because it had nosed at a tempting morsel . . . There was no way out now.'

Detective Sergeant Jack Stallworthy has been accepting backhanders for most of his career. And why not? He's spent thirty years putting villains behind bars, surely he's entitled to a little nest-egg?

Lily, the pretty wife he deeply loves, dreams of retirement on the paradise island of Ko Samui, but Jack will happily settle for a bungalow in Devon.

Until, that is, influential businessman Emslie Warnaby offers him Ko Samui on a plate. Or, rather, first-class air tickets to the island, plus the deeds of ownership to the Calm Seas Hotel. All Jack has to do in return is steal an incriminating file from the Fraud Investigation office at police headquarters – which is, he discovers, as secure as Fort Knox.

As Warnaby's deadline grows ever nearer – and Lily ever more impatient for her life in paradise – Jack plunges deeper and deeper into crime. And soon there is no going back . . .

By the same author

Death and the Visiting Firemen

Zen there was Murder

A Rush on the Ultimate

The Dog it was that Died

Death of a Fat God

The Perfect Murder

Is Skin-Deep, Is Fatal

Inspector Ghote's Good Crusade

Inspector Ghote Caught in Meshes

Inspector Ghote Hunts the Peacock

Inspector Ghote Plays a Joker

Inspector Ghote Breaks an Egg

Inspector Ghote Goes by Train

Inspector Ghote Trusts the Heart

Bats Fly Up for Inspector Ghote

A Remarkable Case of Burglary

Filmi, Filmi, Inspector Ghote

Inspector Ghote Draws a Line

The Murder of the Maharajah

Go West, Inspector Ghote

The Sheriff of Bombay

Under a Monsoon Cloud

The Body in the Billiard Room

Dead on Time

Inspector Ghote, His Life and Crimes

The Iciest Sin

Cheating Death

The Rich Detective

Doing Wrong

The Good Detective

The Strong Man

The Underside

A Long Walk to Wimbledon

The Lucky Alphonse

Murder Must Appetize

Sherlock Holmes: The Man and his World

Great Crimes

Writing Crime Fiction

Crime and Mystery: The 100 Best Books

The Bedside Companion to Crime

H.R.F. Keating

The
Bad Detective

MACMILLAN

2 1 FEB 1996

First published 1996 by Macmillan

an imprint of Macmillan General Books
25 Eccleston Place London SW1W 9NF
and Basingstoke

Associated companies throughout the world

ISBN 0 333 64994 X

1 3 5 7 9 8 6 4 2

A CIP catalogue record for this book is available from
the British Library

Typeset by CentraCet Limited, Cambridge
Printed by Mackays of Chatham PLC, Chatham, Kent

The Bad Detective

Chapter One

Detective Sergeant John William Stallworthy, Jack Stallworthy, gave a groan.

Bloody Monday mornings. And something wrong inside me somewhere. Stomach? Chest? God knows. Probably just how old I am. Fifty-two years of age. Too clapped out for much more of this caper.

No.

He straightened his shoulders, pulled in his belly, raised his head till he could see the incised stone letters *Abbotsport Central Police Station*. And took the steps up at a trot.

All right, getting on if you like. Worse for wear. But still a bloody good thief-taker.

The swing doors thumped to behind him. To his left the old mahogany counter, still highly polished, brass bits gleaming, young Sergeant Evans leaning his uniformed elbows on it contemplating the day ahead.

'Morning, Jack.'

'Morning, Taff.'

On up the broad stairs, heading for the CID Room. Less of a trot now, more of a trudge.

Too old to be showing off to the youngsters. Retirement age. Thirty years' service behind me. Could put in my papers any time, get pretty well the full pension. Full? Full of shit.

Nothing but that measly monthly pay-out to show for it all. The years and years of putting villains behind bars. All right, there's the nest-egg safely tucked away. I've got that to add to the pension. But, damn it, put together it's not enough, not nearly enough, to get me and my little Lily the sort of nest I'm entitled to. Sort of comfy nest she's counting on.

Halt at the turn of the stairs.

So how to get the nest-egg a bit of extra this merry morning? Couple of possibilities. Thank God. Place I tumbled to Friday afternoon. Video Magic. Fancy name, poxy little shop. Dropping in on the unlikely chance they'd have that gardening video I been on the look-out for. *The Lovely World of Lilies*. For when we get the bungalow in Devon, if we ever do. Go for a garden full of lilies there, for my Lily. Least I can do. And that garden, twice the size of the bit we've got out the back now. A garden full of lilies. Pretty as my Lil. Pretty as she is still. Knows how to look after herself, Lily, say that for her.

No *Lovely World of Lilies*, of course, in that grubby place. Forlorn hope asking, really. When I've never seen it anywhere else. Not sure I've even got the name right now.

But what did old sharp-eyes Jack see instead? Lovely world of hard-core porn. That's what. Those unboxed tapes on the counter the slimy shitbag there quickly flipped out of sight.

Not quick enough, though. Not before I'd taken in the labels on them were blank. Bar those tiny letters pencilled at the corners. *S/M, Les, Gk, Ped.* Or, say it out loud, Sado-masochism, Lesbian love-making, Greek (also known as up-the-bum) and Paedophile. Nasty stuff, specially that last one. Little kids involved. So, if there turns out to be nothing else on this chilly March morning – no, April morning, first of the month, isn't it? – then a visit to Video Magic, give it a good spin, put the fear of God into the scumbag behind the counter, and there should be a nice little bit to add to the bungalow fund.

But, no. Shit like that fellow don't deserve to get away with it. Peddling that sort of porn. Kids. Using kids. No, better make that scrote one more for the old arrest record. Put him where he ought to be. Behind bars.

Instead, think I'll take a quick trip see my old friend Jinkie Morrison, criminal activities strictly confined to break-ins on the creep. Spots a place where some dozy citizen's left an upper window a crack open. Checks there's no lights on – bar the one in the hallway, specially left as a certain sign to any-one contemplating entry that there's a householder waiting with a loaded shotgun – shinnies up a drain-pipe like a ruddy spider. In at the window. Picks up whatever's going and waltzes out through the front door. His MO.

The MO all over the smarmy-posh residence of Councillor Arthur Symes last night. *Modus operandi*, poncy Symes'd probably call it, making a meal of it.

Method of operation, I called it from the first, back at Mansfield.

Police Training College. Jesus, that was a long time ago.

A right laugh, really, the business last night. Called out on orders from Detective Chief Superintendent Detch, no less, at damn nearly midnight. Duty bod on the phone. *Listen, Jack, that stupid sod Symes, Councillor Symes on the Police Committee. His place has been done. Been on the blower to old Detchie. Howling blue murder. 'Aren't you doing anything to protect the citizen from these burglarious acts?' What he said, if Detchie was passing it on word for word: burglarious acts. So, listen, get round there toot sweet, eh?*

'I don't know what Abbotsport Police are coming to. A home like ours, fully protected, and when I have to go out to attend a function and my good wife is visiting a lady friend, what does she find when she gets back? The house ransacked. Ransacked. And I'm willing to wager you people never bring the perpetrators to justice.'

'Well, I hope we shall be able to do that in the course of time, sir.'

Could do it tonight, almost for a cert. If I was willing to stay up till all hours doing the paperwork after I'd brought the bugger in. Spotted Jinkie's MO soon as I felt the draught coming down the stairs from that wide open window.

'We shall see. We shall see. What did you say your name was, officer?'

'Stallworthy, sir. Detective Sergeant Stallworthy.'

'Well, I shall remember that. And why are you here on your own? Where is the fingerprints team? The – what are they called? – Scene of Crime officers.'

'Scenes of Crime, plural, we generally say, sir. And they're not actually called out unless it's for a major inquiry.'

'But this is a man. Thousands of pounds worth of property taken. My wife's jewellery, a very considerable amount in cash, some extremely valuable ornaments.'

'Very good, sir. So if you can supply me with a full list, our inquiries will be all the more likely to produce a quick result.'

A sniff of disbelief.

Toffee-nosed sod. And what is he, take away that Councillor? Just some minor official, isn't he?, at the what-d'you-call-it, Fisheries Development Authority place. Pretty tuppenny-ha'penny affair. Not as if he's an executive at Abbotputers, employing half the people in the city now the fishing's down to nothing.

Then, while Councillor Arthur Symes was making a big performance out of producing his list of property stolen – How valuable was a mail-order 'Collector's Item' group of three china budgerigars? – into the room comes his wife. And a right sight for sore eyes she was. Twenty years younger than her old man, if a day. A slinky collection of luscious curves under a clinging satin housecoat, where he was a little stick of a fellow in a three-piece suit. Mass of loosely curled dark hair falling to her shoulders. His narrow skull hardly covered by slicked-down, greying strands. She altogether as sexy as a model, if a bit on the large side. And Symes, no doubt about it, a dried-up pompous little git.

'Two thousand pounds in twenty-pound notes from a locked drawer in my desk. Two thousand at least, plus the necklace I gave Raymonde when she consented to be my wife. Dia— very fine stones.'

'Yes,' sexy Raymonde had broken in. 'That necklace cost every bit of ten thousand pounds. I do hope—'

'No, no. No, dear, not that much. Nothing like that. You know you've no head for figures. Sergeant, I'll give you the full description later. When I've looked out the jeweller's receipt. Now, darling, why don't you go and make yourself a nice cup of tea and pop off to bed? All this has been a shock for you, you know.'

And, good as gold, off she'd gone.

Must be a bit more to Arthur Symes than there looks. Be able to order about that piece of gorgeousness. Hidden talents in the bed line? That what he's got? Certainly what he'll find in the bed when he gets there would be worth exercising the talents on. If he has any.

So, if there's nothing special down to me, as it isn't likely there'll be on a Monday morning, it'll be off to not very magical Video Magic. Turn the place well over, secure the evidence, arrest the toe-rag from behind the counter. But before that Jinkie, and the usual arrangement. Half the cash should be about right, provided Councillor slimy Symes was telling the strict truth last night about it being two thou.

Make-believe to search Jinkie's place top to bottom. Rely on him to have everything bar the money well buried. In that cat-smelling backyard of his as per usual. All out of sight, that necklace – no surprise shifty Symes had 'mislaid' the receipt, probably cost only a quarter what he'd told sexy Raymonde – her other jewellery, the four Staffordshire figures, the three china budgies. If Jinkie didn't toss those over the nearest hedge on his way home. And, this time, old Jinkie can go free as air. Only fair not to put him away too often, harmless little bugger as he is.

After all something's got to be done on behalf of the nest-egg. Still a bloody sight too far off the total I'll need when my time's up, even to buy the Devon bungalow. If that's still for sale. Let alone to cater for the mad notion Lily's got in her pretty head about what she'd really like when I've turned in the warrant card. The sort of sum that'd need doesn't even bear thinking about.

Chapter Two

It was not as simple as he had envisaged. As soon as he entered the CID Room the Guv'nor beckoned him over.

'Got anything on this morning, Jack?'

Show a bit of caution. Don't want to get tasked with some complicated nothing when I've plenty of fish of my own to fry.

'Yeah. Well, I got to follow up that Councillor Symes break-in. Looks as if it may be down to Jinkie Morrison. His MO, more or less. Thought I'd go along to Jinkie's place, St Oswald's Estate. See if he's left any evidence about. Probably too fly, our Jinkie, but you never know. Then there's a video shop down by the docks I happened to pop into Friday. Got an idea the fellow there's doing a line in porn. Some of it paedophile, if I'm right. Worth a look.'

'That's my Jack. You may be old enough to be my grandad, but, by God, you've still got a pair of eyes on you. Go to hire a film for the weekend and come out with a nice likely arrest none of us had a sniff of.'

'Well, I don't know about a pair of eyes. But I have got ears. You weren't asking if I'd got anything on, not without having something up your sleeve you want me to do.'

'No, no. You go off right away, give Jinkie's place a going-over. It's just that I'd like you to take one of the Aides with you. Let a learner see a real old hand at work.'

'If I must. Who is it? That young Spencer? He looks as if he might have the right idea. In about ten years' time.'

'No. It's not him. It's WPC Lane.'

'The woman? Oh, come on now, guv. That ain't fair.'

'Why not? She's a bright kid, Jane Lane.'

'Jane Lane, Jane Lane. Daft bloody name, daft bloody girl, you ask me.'

'No, no. She may still be a bit green round the edges. Thinks it's all playing Sherlock Holmes. But she's bright, she'll learn. And no better way than hanging on your coat-tails.'

'Guv—'

'No, that's an order, Jack.'

From behind him in the big room, at the nearest of the four clumped-together desks, someone of the morning shift – it sounded like Pete Hoskins – gave a donkey-bray of a laugh.

'April Fool Jack.'

'What – what – is this some sort of a con?'

'No way, Jack,' the Guv'nor said. 'When I give an order, it's an order.'

Turning away, the words *April Fool* abruptly jogged something in his mind.

Yeah, horse called that. Running at Uttoxeter this afternoon, two o'clock, if I've remembered the paper right. Would be today, come to think. April the first, All Fools' Day. Owner probably entered the nag just because of that. Still, might be worth putting on a quid or two. Could have been trained for just that race, after all. Odds probably pretty short, lot of silly money on it. But if I get a moment, I'll give it a try.

He looked round the room. Aide-to-CID Jane Lane was aiding the CID in the best possible way. Her back to everybody at the broad shelf running all along the far wall, she was putting on the kettle to make tea.

With a groan of a sigh he went over.

'When you've brewed that, darling,' he said, 'you're coming with me. Do a bit of real detecting.'

'What's this, then?' she asked, accent a bit posh, pretty face, snub nose, clear complexion, sweep of gleaming blonde hair.

He told her what he had worked out at Councillor Symes's place. The current of chill air pouring in from the upper landing window, Jinkie Morrison's invariable MO.

She took it in, no fuss, no stupid questions. The Guv'nor was right. A bright kid. Graduate, hadn't somebody said last week when she'd arrived?

Too bright? he wondered. Would she clock on to what he was up to when he took Jinkie aside for a quiet word? And if she did, or had her suspicions, how would she react? Want her cut? She'd be likely to have a fairly fancy life-style. After university. Probably running a flash motor. Plenty of party-going, and the clothes for it. Constable's pay won't go very far. Or would she get up on her high horse? Middle-class morality. Our duty as officers of the law, keep strictly within the law.

Never mind. I can see a nice neat little way round that if it comes to it.

Jinkie Morrison. Built like a monkey, slightly stooping back, long arms, bandy legs, not much more than five foot tall, round bunched-up nut-brown face. Cautiously opening the door, peering out. No shoes or socks on, trousers half unbuttoned at the front. Strong odour of bed frowstiness.

'Jinkie, me old pal. Want a word.'

'Yeah? But, listen. Listen, I got to go out. Just on my way. Promised the old lady I'd do some shopping.'

'Off in your bare feet, are you? Well, you'll just have to tell the old girl you've got what they call another engagement.'

'But she's out.'

'Doing the shopping, is it?'

'Yes. Well, no. Well, she is, like, but there was something else she wanted extra. I said I'd get it.'

'Come off it, Jinkie. We're going to have our little chat, like it or not. And let me introduce you to this nice young lady, come to visit with me. Constable Jane Lane, just joined the CID. Dare say you'll be seeing plenty of her as time goes on.'

'Miss.' Jinkie ducked her a dip of his head. 'But don't you listen to Mr Stallworthy, miss. I ain't none o' your 'abitual criminals. Take my word.'

'That's right, Jane. Believe every syllable our Jinkie breathes. Then do the other thing.'

'Mr Stallworthy.'

'Come off it, Jinkie. Less of the innocent. You know why we're here, don't you?'

'Me? Know? Why should I? How should I know what Abbotsport CID takes into their heads to do?'

'How about because someone went inside Councillor Arthur Symes's place last night?'

'That wasn't me, Mr Stallworthy. Straight it wasn't. Don't even know where his place is.'

'But you know who he is, don't you, Jinkie? Recognized the name right off, didn't you?'

'Well ... Well, why shouldn't I, then? Councillor, ain't he? Name in the paper an' everything.'

'Oh, yes. Name in the *Argus* often enough. And address in the phone book. Not to speak of the *Argus* saying there's some big bash, Sunday evening. Whole Council on the invite list. So anyone planning to pay Mr Symes a visit can be sure no one's at home.'

'Yeah, but, Mr Stallworthy, that's no time to go in there, Council affair. Got a wife, ain't he, Councillor Symes? Fancy bitch, half his age. You go in there when he's out on Council business, an' you find you're face to face with some big hunk of a lover boy.'

'So you know all about Councillor Symes's home life, Jinkie? Wonder why that is. Suppose you're going to tell us you didn't keep an eye on his house Sunday evening? Waiting to see if the lady wife was going to trot off to that lover boy. Or to one of her girl friends, believe that's what she told her old man.'

'And bloody cold it— No. No, Mr Stallworthy, I never done nothing like that.'

'Oh, no. Never, never, never. So why don't we come in now and take a look-see. Just in case you happen to have three fine-china budgies about somewhere, or four Staffordshire figures, shepherds and shepherdesses. Or even a necklace, may or may not be real diamonds?'

'You can't come and turn over the place just like that.'

'No? Done it before, haven't we? Don't know how many times. Now, out of the way. There's a good lad.'

And as soon as they were inside he turned to Jane Lane.

'Suppose you go up to the attic, love. Likeliest place for our friend to have stashed away all those ill-gotten gains of his.'

'Not the bathroom, skipper? That necklace you talked about, tucked in the loo cistern?'

'Learnt your stuff, haven't you? Every word you were told in training. But, trust me, I know Jinkie's little ways. I've been up in his attic myself, more than once. Don't let all the dust there put you off. Give the place a right spin. And I wouldn't be at all surprised if you don't come down with half the stuff on that list old Symes made out.'

'Okay, if you say so, skip.'

And off she went. Keen as mustard.

He turned to Jinkie. Still looking pretty uncomfortable. Even more than he ought to be.

Surely he can't have left some of the stuff lying about somewhere?

'Right, now, old son. You and I have got to have a little talk, eh?'

'Well, yes, Mr Stallworthy, but . . .

'But nothing, mate. Listen, we've played this game before, haven't we? All right, let's be clear about it. Today's going to be your lucky day. What you going to put up as an alibi, eh? Playing cards with some well-chosen friends? Out with the old woman somewhere?'

Jinkie looked suddenly deeply embarrassed.

'Well, no, Mr Stallworthy. I never got nothing like that fixed up. It'll have to be the telly. In all night, watching the box. I could tell you all about the programmes.'

'You got the old woman to do her stuff then? Give you the full details?'

'Yeah, yeah. That'll be all right, Mr Stallworthy. Promise you that. But—'

'Right. Well, it's about as iffy as April Fool for the two o'clock at Uttoxeter today, but it'll have to do. My report: *I have thoroughly checked this alibi and the suspect was able to give a full account of that night's programmes*. And you make sure the wife gives 'em you, in case anybody else comes to check up. So, okay, now there's the matter of four or five thousand quid taken from a desk drawer.'

'Four or five thousand! He was having you on,

Councillor Symes, if he told you that. Two thousand in twenties, and not a penny more. All counted and correct.'

So old Symes was telling the truth about the cash. Even if he was lying his socks off about the necklace.

'All right, then. Better be a thousand for me, thousand for you.'

'A whole thou? Mr Stallworthy, I couldn't make a decent thing out of it any way if you take that much. You know how little I'll get for that necklace, even if it does turn out real diamonds. And those Staffordshire figures, I won't be able to get rid of them till the heat's well off. It may be months, years. I ain't no Harry Hook, you know, got the muscle to make a fence take what he asks for, or find half a dozen of the lads duffing him up.'

A thousand, he thought. Well, not too bad, with what I've got nicely buried in my garden, Jinkie fashion. Add 'em together and I'll not be far off putting down the deposit on the Devon bungalow.

April Cottage. Getting the last bit for the first payment on April the first. Could be a good sign that. Silly bloody name though, April Cottage. But quite a decent little place, brand new after all. April Cottage, one of twelve. April Cottage, May Cottage, June . . . Up to October, then Autumn instead of November and Christmas instead of December. Hardly hope to sell a bungalow called November Cottage. And the beginning ones, First Cottage, Spring Cottage – spring in February, what a con – March Cottage, and then our home sweet home. If that builder ain't sold it by now. Not much, but best we can hope for, Lily and me. And a good big garden, that'll be something.

'Not your day, Jinkie,' he said implacably. 'Two-way split for the cash it's got to be. Remember, they're not going to be notes I can flash about tomorrow. And you'll get quite a sum for those Staffordshire shepherds and shepherdesses. I know. My missus wanted one for her birthday couple of years ago. Way out of my range. You let the four of 'em stay nice and buried in your stinking bit of a backyard six months or so, and you'll—'

'Mr Stallworthy, that's not the trouble. You see—'

'Don't ponce me about, mate. Half those notes I've got to have, and there's no two ways about it.'

'But them, they're all old ones, Mr Stallworthy, and mixed. No running numbers. I checked. You could pay for anything with them any time. Make it five hundred for you and the rest for me. Please.'

'Sorry, me old mate. A straight thou. Or I shan't believe that tinpot alibi of yours. Watching telly all night. Your old woman swearing you were here.'

Then he realized. The door behind him had just been thrust open. Jane Lane was there. Dust-covered head to foot, and with, cradled in her arms, four Staffordshire figures. Shepherds and shepherdesses.

Chapter Three

So Jinkie Morrison got arrested.

For a minute, as Jane Lane had stood grinning there, the Staffordshire figures clasped to her dust-smeared bosom, Jack had contemplated cutting her in on the deal.

'Well, Jinkie,' he had said, by way of fishing for her response, 'I guessed you'd been a naughty lad, but I didn't think you'd have been stupid with it.'

'But, Mr Stallworthy, it was bloody cold last night. I was frozen stiff when I got home. Frozen. I couldn't of gone out digging there in the back. Never thought one of your lot'd be round first thing. You can't blame me.'

'You've blamed yourself, me lad. Looks like you'll have to do a stretch for this lot. Two thousand quid in loose notes somewhere about too. You're a right berk, you know.'

He had flicked a quick glance at Jane Lane as he had mentioned the cash. But not a gleam of interest showed on her smoothly pink face.

'Of course,' he had gone on, risking taking things a little further, 'there'd be some officers who'd have a bit of that cash off of you. Sort who take a few quid here and there. Not what you'd call corrupt, you know. Just blokes who like to do things.'

Another glance across out of the corner of his eye. And still not a flicker of response. Unless there was a faint hardening of those pretty lips.

So he gave up.

'But don't you start thinking you've landed up with any of that sort, me lad. Not here, not now. You're for it, and no mistake.'

He turned to clever-clever, straight-out-of-nursery-school Jane Lane. Daft name, daft girl.

'Right, darling,' he said. 'You found the stuff, you make the collar. And don't forget to caution the bugger, he's fly enough to take advantage.'

She darted him a scornful glance.

'Mr Morrison, I am arresting you on suspicion of burglary, and I caution you: you do not have to say anything unless you wish to do so but what you say may be given in evidence.'

'There you are, Jinkie,' he said, to pay the bitch back for that don't-teach-me look. 'Bet you've never had it done so much by the book before. *Keep your mouth shut, you're in trouble.* What you've heard from me more than once, ain't it? And hundred per cent good in law, too.'

But then he had to watch, inwardly seething, while Jane Lane, besides noting down in her pocket-book the Staffordshire figures she had recovered from the dusty attic and the necklace and other items Jinkie had reluctantly produced, meticulously counted the two thousand pounds in notes, licked forefinger flipping up the twenties one by one.

But, as he had planned when he let her make the arrest, in the end she paid for her lucky find. He left her at last in the nick ploughing through all the follow-up paperwork on her own.

She'd learn one day not to be too cocky. Perhaps.

He thought then suddenly, as he slipped away, of his own early years. Not in the CID, but as a probationer constable, when he'd believed he was going to devote all his energies simply to catching criminals. In the days – still bright in his mind – when he'd caught out, as a boy of ten at school, his thieving classmate, Herbie Cuddy. Proud as Punch he'd been when he'd worked out, by keeping tabs on boys – and girls come to that – asking in class 'to be excused', who it had been who was dipping into the pockets of the coats hanging outside. And, after his process of elimination had produced the only possible perpetrator, he had got together a gang to beat up Herbie in the playground. Little had he known then that Herbie was one of the notorious Hook family, pirates in the olden days, so it was said, and Abbotsport criminals ever since, generation after generation.

His start as a detective. And, by Christ, when he'd first joined the force he'd carried on in the same boy-wonder letter-of-the-law way. Behaved, in fact, just like Jane Lane. Or even more prissy.

There'd been the time when, back in the canteen out at the old Mussel Street nick, demolished now, the sergeant he'd been on patrol with had leant across the table and slid a pound note into the top pocket of his regulation heavy serge, high-buttoned jacket.

'What this for, Sarge?' he had actually asked.

'For you, laddie. No questions, eh? No pack drill.'

'But what's it for, Sarge? Where did it come from?'

'Oh, God, laddie. Didn't you learn anything at Mansfield? Not even how to keep your eyes open? Looked into three pubs this evening, didn't we? Did you think the gaffers in them were happy to see us because they liked coppers?'

Payment for turning a blind eye to minor infringements of licensing hours, for coming quickly to the rescue if customers cut up rough. At least he had had the sense to shut up when eventually the penny had dropped.

But on his way back to his bachelor bed at the station-house that evening he'd thrust the pound note – drinking money for a week or more in those days – into the first dustbin he'd come across.

Then, next morning, what had he done? Actually left the station-house ten minutes early in the chancy hope that the note would still be there in the bin, for all he knew – routines of his beat well learnt – that the binmen would have been round at first light that day.

But really, he thought as he watched Jane Lane march Jinkie off to his cell, that incident in the old Mussel Street nick had been the beginning of it all. Not that he'd ever done much in those early days. Not until he absolutely needed to. Not till he was married to

Lily, and mad about her. Lot of water under the bridge since then.

So no question now of Jane Lane coming with him to Video Magic. She still had plenty of paperwork to do before she had finished booking in Jinkie.

No, it's off on my own to the docks and that nasty shop. Where that unsavoury object behind the counter is going to have to do what clever-boots WPC Lane by chance prevented Jinkie Morrison doing. Make a fat contribution to the nest-egg.

Nothing else for it. Allow the shitbag to escape the cell he – much more than Jinkie Morrison – deserved, and let him cough up some of his nasty earnings instead. Not that whatever sum he's likely to shell out will provide a tenth of what I really need. For what Lily, above all, wants.

With a bitter taste in his mouth, he set off for the docks area.

Video Magic, sharply illuminated in the bright spring sunshine, looked just as grimy as when, passing by on Friday, he had gone in to see if, however unlikely it was, there might be a copy of *The Lovely World of Lilies* on its shelves. The man leaning on its bubbled plastic counter, the thin white stripes of his drooping brown suit almost lost in its general greasiness, seemed every bit as repulsive as he had been before. The cigarette dangling from his mouth might have been the identical fag he had hanging there earlier.

But now there were no blank-label unboxed videos on the counter beside him with those tell-tale letters on them, *S/M, Les, Gk, Ped*.

Jack got straight down to business. No messing about. Out with the warrant card, flick it open in the fellow's face.

'Detective Sergeant Stallworthy, Abbotsport CID.'

And, at once, a look of wariness in the eyes in that narrow face.

'What you want? Ain't nothing for you here.'

'You the owner?'

'Suppose I am?'

'I asked: you own this place?'

'What if I do?'

'You got a name, I suppose?'

'What you want to know for?'

'I asked you your name.'

A moment's battle of wills. But a moment's only.

'Teggs, if you must know. Mr Teggs.'

'I suppose you put something in front of Teggs. What is it? Fauntleroy? Marlene?'

'Norman.'

A two-syllabled grunt.

'Right, Norman.'

Without more questions, Jack went round the side of the narrow counter to the doorway to the back premises and brushed apart its curtain of multi-coloured, tatty plastic ribbons.

'Hey, you can't go in there.'

'Just watch me.'

He stepped through. A small room, in almost

complete darkness by contrast with the sun-splattered shop itself, the only light coming from a dust-thick window high up on the far wall. In a moment he made out a rickety table and on it an electric kettle, a half-empty milk bottle, and a battered radio. Round the rest of the walls racks were stacked with boxed videos.

He peered at the nearest rack, conscious of Norman Teggs at the doorway behind him, thin face poking half through the plastic ribbons of the curtain. Moving closer, he was able to make out, on the dust-rimed spines of the boxes, popular film titles.

'All bought regular from the wholesalers. Show you the receipts.'

He ignored that.

Further round, Bruce Lee kung-fu movies. Then horror films. And a section of James Bonds. Some science fiction.

But then, down on a bottom shelf, he spotted, on a half-hidden label, two semi-naked intertwined bodies. He stooped, pulled the box out. *Cousins in Love.* Never heard of it, but a regular film by the look of it. Bit naughty, but hardly what he'd come to find.

He moved on.

'That's just kiddies' stuff there,' came the whiny voice from between the plastic ribbons.

'Oh, yes? And what else've you got with kiddies in 'em?' He managed his swing round to a nicety. Just in time to catch on the narrow, cigarette-dangling face the look not of wariness now but of plain dismay.

'What you mean? You saying I got porn stuff?

Got him.

'You had Friday, when I was in before.'

But the fellow had recovered. A bit.

'So that was you? Pretending to ask for some poxy gardening video. Thought you was familiar.'

Poxy? Take the bugger down a peg.

'All right, that was me. And what did I see on the counter out there, just before you stashed them away underneath? Not bloody Walt Disney's *Fantasia* they weren't.'

'Listen, mister, they were just a few tapes I was keeping for a friend. Nothing wrong with a grown man watching stuff like that, is there? Not if it takes his fancy. That ain't illegal.'

Without answering, he went over to a narrow wooden cupboard in the wall opposite the table, which in the dim light he had not seen at first.

'Right, what's in here, then?'

'Nothing. Nothing. Just some stuff. Old stuff. Things we got no use for.'

But the door had a Yale lock, and, close up now, he could see round it smears on the dusty surface.

'Key.'

'Ain't got one.'

'Come off it.'

Norman Teggs stepped fully through the dangling curtain.

'Listen, mate,' he said, 'I got friends. How about you call all this off?'

'Friends? You? You surprise me. Now, give us that key. And quick about it.'

'Just you watch out, I'm warning you.'

'You and who else?'

'You'll find out. You'll find out all right, if you don't just buzz off.'

'Oh, I'll buzz off all right. Just as soon as I've had my look-see in here. Now, that key.'

'Dunno where it is. Ain't put anything in there for years. It's just an old storage place. Why d'you want to look in there?'

'Because I do, mate. So, the key.'

'I told you, dunno where it is.'

'You'd better think, then. Unless you want me to call up a support team. With a crowbar.'

'No, no. No need for that.'

Norman Teggs stuck a hand in the trouser pocket of his droopy brown suit, pulled out a ring of keys, held it out with one of them, a Yale, to the front.

'This should be it. I was sort of – I forgot I had it, that's all.'

Jack took the offered ring, slid the Yale key into the lock, turned it, pulled the narrow dusty door open.

What he saw inside was more than a cupboard. As far as he could make out in the murky daylight coming from behind him, it was another small room, windowless.

'I suppose there's a light.'

'Yes. No. No, you can't never see nothing in there. I told you it's just a store place. Stuff we don't want.'

'Oh, yes?'

He groped along the wall beside the door. Eventually found a switch.

A neon tube came flickering to life. Except for more racks jammed with videos, most of the confined space was taken up by a bench on which stood a grey-painted machine with a little VDU above a complicated set of controls.

Not hard to guess what it did. Copy tapes.

Norman Teggs had come to peer in from just outside.

'Well now, Norman, looks as if you're in a spot of bother, don't it? What are all these, then?'

From the rack beside him he pulled out the first tape that came to hand. No tiny discreet letters on this. Instead a fuzzy black-and-white photograph of two jutting female backsides and a luridly printed title *Hot Bottoms*.

'Well, mate, you're in big trouble, ain't you?'

Norman Teggs, hovering at the narrow doorway, looked as if he knew he was.

'Listen . . . ' he said, and came to a stop.

'All right, I'm listening.'

'Look. Look. Well, I know those are a bit dodgy. But they don't do no real harm, do they?'

'Not to your pocket, they don't. That's for sure.'

'Yeah, well, most of that sort of thing's faked, ain't it?'

'Is it? You going to give me a bit of a film show, then? We see how faked it is?'

'I could do that. If you like, I could show you some as'd make the one you got there look like a fairy story.'

'No way, my son. You ain't going to get out of this just by giving me a hard-on.'

Was the fellow sharp enough to take the hint?

Seemingly not.

'All right, if that stuff's not what turns you on, maybe I can find you something else? What you like? Lezzies at it? Or is it nice little innocent kiddiwinks?'

'Got some of that, have you?'

He kept his voice hard into neutral.

Norman Teggs sidled in and picked up a cardboard carton from the floor. He ripped off the shiny brown sealing tape, dipped in and came out with a video marked only with a title on a plain white label.

He thrust it towards Jack.

Two Little Darlings Get A Lesson in Love.

For a moment Jack was tempted just to put his fist hard into the stomach opposite him. But he reminded himself there was something else he wanted.

'You lousy bugger,' he said. 'That's the very last thing to give me a hard-on. Christ, I'd like to . . .'

Norman Teggs stepped back. The tip of his tongue went sliding from side to side of his pinched-up lips.

'Could give you something better than a hard-on,' he said at last.

'What's that, then?,

Landed the scrote. Surely.

'Bit of dosh. Look, I ain't doing nothing really wrong, am I?'

'Kiddy porn. You're doing kiddy porn, and you're doing nothing wrong? Don't make me laugh.'

'Well, all right. Some o' that goes a bit far, I grant. But I could take that into account according.'

'I should bleeding well hope so. Don't try and blind

me you don't make a hell of a lot every time you sell a tape like this.'

He could see relief slowly rising up in the nasty little shit. A straightening of the back. A puffing-out of the narrow chest.

'Couple o' hundred notes be any good to you?'

'Two hundred? Don't make me laugh.'

'Well, no. No. That was just a figure, like. I mean, I'd go to five. All the way to five.' A sudden spurt of pale-flame courage. 'But I couldn't go to no more. Five's your limit. I ain't no big-timer, you know. I ain't no Harry Hook, nor no one like him.'

'Never mind Harry Hook. It's you we're thinking about. You and the three-stretch you'll likely get if you come up before the Bench. They're downright hard on porn, the magistrates here.'

'Well, I suppose I could . . .'

'A straight thou. Don't tell me you ain't got that much stashed away somewhere on the premises. Your sort don't go toddling round to the bank, put it all in National Savings.'

'But I haven't got anything like that much, mister. Honest I haven't.'

'No? No more than what you didn't have the key to this little copy-shop. So just cut it out. I haven't got all day, you know, and I'd just as rather have a shitbag like you on my arrest sheet as have your filthy money. So, quick about it.'

The look of overwhelming fright firmly back in place.

'All right, all right.'

'That's a bit better. And one other thing . . .'

'What you want now?'

'Those videos. The kiddy ones. In the fire, every last one of them. And I'll be back one day, see it's done.'

'Okay, okay, I'll do it. I never much liked 'em, if you must know. Sickening really. Downright sickening.'

'Yes, that's what they bloody well are. Whether you say so or not. So get them burnt. Right?'

'All right, all right.'

'And don't forget what we agreed neither. Come on, cough up.'

Five minutes later, folded wad of notes stuffed into the inner pocket of his coat, Jack stepped out again into the chilly bright sunshine.

He took a long, deep breath.

Chapter Four

After stopping off at a pub for a bite to eat – he had needed a couple of whiskies with it to wash away the taste of the Video Magic transaction – Jack found himself going past a betting shop. At once he thought of April Fool for the two o'clock at Uttoxeter.

Two o'clock. Good God, must be almost that now. Or past it. Missed my chance?

And, even as he pushed up the sleeve of his coat to see his watch, he became convinced April Fool would by now have romped home an easy winner. Or would be in the act of doing so that minute, moving to the front, jockey's whip flailing.

No. All right, by Christ. Five minutes to go.

He swung round, banged his way into the shop. Darting glances to left and right, he saw the monitor screens high up along the walls were still showing the prices for the two o'clock at Uttoxeter. And there was April Fool at 7–1.

Bloody good odds.

He snatched a paper slip from the nearest dispenser, and, hardly allowing himself to think, scribbled down *2 o'c Uttoxeter – April Fool –*

And, knowing in an instant flash of feeling that this was what he had to do with Norman Teggs's ill-gained money, he scribbled down a final *£1,000 to win*.

From his inner pocket he snatched the wad of notes he had stuffed there and strode across to the counter.

Perhaps I'll be too late. Be stopped from taking the risk.

But, when he thrust the money and the slip across, the comfortably plump lady clerk behind the grille seemed only a little taken aback at the size of this last-minute bet. Looking up for a moment at the clock on the wall beside her, she then simply pushed the slip into the slit on her till and registered the bet.

Christ, what a fool I've been.

Madness. A thousand quid. There in my pocket. In an hour from now I could have been squatting down there in the garden, shoving my trowel under that clump of aubrietia. Should be coming into flower soon, makes a lovely show every year. Then haul out the old Cadbury's Roses tin and put in almost a quarter as much again as I've got there already.

Something a bit better than those chocs and sweets old Lily gobbled up that Christmas I gave her the big round tin. Coloured wrappers all over the place.

God, and now I'm risking that much bloody cash on the chance of a horse at seven-to-one getting first past the post over at faraway Uttoxeter. Don't rightly know where that is, even. Christ. Madness. Total bloody madness.

Sick with his own stupidity, he stood where he was,

staring at nothing, oblivious of the other punters studying the racing pages of the papers pinned along the walls, filling out slips or waiting to see the results on the screens. He sensed nothing of the grey layer of cigarette smoke all round. He heard nothing of the monotonous voice from the TV announcing changes in the odds at other meetings.

'Bloody April Fool, might have known.'

The sharp voice from somewhere near came to him like something in a dream. But *April Fool*, the name had brought him back to life.

What had that bloke meant? That April Fool, as he should have known, had never been in with a hope? If that was the result, perhaps it was all for the best. Bloody tainted money.

Or had that comment meant . . .?

He looked up to the nearest screen. And there it was.

> Uttoxeter 2.00
> 1st   6 April Fool (7–1)
> 2nd 3 Bouncy Boy (6–4 Fav)
> 3rd 8 Mr Frisby (4–1)

Seven thousand quid. I've won seven thousand quid, give or take a little for tax. Seven thousand. Jesus, enough to put down the deposit on the bungalow, and with a few quid over. No, on the cottage. I'll definitely call it a cottage now. April Cottage. Call it that to Lil. Make her see it as the home she's always wanted. Go on about roses round the door, and, yes, by God, garden full of lilies. Lilies all the way. Every variety, every colour.

Waiting till he could go over and collect his winnings, a shadow passed over the glittering fairy castle he had just built up. All right, he'd got enough to put down the deposit on a bungalow in Devon, and he'd hardly managed to accumulate that much in all the years he had been adding to the nest-egg. But the whole total he had now, putting the two sums together, was far from what he would need to complete the purchase. Which meant a heavy loan round his neck more or less for the rest of his life. If he could even get the loan.

And as for that dream of Lily's about some Pacific island . . . for God's sake, pie in the sky if ever there was.

In the end it was a good deal more than an hour later before Jack reached home and went out to dig under his clump of thick-growing, ground-covering aubrietia where he hid away the Cadbury's Roses sweets tin with its cache of slowly collected nobody-knows-about money. First, he had visited, as he had in no way expected to do, the branch of the estate agency where months ago he had first seen the Devon bungalows advertised. There he had found – my lucky day, definitely – April Cottage still unsold.

But as soon as he had got home, he went out, while the daylight lasted, with no more than a called-out greeting to Lily, and lifting up the thick tangle of aubrietia, he added to his nest-egg several hundred pounds left after handing over the six thousand deposit.

Pity, he thought as he scraped the damp earth off the top of the Roses tin, that all the lolly has to get put away here. The really good thing to do when you'd got more cash than your police pay warranted was have a wife with a business of her own. Far better than the risk of keeping bank accounts elsewhere, with all the complication records and procedures create. There were always rumours about officers, high-ups often, who had set up their wives with a hairdressing establishment or a little restaurant. Employ just a bit of what's called creative accounting and you could absorb into a business like that thousands of pounds with no one ever needing to know anything. All ready when retirement days came for the pair of them to live on in style.

But Lily, bless her, too much of a birdbrain even to run a newsagent's. She'd just sit there all day, looking pretty as a picture, reading the fancy magazines from the stock and dreaming of all the nice things she'd like to buy. Place'd be bankrupt inside a year.

He eased the tight-fitting lid off the tin, took a look inside just to reassure himself the bundles of notes were still in place – no need to count them, he knew almost to a penny how much, how little, there was – stuffed the new batch in on top of the old, thumbed the lid firmly back down, pushed the tin deep into its hole and trowelled the earth over it once more.

With a groan he straightened his back, got to his feet.

A wave of sick-feeling came and went. Yes, he really was beginning to get too old for this lark.

Or so he thought sometimes.

Carefully he scraped the wet earth off his trowel, took it to the shed, wiped it well. Tools rusted all too easily. Let a bit of damp slimy earth cling to them and before you know it a little patch of rust starts up somewhere. And then, carry on being careless, and all too soon it's too late to do anything about it. Rust spreads, bit by bit, and one day rivets to the handle go all loose. Then all you can do is chuck the thing away.

Heavily, feeling the ache in his back, he made his way indoors.

Lily was there in the lounge.

Jesus, how pretty she looked, curled up in a corner of the big armchair she specially liked. Box of chocs on the little table beside her. As per usual. But, pop them in as she might, she hadn't lost her looks. Or, hardly. Little bit plumper than when he'd courted her – and, by heck, she'd been hard to get, what with all the competition – but still a fine figure of a woman. Petite. Be forty-nine next birthday, July the tenth, but you'd never know it. Curls as golden-yellow as they'd been when, at last, ruddy besieging her with presents, he'd chased off the opposition.

All right, there's a bottle of stuff on the bathroom shelf she uses on her hair sometimes. Well, once a week. But that's only for touching up here and there.

And her skin. Even in bed at night, when she's creamed her bit of war-paint off, she still looks like a thirty-year-old. That pink-and-white. Like coconut ice, that's what I used to say. Till she told me she didn't like being made to sound like a tray of sweets in a shop window. When I switched to calling her *my little English rose*. But still sometimes feel I could eat her. Sometimes? Nearly bloody always.

And in bed. In bed, when she wants to be nice, things better even than they were that first time. More than better.

When she wants to be nice . . .

Because, by Christ, she can use that, old Lil. First car we got. On and on at me for it. Just not listening when I told her there simply wasn't the cash.

'You could get a bank loan. Banks are always happy to lend to the police. Mike Mellish told me that.'

'Yes, and look at Mike. Always trying to borrow the odd fiver even from blokes just come into the CID like me. And never ever paying anything back. The banks'll lend you all right, but they want their interest. Police or no police.'

'Well, Sergeant Mellish seems to manage. That motor of his is a lovely job.'

'Yes, and you know how he paid for it? By being on the take. That's how. And, mark my words, he'll come to a sticky end one day over that.'

But Detective Sergeant Mike Mellish never did come to a sticky end. Or not as far as I heard. Away in another force somewhere. Probably retired already. Living on the fat of the land.

So then there came the Strike. Nothing whatsoever in the way of bed. Not so much as a kiss or a cuddle. Week after week. And no way I could take what I wanted by force. What they call marital rape now. And well she knew it, my little English rose.

So in the end it was getting hold of some real money, the Mike Mellish way. And Lily got her car. Learnt to drive, too. In about a month. Probably sweet-talked the test examiner into passing her, come to think of it. Well capable of that.

So it had been *I ain't never going to go in a bus* ever *again*. And reward between the sheets. All over the bedroom, and out on to the stairs too, truth to tell. Lucky we never had kids. Wake up and find Mum and Dad at it up against the banisters.

My Lily.

'Hello, darling, there you are, then. All finished in the garden? Bit more popped in the old Cadbury's Roses?'

'Yeah. Just about.'

When he had first come home he had been careful to avoid saying anything about April Cottage. For one thing, it would have meant mentioning his big bet, and Lily never liked him putting money on the horses. Or drinking very much, come to that.

There'd been a bit of a strike about that too, one time. In the days when he'd still been a twelve pints a night man. And she'd won that one as well. Quicker than with the great car strike.

One thing, though, giving up drinks with the boys end of the day, almost expected of you after you got married. But quite another matter deciding to get that car cash, in whatever way it had to be got.

God, but that was a long time ago. Married nearly twenty-nine years now. Twenty-nine bloody years. And I'm still dead struck on her. Got to admit it. Only been over the side a couple of times. Or maybe three. Well, four, say. And that only when it was pushed in front of me, in place of hard cash. Fair enough then, take what was offered.

But the real reason why he had decided to say nothing to Lily just yet about what he had done that afternoon was that, by the time he had turned into his own street, he had ceased to feel at all sure that putting down the deposit on April Cottage would be something that delighted her. So he had just called out he was back and needed to go out to the garden, and then had gone straight through and into the shed to collect his trowel.

So all he did now was to reply to her with much the sort of say-nothing question she had greeted him with.

'How about you then, ducks? What sort of a day you have?'

'Oh, all right. Bit boring. Had my hair done, that new place. Bet you never even noticed.'

'Oh, I did. Straight away. Only I wanted to get out to the garden, before it got dark.'

'So, what d'you think?'

'Think? Oh, your hair. Looks very nice. I was saying that to myself when I was in the shed, cleaning up the trowel.'

'You and your old trowel.'

Yes, right not to mention April Cottage and a garden full of lilies. Likes flowers all right, my Lil, but mostly if they come wrapped in shiny paper.

'I got something tasty for supper, Jackie. Popped into the supermarket, bought a couple of those Chicken Kievs.'

'Very nice.'

'And you? What sort of a day you have? Caught any more criminals?'

'Well, as you reckoned, I did get meself a nice little contribution to the nest-egg.'

'Nest-egg, nest-egg. I wish you wouldn't call it that. Makes it sound all titchy and cosy. No romance in it.'

Tell her after all the nest-egg was not as titchy as it had been? Or tell her, rather, what I've done with what I could've put in that tin? Show her it's all a bit more romantic than she thinks?

Only it ain't. A bungalow in Devon won't be Lil's idea of romance. No way. That sodding Pacific island she's got on the brain. That'll be what she wants. What she saw on telly. Bloody tourist programme. That place. Ko Sammy whatsit.

No, wait till the right moment. If it ever comes. Or at least wait till there's nothing else for it but to bring out the bloody truth.

'Yeah, well, it still is pretty titchy, the nes— I mean, there's no getting past that.'

'But what about that Councillor Symes burglary? Was what you got today from the fellow who did that? You told me, soon as you got back in Sunday night,

39

you knew who it was. Fancy calling you out to that at almost midnight. The cheek.'

'More like Monday morning when I got back. And, yes, I was right about who it was. But I had to go to his place with a ruddy woman aide, and, damn it, she went and found the loot in the attic there. So Jinkie Morrison's tucked away in a cell now. Poor sod.'

'Well, I don't know about any poor sod. He had laid his hands on all that stuff from Councillor Symes, after all. His wife's jewellery and everything. Wasn't that what you said?'

'Yeah. Well, old Symes has got it all back now. Or will have when they've put Jinkie away and the evidence ain't needed no longer.'

'You know, you might get a word of thanks from Councillor Symes, clearing it up so quickly, getting him everything back. Be nice for you. By rights he ought to give us a dinner invite or something.'

'Dinner invite from him? He wouldn't invite us to share a packet of crisps. Toffee-nosed sod.'

'Well, you never know, you know. Be nice if he did convey his thanks.'

'Thanks but no thanks. I'd be happy if I never heard another word about that stuck-up bastard.'

But Jack did hear another word about Councillor Symes. It was something over a month later, just after Jinkie Morrison had been sent down for an eighteen month stretch. And it was a word that astonished him.

Coming into the CID Room on the Wednesday

morning he saw on his desk a big, stiff-paper white envelope with his name *Detective Sergeant J. W. Stallworthy* neatly typed on it. Wondering what the hell it could be, he slit it open, pulled out the sheet of thick white paper inside.

Abbotsport City Police
From the Chief Constable's Staff Officer
Dear DS Stallworthy, I am directed by the Chief Constable to convey to you the earnest thanks of Councillor Arthur Symes, of Abbotsport City Council, for your good work in swiftly recovering the personal property stolen from his residence on the night of 31 March last. Councillor Symes particularly praised your work in conversation with the Chief Constable at yesterday's meeting of the Police Committee. I am happy to inform you that, although the Chief Constable feels that Councillor Symes's request that you receive a Commendation at a public ceremony at which he would be present is one that he cannot pursue in justice to other officers, Councillor Symes's praise for your work on the case is being entered on your Record of Service.
Yours faithfully,
R. J. Parkinson, Chief Inspector

He almost laughed aloud.

Councillor Arthur Symes. Pompous git. Still, do no harm having that on his record. Might come in handy one day, if ever he found a Misconduct Form on his desk rather than a fancy notepaper letter from the

Chief Constable's Staff Officer. Allegation of something like *improperly receiving financial reward in consideration of failing to carry out an investigation to its fullest extent*.

And the letter'll be something to tell my Lil about when I get home tonight. Always likes hearing about any bits of good come my way.

Sometimes, he added to himself gloomily, things like that help when she gets to feeling, if she did have to have married anyone in the police, she ought to have fixed on someone who'd go shooting up higher than I ever will. What she'd like, perhaps, would be to be someone like Mrs Chief Constable's Staff Officer. Or, maybe not married to a high flyer like that – just come from the Met, hadn't he, CI Parkinson? – but at least to be the wife of someone taking home an inspector's pay. She might have some hope then of retirement days on her Pacific island.

Well, she ain't never going to get to anywhere like that with Detective Sergeant Stallworthy. Not when about the best I can do is take a thousand quid off a shitbag like Norman Teggs, Video Magic. Christ, wouldn't it be good to have a nasty piece of work like him bang to rights one day, with maybe a whole firm along with him, and not to feel then I'd got to lay my hands on whatever I could squeeze out of the sod. Just for once to carry out a major investigation right to the end. No mucking about. Put Norman Teggs and all his mates, whoever they might be, where they deserve.

And – if you're going to have a nice pipe-dream, have a good one – at the same time, in some mysterious way, I could find coming down from heaven the really big sum I need. Real Pacific island stuff.

Only, that'd more likely be coming up from hell.

And now there's poor old Jinkie Morrison doing time once again. And smug bugger Symes particularly praising what I got tricked into doing for him.

It was thoughts like those that made it all the sweeter when, just a fortnight later, he heard that the big boss, Detective Superintendent Detch himself, had gone to arrest Councillor Arthur Symes and had charged him with a long list of financial irregularities at the Abbotsport headquarters of the Fisheries Development Authority where he held the post of Chief Purchasing Officer.

This time, when always-joking DC Hoskins told him the news, he did laugh aloud.

Chapter Five

Jack had thought such dealings as he had had with Councillor Arthur Symes must now be at an end. But, a few weeks later, he found he was wrong.

It was the evening of 15 June, his twenty-ninth wedding anniversary. Rather than dipping into his nest-egg to pay for a night out, he had persuaded Lily to agree to a special supper at home, bottle of champagne, supremo pizzas from the take-away plus big sticky frozen dessert, candles on the table. He found, however, when he reached home that the economy nature of the celebration had not stopped Lily making a special visit to her new hairdresser's. 'Very nice lady in the next chair, knew all about Ko Samui.'

His heart sank. Bloody Ko Sammy. That sodding island paradise would come up now. When this was at last going to be the time, soon as the bubbly had softened Lily up, to mention what, week after week, he had not found the right moment for. That he'd paid the deposit – have to confess to that seven-to-one bet – on April Cottage.

But he couldn't put off telling her much longer.

Wouldn't be an opportunity as good as this for weeks to come.

So, as they ate, he chatted cheerfully about this and that. And all the time watched the reactions on the opposite side of the table as sharply as if his English rose was an Interview Room suspect.

At last he judged the champagne had done the trick. Lily was a mass of giggles over his tale of how the night before, driving home, his eye had been caught by a row taking place outside one of the city's smarter restaurants. He had pulled over and gone across. From all the yelling and swearing he'd pretty soon grasped that a yuppie-looking type, who'd obviously had more to drink over his meal with his girlfriend than he could take, had objected to another man and his wife staring at his table. In the end all four had been put out on to the pavement.

'Just up my street,' he said to Lily. 'Section Five, Public Order Act, *Abusive behaviour likely to cause a breach of the peace.* You can pile anything you like on to that, case comes to court. Young rich git likely to be sent down for fifteen days. Maybe more. Not at all what Mummy and Daddy would like. So it's quieten them down a bit and lead little yuppie round the corner on his ownio. Put the facts to him. Facts plus, really. And then it's *Look, Officer*-time, and fifty notes for the old nes— for Cadbury's Roses under the aubrietia.'

'Oh, Jack, you are a one.'

And then the phone rang.

He went over to it cautiously. Call to some urgent case? Murder, even? At just this of all moments.

'Hello?' He fought back a champagne belch.

'Detective Sergeant Stallworthy?'

A woman's voice. Not one he recognized. Young, but no schoolgirl. Definite hint of seductiveness there.

'That's me.'

'I understand you were the officer who investigated a burglary at the home of Councillor Arthur Symes recently. Am I right?'

'Who are you? What's all this about?'

'Nothing to be worried over, Sergeant. All perfectly simple. I have got some information about that business I think you would find of interest.'

'Oh, yes?'

'Could you drop in on me? Say, tomorrow evening? And I'll tell you about it.'

This has gone too bloody far.

'Madam, if you have information concerning a criminal act you should report it to Abbotsport Central Police Station.'

'But it's not really as important as that, you see. Just something I think the detective who went to Councillor Symes's house might be interested to learn. Couldn't you really just drop by for a few minutes tomorrow evening?'

What is this? Can't really be a woman wanting a bit of off-the-ration how's-your-father, even if it sounds like it. Certainly not if she's got any idea what I look like, sight fatter than I ought to be, permanently red in the bloody face, puff and pant at the least effort.

But she does know I'm a detective sergeant, and

that I went out to old Symes's place that time. So she must know a bit about me. Must have got to know something about me, though God knows why she'd want to.

'Look, madam, what is this?'

'But I told you, Mr Stallworthy. It's just the most trifling thing. But I think you'd be interested. Please, just pop in tomorrow. It's a flat in a block called Seaview. Number fifteen. That's on North Esplanade.'

'Yeah, know it.'

'Then I'll see you tomorrow. Any time after six.'

'Wait. Wait. What's your name?'

'Oh, you won't know me, Sergeant. But it's Foxton. Anna Foxton.'

And the phone was put down.

'What was all that?' Lily asked.

'Oh, just something. Informant. Sort of.'

'You haven't got to go out, have you, Jackie? Not tonight?'

'No, no. No, let's finish the bubbly, enjoy ourselves.'

But, he saw, the bubbly was finished already. And somehow the atmosphere had changed.

It no longer seemed anything like the right time to tell Lily that after retirement it would never be far away, exotic, financially out-of-reach Ko Whatsit. Just a new-built bungalow in a cluster of others on the edge of Torquay. For all that it went by the name of April Cottage.

*

All next day he was in two minds about going to see this mysterious and mystery-making Anna Foxton. How could she know anything worth hearing about Jinkie Morrison's break-in at Symes's place? Or was it that she knew something about Symes and the business at the Fisheries Development Authority? About what had led to his arrest? Well, if she did, it was Detective Chief Superintendent Detch she should be trying to contact. None of that was anything to do with him. And she had asked if he was the one who investigated the Symes burglary. No, she must just be some sort of a nutter, little though she'd sounded like it.

If something comes up and I'm busy, he told himself eventually, I'll forget all about going to see her. Silly cow. Almost for a cert there's nothing in it. If anyone says *Come for a pint* at five o'clock, that'll be it definitely.

But no one did and he was tasked with nothing all afternoon. So, just after six, he was ringing the bell of Flat 15 in Seaview Mansions, North Esplanade, perched up above the port. A reasonably well-kept block, if not exactly the peak of luxury. Strip of carpet along the corridor. Lift had been in order, thank goodness. Even climbing a couple of flights of stairs was more than he liked these days. One-bedroom flats, from the look of it. Doors along the passage pretty close together.

So what's this Anna Foxton going to turn out to be? Secretary somewhere? Able to support herself, if not in much style. Almost for a cert unmarried, small flat like this. So probably that voice on the phone last night sounded more sexy than the woman I'll get to see in just a moment.

He was on the point of putting his finger on the bellpush once more when the door opened. He saw at once he had been wrong. The woman who stood there, an enigmatic smile on her face, was dead sexy.

Although she was a brunette with a cloud of loose hair surrounding an ivory pale, pointed-chin face, she reminded him instantly of Lily as she had been when he first knew her. Not at all like her, really. She was somehow more together than bubbly, don't-give-a-damn Lily had ever managed to be. Svelte, that was the word for this lady. No golden curls like Lily's, of course. No coconut-icing complexion either. Not much in the way of any likeness in the face, come to that. But small-built. Petite. If not quite the same build as Lily, but— this was it, this was what made him think of Lil – giving out from every inch of her the feeling Woman.

He felt a rush of sweat spring up.

Was this going to be some sort of seduction scene after all? But why? What had he got, what could he possibly have, that could have made a woman like this determined to get him into bed?

'Mr Stallworthy, I presume.'

A hint of laughter in that. Somehow he knew then that the seduction of Jack Stallworthy was not what was on the agenda.

'Yep. I'm Detective Sergeant Stallworthy.'

Make it plain he was police. That there was going to be no mucking about.

'Well, come in, then. It's good of you to have made the time.'

She stepped back and preceded him through a tiny patch of hallway with closed doors to either side and on into the flat's sitting-room.

He took in the furniture. Nothing very much, but reasonably decent. Sofa and two smallish armchairs in some sort of brown velvety material. A table, presumably to eat at, up against one wall. A matching sideboard, with on it, he was glad to see, an array of bottles on a tray. Low tables beside the armchairs. Nice big picture window with a view out across the sea.

'Right,' he said. 'Now what's all this about Councillor Symes?'

She smiled. More warmly than before.

'Sergeant,' she said, 'I'm afraid I've brought you here on false pretences. The fact is that there's someone waiting who particularly wants to meet you.'

He felt a prickle of something between suspicion and fear.

'Yes?'

'It's Mr Warnaby, Emslie Warnaby. I dare say you know him. Know of him.'

Of course he did. Something about Emslie Warnaby almost every day in the *Argus*. The boss of Abbotputers plc, the enormous outfit that twenty years before had rescued the city from dying on its feet when the fisheries began to fail. The personal computers it churned out by the thousand now gave employment, one way and another, to half the town. With yet more to come when the firm launched some big new system it had been going on about in the press for the past year or so.

And it came to him abruptly what Anna Foxton must be. Of course. Emslie Warnaby's mistress. This was why she was living in a flat in this particular, anonymous block. And, yes, *mistress* was the exact word for her. Not girl-friend, not secretary having it off twice a week, but mistress. Substitute wife.

'Emslie,' she called. 'Come through.'

Behind him, the door on the right of the mini-hallway opened and Emslie Warnaby stepped out and came into the room.

He looked no different from the photos in the *Argus*. Heavily built. A dark suit that shouted out to the last stitch: tailor-made, best cloth only. A sombre-looking face, dark with good living. Every one of its thickly blunt features, short nose, jutting chin, touring black eyebrows, saying power. A presence.

Easy to see how someone like this would have pushed and fought his way to success. Pushed and fought Abbotputers to its commanding share of the market for small computers, in Britain, in Europe.

'Good evening, Sergeant. I expect you're wondering what all this is about. How I got to know your name? How I knew you had been the investigating officer when Councillor Symes's house was burgled?'

51

He stopped, indicated the bottles on the sideboard.

'But won't you sit down? Can Anna get you a drink?'

For an instant Jack was undecided.

Something odd here. Best just to say I'm sorry but I've got to go? Fuck the drink.

But at once he knew he would stay. For all that instinctively he distrusted everything about the Abbot-puters boss, he could not leave without hearing the answers to the questions Emslie Warnaby had put into his mouth.

'Thanks very much,' he said, taking the nearer of the two armchairs. 'I wouldn't mind a whisky. Small one.'

He looked at little Anna Foxton as she hurried over to the sideboard – plain that Emslie Warnaby gave the orders, and expected them to be instantly obeyed – and poured the whisky, just turning to him as she did so with another of her edge-of-mocking smiles.

J&B Rare, he noticed.

'Emslie?' Anna asked.

'Not for me. Not just yet. You pour yourself something.'

'No, I'll wait too.'

Emslie Warnaby did not sit down.

'Let me get the matter of knowing you out of the way first,' he said. 'Then you'll see more clearly why I wanted you here.'

So this was a summons from the big boss. However eager to get him Anna Foxton had made herself sound.

Emslie Warnaby pursed his heavy lips for an instant.

'I first happened to hear about you,' he said, 'from Chief Inspector Parkinson, your Chief Constable's staff officer. It so happens that Richard Parkinson has the cottage at the end of the grounds out at my place in Chillingford. I was dining your Chief a few months ago and he told me that Parkinson, who'd just come up from London, was having some difficulty finding somewhere decent to live. So we offered him the cottage.'

Another bloody world, Jack thought. What if old Lil had managed, after all, to marry some high-flyer like CI Parkinson? Being talked about at dinner by the Chief and this top dog? Having a cottage in his grounds – grounds, for God's sake – offered to her? She wouldn't have lasted six months, poor Lil.

But he said nothing.

Emslie Warnaby went on.

'We've had Richard and his wife for a meal once or twice, and on the last occasion I happened to mention that Arthur Symes – this was before he ran into his current piece of trouble – had been telling me how he had secured a commendation or something of the sort for the detective sergeant who, the very next morning after his house had been burgled, had caught the man who did it.'

A sniggle of puzzlement ran through Jack's head.

All right, thanks to bloody Jane Lane's interference, I did get a quick result on the Symes break-in. But anyone in the police must know that'd be as much by luck as anything. So why all this about telling CI Parkinson about it?

'When I mentioned the matter,' Emslie Warnaby went on, 'Richard simply laughed. Oh, yes, he said to me, that idiot Symes made such a fuss about Sergeant Stallworthy that we had to do something. So we sent Stallworthy a nice letter. But the fact of the matter is, that, as I found out as soon as I looked at his record, Stallworthy's an absolute disgrace to the force. No one's ever been able to catch him out, but it's perfectly clear he's dishonest as the day's long. As rotten an apple as we've got.'

Jack half rose.

He wasn't going to sit there and take this. Whatever it was somebody had put in his confidential records, he was still a damned good detective. A tally of arrests long as your arm to prove it.

'No, no. Don't take offence, my dear chap. That isn't my opinion of you. I don't make any judgement. Far from it. I'm only telling you what Richard Parkinson happened to say one evening. However, just a few days ago, your name came back into my mind. When, due to certain circumstances, I saw that I might have need of someone in the Abbotsport Police who – what shall I say? – doesn't possess too many scruples.'

Jack sank back in his chair.

No use shouting and protesting. What CI Parkinson had said was pretty much the truth, after all. Truth of one side of him.

He waited to see what would happen next. Took a relaxing sip of his whisky. Yep, good stuff.

'So then I got my good friend Anna here, who's a very intelligent and persistent little lady, to make a few inquiries about you. Not hard to find where you lived. Not very hard to find out where your wife goes to the hairdresser. Not too hard, in fact, to get herself in the chair next to her, even if it did mean sacrificing an expensive coiffure in the hands of, Anna tells me, something of a lawnmower-wielder. In short, not very difficult to discover that you are due for retirement in a year or so, and that it's the dearest wish of your wife to spend the rest of your joint days in an island off the coast of Malaysia called Ko Samui.'

Christ, yes. It links up. It fucking links up. Lily and – what was it she said yesterday? – the very nice lady in the next chair at the hairdresser's knew all about Ko Samui. No. Just this bitch here finding out all about yours truly.

What've I got myself into?

'I see you're upset about all this,' Emslie Warnaby went smoothly on. 'I can't say I blame you. But I hope in the end you'll see that whatever Anna has done on my behalf will prove to be in your own best interests. You see, there's a small task I'd like you to undertake for me. Nothing, in all probability, that should tax you unduly. But of some importance to me, and so carrying a reward. I venture to say a reward more than commensurate with what I shall ask.'

'Oh, yes?'

Butter wouldn't melt . . . More than meets the eye here. That's for sure.

'Yes. It's something that has arisen as a consequence of that unpleasant fellow Symes getting himself arrested. I dare say you know that the charges against him concern a variety of comparatively minor matters to do with goods obtained on behalf of the Fisheries Development Authority, where he was chief purchasing officer or something of that sort. A question of persistent falsification of documents. So, naturally, when he was arrested a large number of files were seized from his office.'

For a moment Emslie Warnaby seemed at a loss about how to go on. His lower lip came thrusting forward as he thought.

But he was not silent for long.

'The fact of the matter is,' he began again, 'that among the documents seized, as Symes who is out on bail told me a few days ago in an effort to obtain financial assistance over his defence – an effort, I am afraid to say, that met with no success – among those documents is a single file of letters relating to my firm.'

He paused again, and Jack wondered whether he was making up his mind how far he need go in saying what exactly the letters were about.

Then, in a zip of memory, he recalled something he had happened to read in the *Argus* months ago. Abbotputers plc had landed, the paper had said, a contract to supply the Fisheries Development Authority with a new computer system, the one the firm's research department had just invented.

The Maximex System. He even remembered the name.

And hadn't Warnaby implied that Councillor Symes, unpleasant fellow as he'd called him, was someone who knew him well? Well enough to go asking him for 'financial assistance'? Get hold of some expensive crafty defence counsel. So wrong 'un Symes, very likely, knew the Abbotputers boss well enough to have been persuaded – bloody domineering Warnaby, you could just see him at it – to accept the Maximex contract for the Fisheries Development Authority without letting any other tenders go forward. Something of that sort.

Everything beginning to add up now.

But why was he being told about this file of letters?

'Now those particular papers,' Emslie Warnaby boomed out, 'had no business to have been seized. They have no relevance whatsoever to the offences Symes has been charged with. However, it would be awkward – yes, that's the word, awkward, no more – for Abbotputers if that file should chance to fall under the wrong eyes.'

He took half a step forward. Loomed over Jack.

'So this is what I want you to do. I want you to get hold of the file and bring it to me. It's – so Symes tells me – quite a slim folder, pale blue in colour. One he bought himself for this quite private business. So the only one in the whole batch of that particular colour. You should have no difficulty in finding it – it has the word *Maximex* on it in Symes's handwriting – and, when you have, it ought to be no trouble simply to take it out of the building, whatever building it is where your Fraud Investigation Branch is housed. And for that simple operation I propose to offer you a very substantial reward.'

And, inwardly, Jack revolted.

All very well this geezer talking about those papers having *no relevance* to the offences Symes is charged with. All that stuff about *no business to have been seized*. But it's plain as the nose on my face he and Symesie were up to something. Both together. Getting that Maximex system approved, spite of it costing more than some rival. Be about the size of it. And if that comes out, as it's bound to do, really, once DS Mac-Allister in Fraud Investigation starts beavering away, then, big boss or no big boss, Emslie Warnaby's going to be in dead trouble.

And serve the bugger right. What's a fat cat like him want with even more money?

No, all right, there may be items on my confidential record up at Force HQ, that don't look too good. I may have done some naughty things in my time. Right up to taking that thousand off that out-and-out bad bastard Norman Teggs. But I joined the police to catch criminals, the way as a kid I caught fat Herbie Cuddy, and I'm not going to let this sodding criminal get away scot-free just because he's got the money to lay on a big payment for me.

No, there's a sticking-point. There's got to be. And this is it.

'Now,' Warnaby was going on, 'I realize that, although there should be no great difficulty in what I have asked you to do, there is a certain risk involved.

For you. Something may come out later on. I don't think that's at all likely, but I haven't got to where I am by leaving out proper provision for unlikely contingencies. So I am not proposing to do anything like paying you a large sum. I imagine, in any case you would have more than a little trouble concealing any such sudden access of funds. No, I propose something altogether different.'

And Jack knew what it was going to be.

He almost said it out aloud, flung it into Warnaby's face. Only, he knew at the same instant that this was something he could not fling into that face. That it was something he would have to think about.

Something – he felt as if iron-sheeted walls were cramming him in on both sides – which he was almost certainly going to agree to.

'What I propose is simply this,' Warnaby steamrollered on. 'I have recently been looking into a joint venture with a major concern in Singapore. I took a yachting holiday in the region last year to assess the possibilities. Arthur Symes came along as my guest, as a matter of fact, with that wife of his, and he expressed an interest then in taking over, when he left the Fisheries Development Authority, a small hotel I had purchased out there. Somewhere for my senior staff to relax. A hotel on the island of Ko Samui.'

Yes, as he had somehow known.

'Well now, there is, of course, no question any longer of Symes having the place. So I propose to make it over to you. It should give you, and your wife, many years of happiness and prosperity. And, of course, far away out there, complete assurance of no unpleasant proceedings arising from those matters my friend, Chief Inspector Parkinson, spoke about.'

Chapter Six

Caught. Jack knew he had been caught. Like a fish jerked all in a second out of the water where it had been contentedly swimming. Just because it had nosed at a tempting morsel and then snapped its jaws.

But there was no way out now.

Lily had gossiped to the lady in the next chair at the hairdresser's. She would have poured out her longing for her island paradise. Ko Sammy, blast the place. And now a life out there was being put on a plate in front of him. Even if he did have the strength to chuck the plate back at Emslie Warnaby, the Abbotputers boss still had him where he wanted him. He had only to send svelte little Anna Foxton to that hairdresser again on the day of Lily's next appointment and Lily would learn soon enough what had been offered to him. What, it would be made clear, was still on offer. And then she would beg him just to say yes. And if he said no, there'd be another long, long bed strike. Or, worse, she would tell him it would break her heart not to snatch at this gift offered them out of nowhere.

In the end he would not be able to resist her. Not possibly.

For a long time – or what seemed to him a long time – he sat there in the little brown armchair, the whisky he had only once sipped at untouched on the table beside him, and allowed the full misery of it all to swish like dirty washing-up water to and fro in his head.

Then he looked up at Emslie Warnaby.

'Okay,' he said.

'Good. I hoped you would see the sense of it. And, remember, there's to be no nonsense about going off in secret to your superiors. That simply wouldn't be practical, you know. I've had to allow you to become aware that I happen to be in a position I would frankly rather not be in, but your situation in my hands is hardly less uncomfortable. I would have only to say it was you who had proposed the deal to me, and with your reputation ... But we won't talk about that. You have very sensibly agreed to my proposal, and we'll go on from there.'

Emslie Warnaby sat down now, leant forward on the sofa with an air of colleague discussing with colleague. An informal board meeting.

'There are one or two points still to clear up. First, there's to be complete secrecy until you have handed me the file I want and have received your reward. If I get any hint that you've spoken to anyone, even to your wife, let me say – explain your good fortune to her afterwards in whatever manner seems best to you – I shall have no hesitation in calling the deal off and taking appropriate action. Action you would find extremely unpleasant.'

Looking at those blunt features and the steady stare confronting him, Jack had no illusions about the ruthless measures Warnaby would take if he was crossed. Easy to see how Abbotputers had been driven over the years to where it was at the top of the tree. And, come to that, how Warnaby must have used slimy Councillor Arthur Symes as if he was no more than a piece of wet string to be tied and twisted in whatever way suited him.

'I can hold my tongue if I have to,' he answered, cursing himself at once for the abject way the words had come out.

'As to the payment,' Warnaby went on, one item on the agenda dealt with, on to the next, 'the day I receive that file from you, you will be handed two first-class air tickets for Ko Samui together with the deeds of ownership of the Calm Seas Hotel. It's not a big place. You should have no difficulty running it, making a reasonable living out of it.'

'All right.'

He knew he was still sounding like a whipped dog. Or, worse – the image came into his mind with piercing vividness – like some cheap criminal of the day before yesterday, cringing there in the Interview Room expecting at any moment to get a slapping.

'And one final point.' Emslie Warnaby winding up the meeting. 'There's a certain time factor involved. I gather from Symes that there's no question of the proceedings against him commencing for at least three months, if only because of the sheer mass of documents he says were seized. However, from my point of view there is rather more urgency. I won't bother you with the details. Suffice it to say my wife is due to spend her annual holiday with her parents in the south shortly, and Anna and I want to get away for a brief holiday then. So I must have the file by this day month at the very latest. The sixteenth of July, not a day later. Is that understood?'

'All right.'

But he sounded to his own ears every bit as beaten-down as before.

He did not go straight home. He got into his car and drove – too fast, he knew – down to the bottom of the hill into the docks area. The first pub he saw, he parked and marched in.

'Whisky. A double.'

He took a deep gulp. Rot-gut it tasted like after his single sip of J&B Rare.

The memory of that made him all the more inwardly furious.

'Same again,' he snapped at the barmaid.

She gave him a quick, assessing look, but took his glass over to the optic and put in two more measures.

The time it took her was just enough to let him get hold of himself. He picked up the refilled glass and carried it carefully over to a vacant table.

But, sitting on the narrow green plastic bench

there, he let his simmering rage re-occupy his whole mind.

Why should I be caught like this just because bloody Emslie Warnaby chooses to whistle? What've I done to deserve it? Why should I be sent away to that sodding island after I've done what he wants, like a bleeding convict shipped off to Australia? Just because it suits Mr Warnaby to have me out of the way? What's it matter to me that the fellow's got himself in the shit over his damn blue file? Why should I have to help him climb out it?

But all the time underneath he knew there was a chill answer to his every question. He had to do what Emslie Warnaby wanted, however much it meant he became involved in some huge shady deal, because Emslie had him by the short and curlies. He had been offered that hotel on Ko Samui, the very thing Lily had dreamt and dreamt of hopelessly. It had been put there in front of him. The big bribe, the one he had never really dared to think about, the one that would solve all the problems of a lifetime. He had to take it.

He had been cheerful enough about passing up Jinkie Morrison's contribution to the nest-egg when that stupid Jane Lane had mucked things up. He had even hoped, the moment after he had put Norman Teggs's tainted money on April Fool, that he would lose it all. Somehow not have been paid off by a shitbag like that. But the offer from shitbag Warnaby was something he would not be able to refuse.

For a few moments, though, he contemplated what it would be like if he did get on to Warnaby – ring him at his bloody Chairman's office – and tell him he could stuff his Ko Samui hotel up his arse. Be free of it all.

But Warnaby would simply take the action he had promised. Invent something to accuse him of? Go sneaking to that precious tenant of his, Chief Inspector Parkinson. Lay it on thick.

Then, with the reputation he had got, listed there on his confidential record, almost for a cert he'd pretty soon find himself suspended. Might even end up, however much of a concoction Warnaby's story against him was, wearing a tall hat again, plodding along on the beat, reduced to a constable's pay. Even April Cottage would be out of his reach then.

But, even if he did reject the offer and still somehow manage to stop bloody Warnaby coming down on him, in no time at all, of course, that little bitch Anna Foxton would be there smarming her way into Lily's confidence. Would, despite Warnaby wanting complete secrecy now, tell Lily just what her husband had to do so as to get that hotel for them both. Make it sound almost nothing. And then, when he had agreed, as he could not but do in face of Lily in tears, bed privileges withdrawn once again, Warnaby would be laughing.

And I'd be back just where I am now.

But, if I do what Warnaby wants— when I do what Warnaby wants, how am I to go about it? I've only got a month, a bleeding month, to think up some way of getting hold of that file and carrying it away. And, bugger Warnaby's *no great difficulty*, doing that'll be one hell of a problem.

No doubt somewhere in the Fraud Investigation Branch office up at Headquarters that precious pale blue file is just lying there. For the taking. In theory. But that office, I well know, is going to be locked up solid whenever Detective Sergeant Mac MacAllister's not sitting there like a hunched-up old watchmaker, working his way through his papers and figures, building up his cases for the Crown Court. So what possible chance is there of even setting eyes on the file? Let alone of waltzing off with it, bold as brass, out of Headquarters?

All very well for bloody Warnaby to talk about a simple operation, but it ain't bloody simple. In any way. It's near enough fucking impossible.

He found he had not touched his second whisky. And that he did not even want it.

He stood up, feeling his body like a sodden sack hanging from his shoulders, and made his way out. Good thing, probably, not to have gulped down that second double. Be just his luck to be stopped by some PC fresh out of Mansfield, waving his breathalyser like a bloody kiddy's toy. Totally deaf to any attempt to work the old pals' act.

And at home he would have to stop himself saying a word to Lil.

Waking early next morning and lying there wishing he would never have to get up, suddenly a possibility appeared in his mind. A little scene between himself and Mac MacAllister. A conversation in which he would – details were vague – end up knowing exactly the whereabouts of that blue folder Emslie Warnaby was prepared to pay so much for.

Coming nearer to common-sense daylight, he lay on, thinking about the notion his half-awake brain had put in front of him. It seemed too good to be true. Somewhere, surely, the plan would go off the rails, the rails he had seen, as he woke, running glistening away into the happy distance. There would turn out to be some total logical impossibility somewhere. Bound to be.

But, as he went through it all again and again – he could hear Lily down in the kitchen trotting about getting a cup of tea – no snag whatever came into his mind. It would not be the total answer. The conclusion he had imagined for it was not going to see himself marching out of HQ with the blue folder neatly tucked under his arm and no one taking a blind bit of notice. Far from it. But it did seem to be a chance of discovering exactly where that folder was. And just perhaps more.

So, as soon as he had arrived at the CID Room he booked himself out 'on inquiries' and drove up to Palmerston Park. Important to get there in good time, if he wanted to be sure of catching old Mac at his desk. Because at precisely two minutes to eleven Mac – he'd been doing this for years – would come out of his room into the outer office, and give a minimal nod to the one civilian clerk allocated to Fraud Investigation. Then they would go out together, with Mac carefully locking the office door. Mac would stalk along next to the canteen, arriving precisely at eleven. There, sitting alone, he would drink one cup of coffee and – the big black lady, Mrs Alexander, the head cleaner at Headquarters who had once run the canteen at Abbotsport Police Station, had told him this – eat one single-portion packet of Scottish Petticoat Tail shortbread biscuits. Leaving the canteen at exactly thirteen minutes past eleven he would unlock the office, let his clerk back in and resume work at eleven fifteen on the dot.

'Hey, man,' Ma Alexander had said, 'if ever those shortbread packets run out there's big, big trouble. Mr Mac he don't say nothing, but, man, the look he give you if you're behind the counter. Freeze you up, more than any damn Abbotsport winter.'

Plenty of excuses, of course, to visit Headquarters. Looking up something in the old records, finding out from Fingerprints whether some dabs lifted from somewhere were worth pursuing. A dozen reasons. And in any case no one was going to ask him what he was doing up there, once he had shown his warrant card at the main doors.

But in his waking dream, as he had stretched out there half hearing Lily making the tea, a reason to visit Fraud Investigation Branch itself had come into his head. And a reason he would need. Though he had known Mac MacAllister for years, they were hardly bosom pals. Old Mac too dry and unforthcoming. A proper Scotchman. So no question of just popping into his office for a bit of a chat.

And – not to put too fine a point on it – he had a nasty idea that somehow Mac knew about him. Knew that, from time to time, he 'did something'. Nothing like definite evidence that he was on the take. But he had always had the feeling that Mac had some sort of an instinct. An idea that he was not exactly scrupulous when it came to being offered cash in hand. Being offered, or asking for it.

No, spending a few moments in friendly banter was definitely not on.

It was just before ten when he put the drowsy-thoughts plan finally into action.

He poked his nose carefully round the Fraud Investigation Branch door. Mac's clerk, an oldish black guy called, of all things, Horatio Bottomley, looked up from the keys of the computer his stubby fingers had been dancing across.

'Mac in?'

'When he ever out, Sergeant, 'cept coffee break an' tea break?'

'Right you are.'

He went across and pushed open the half-closed door of the inner office.

'Hello there, Mac.'

Mac MacAllister looked up from his papers-covered desk where, just as expected, he was sitting hunched up like an old watchmaker.

'Hello, Jack. Something I can do for you?'

Not exactly welcoming. But he went right in and placed himself with his hands on the corner of the desk, leaning his weight on them.

'No. Well, it's what I can do for you, Mac, really. Nothing much, just something I think might interest you. But how are you?'

'Canna complain.'

'Going on holiday soon?'

This was a bit naughty. It was a well-known thing that Mac MacAllister, wedded to poking about among his files and figures, deeply disliked taking his annual leave.

Mac sighed.

'Ah, weel, no. I canna go just yet. I've a mountain of work. You know, they've arrested that Councillor Symes fellow. Improper procedures at yon Fisheries Development Authority. I've all that to look into. That is, once someone's located an FDA technical manager, former technical manager I should say. And those papers won't be dealt with in five minutes.'

'Former technical manager?' Jack asked, spinning things out as hard as he could now that Mac had begun – piece of luck – to talk precisely about the seized Symes files. 'What's a former technical manager got to do with anything?'

'Ah, weel, it's a terrible shame. You see, apparently that fellow – he goes by the name of Turner, so they tell me – went to the top man at the FDA some months ago protesting that Arthur Symes was overriding his decisions. As he may well have been. With the unprincipled object of giving some wee contract to a person or persons who had offered a corrupt inducement.'

'So?'

Had Mac at those words *corrupt inducement* shot

him a quick, assessing glance? No, seemed to be all right. For once.

'Weel now, what d'ye think happened?'

'Search me.'

'Our technical manager laddie got just precisely nowhere. I don't doubt friend Symes managed to put in a bad word about him somehow or another.'

'And then?'

'Why, then yon brave Mr Turner decided the Fisheries Development Authority and Abbotsport itself was no place for the like of him. Nor the real world at all. So off he went to be what the papers call a New Age traveller. Going about the country in some broken-down vehicle or other, living the righteous life without any nasty money, except for the generous provisions of National Assistance.'

'And – I get it – no bugger can find him now to give evidence against old Symesy.'

'Aye, they're looking, but they're no' finding.'

Jack could hardly believe his luck. As long as Mr Turner could not be laid hands on, the Symes papers were almost certain to lie where they were untouched. The blue folder that would bring him and Lily a life of ease on that island of hers would be there for the taking for weeks to come.

As much to hide the grin he felt beginning to force its way on to his face as to establish himself more solidly in Mac's office he swung round and perched one buttock on the corner of the desk.

'Well, well,' he said, 'it's actually about that same Symes business I came to see you.'

'Oh, aye?'

'Yep. What you might call another aspect. Sort of coincidence. I was round at Symes's house a few weeks back. When he was on the other side of the fence, making a meal out of calling in the law because someone had done his place.'

'And . . .?'

Mac's eyes were straying back to the document in front of him.

And so far, though he had learnt that he would at least have the full amount of time Emslie Warnaby had allowed him to get hold of the file, he had not really got any nearer seeing how that might be done.

The glistening rails of his morning daydream beginning to get a bit buckled?

'Yeah,' he said hastily. 'It was like this. Old Symes was creating about all his valuable family heirlooms being nicked, three china budgies, the lot, and, just as he came to tell me about his wife's jewellery, in she came. Bit of all right, too. God knows how a poncy git like Symes came to get hold—'

'I heard something about that break-in,' Mac interrupted, once again glancing towards the rows of figures on the sheet in front of him. 'Jinkie Morrison, wasn't it? Not much detecting needed there, if what I heard's right. His MO stamped all over the place.'

Jack felt a flush of uneasiness. How much had Mac actually heard? Could he possibly know, or have guessed, that it had been as near as damn it that he had accepted that half-baked alibi of Jinkie's? And its price.

'Yeah, it was Jinkie. Got him bang to rights next day.' He attempted a laugh. 'Silly old idiot actually tried to swing an alibi on me. Watching TV, would you believe?'

'Oh, aye?'

Mac said no more. But there had been a note of definite suspicion in the stretched-out vowel of that *aye*.

Quickly he went back to what he had noticed when Raymonde Symes had come in that night.

'Yeah, well, look, this is what I dropped in to tell you. When old Symes mentioned a necklace he had given that luscious wife of his to get her to agree to let him have his filthy way with her—'

'Jack, I just havna time to listen to suppositions anent Councillor Symes's love life.'

'Yeah, yeah, sorry, Mac. No, but the thing was, no sooner had Symes mentioned the necklace that the lovely— No sooner had he mentioned the necklace than his missus chimes in with it's diamonds and worth every penny of ten thousand. And what does old Symes yack out? *No, no, you've got it all wrong, not worth anything like that much, women have got no head for figures, blah, blah, blah.* So what d'you think, Mac? Piece of yum-yum like our Raymonde would never have agreed to marry someone like Symes, not unless he came up with a really big offer, cash or jewels, right? So, at the time they were married, which was about five years ago, one Arthur Symes, no more than a purchasing officer at the Fisheries Development place was able to lay his hands on ten thousand nicker so as to— Here, this is good. So as to be able to lay his hands on the luscious Raymonde.'

Mac MacAllister looked up at him.

'Aye, you may be on to something there, Jack. You're right. Thanks for the information. When they find Mr New Age Turner and I get round to examining the Symes figures, I'll know what to watch out for. Thanks.'

'My pleasure.'

He took advantage of the slight thaw in the atmosphere to give a careless glance round Mac's domain. Green-painted filing cabinets ranged along three of its walls. Dusty old cardboard boxes of finished-with papers, tied up and labelled, above them. A big trade calendar advertising a brand of mobile phone, the days below the glossy picture meticulously crossed off. And, behind him, a battered wooden cupboard, its doors an inch or two open and on its shelves, crammed in, a jumble of new-looking files and spring-lock boxes.

Could they be . . .?

'All that clobber come from the Fisheries Development place?' he asked, swinging round and extending a casual foot in the direction of the cupboard.

'Aye, that's the stuff. I had to requisition that cupboard for it all. And look at the terrible old affair they dug up for me. Not even a key to it. But I had to put what they brought in somewhere. I dinna suppose one half of it'll be any use. Those fellows who made the arrest had no idea at all. Took hold of anything that looked like a wee piece of paper for fear they'd be in trouble for missing something.'

He gave another massive sigh.

Jack sat where he was on the corner of the desk, staring at the crammed shelves behind the cupboard's leaning open doors. And, after a moment, he saw – he was certain of it – jammed between two other files just the edge of a slim folder. Coloured pale blue.

Chapter Seven

Mac MacAllister had seen him looking for longer than he really ought to have done at that doors-apart crammed old wooden cupboard. But, mistrustful though he was, it seemed as if he had read nothing into the deep, far-away stare the sight of that actual pale blue folder had betrayed him into.

'Oh, aye,' Mac had abstractedly answered his query about what the contents of the cupboard were, 'every file in that cupboard, every last paper, will have to be gone over, checked and re-checked, before I get away for my holiday. I've got DI Cutts hovering over me, you know.'

Oh, no, you haven't, Jack thought, pulling himself together.

Detective Inspector Cutts – 'Noble' Cutts as the youngsters in the force had taken to calling him when his willingness to 'improve' evidence, the so-called 'noble corruption', had got him relegated to Admin – would not stir himself an inch to urge on the investigation into the Symes case. He would have no need to. Once Mac had taken up the documents he would grind away at the figures till they had been added up, subtracted, multiplied and divided and the last trickery involved had come to light. In plain fact, he could take his due leave at any time, come back refreshed and get down to it all again. But with the fine excuse of the files from the Fisheries Development Authority waiting to be opened up he would never forgo his eleven o'clock ration of Petticoat Tail shortbreads, not even for a single day.

No, Jack said to himself with a thump of gloom, the bugger'll be here just as he is now, carefully locking his door each time he sets foot outside it, for weeks and weeks to come.

But if . . . If that mass of stuff in the cupboard doesn't get hoisted up to the desk to be looked at . . . If that FDA technical officer stays missing . . . Then . . . Then there's always the hope I'll somehow work out a way of lifting that folder – God, yes, that can only be the one, that bloody blue colour – right from under old Mac's sharp eyes. Somehow.

God knows how, though.

Mac looked up from the document he had already gone back to examining.

'Ah, weel, be seeing you, Jack.'

In other words, *Get out from under my feet*.

'See you, Mac.'

But when the hell will I get to see that folder in that specially requisitioned old cupboard of yours?

For the next three days it seemed to Jack he did little but think of possible ways of getting at the blue folder without Mac MacAllister knowing. If, he thought, he could slip into the Fraud Investigation inner office for even just a minute while Mac was out, he could whip that slim file out of that grotty old cupboard without Mac ever realizing anything was missing. He had spotted the thin strip of pale blue jutting out between two ordinary files himself only because it was totally in his mind.

But what chance was there of finding himself in the office without Mac's ever-suspicious gaze fixed on him?

Bloody none.

The deeds to the Calm Seas Hotel, Ko Samui, the life that Lily wanted so much, it was all as far away as it had been before that phone call during their wedding anniversary meal. Svelte little Anna Foxton fixing up the secret meet with bloody Emslie Warnaby.

What he had to get hold of and hand over to Warnaby before he got his reward – before Warnaby paid him his bribe, say it – was totally and absolutely out of his reach.

Or . . .?

It had taken him another whole day before he could bring solidly to mind the glimmer of a possible solution to his problem that he had begun to see. How to get into the Fraud Investigation offices without Mac knowing? Ridiculously simple first step: by going there when Mac was not present. Good and early in the morning. Well before nine when Mac and his clerk, the comically named Horatio Bottomley, arrived. Both of them always absolutely prompt.

As soon as he had hit on this elementary piece of reasoning he realized that the next, seemingly impossible step, actually getting into Mac's room, might even be in his grasp.

Mrs Alexander. She and he had been on good terms for years, starting from her time as canteen lady at the main city police station. And, since she lived not far from his own place, even when she had moved on to become head of the cleaning staff up at Palmerston Park Headquarters he had kept up with her. Palmerston Park head cleaner. There she was now, with, of course, her own set of keys to every locked room there. Her work, and that of her fellow cleaners, had to be over before any of the top brass got in.

So, Day One. Get up early, walk round to within sight of the bus-stop for Palmerston Park before the first bus rolled up. Double check the time on the notice in the bus-shelter. Retire to where he could watch without being seen.

Reward, that very first morning: Mrs Alexander arriving at the stop a good ten minutes before the bus was due, worn beige coat firmly buttoned round her, shapeless reddish hat well jammed down on her head, green-and-yellow check umbrella under one arm. He watched then as she tugged her heavy purse from her coat pocket and took out the money for her fare. At last the bus, all of five minutes late, appeared. He stayed where he was until Ma Alexander had clambered aboard, cheerfully abusing the conductor for being behind time.

So next day who should come driving slowly

towards the bus stop shortly before the bus was due – extra piece of luck: a drift of penetrating rain – but Detective Sergeant Jack Stallworthy. Just as Ma Alexander, marching along under her green-and-yellow umbrella, came into view. Jam on brake. Lean across to the nearside window, wind it down.

'Hey, Mrs Alexander. You on your way to HQ? Going there myself. Give you a lift if you like.'

'Oh, ho, Mr Stallworth,' – she had never properly mastered *Stallworthy* in all the years he had known her – 'Grace o' God you come by. This damn rain don't do nobody no good.'

She lowered her umbrella, gave it a good shaking, closed it up and heaved herself in beside him.

Tempted though he was to begin operations as they drove along, he restrained himself. As much softening up as possible was what was wanted here.

So he chatted about the weather and about his garden and hers – she had just picked her first crop of broad beans; the Day Lilies he had split into two clumps last autumn were giving a fine show now – until he drew up at the back of the big Headquarters building, silent as if it was still crouching under the bedclothes in the early morning drizzle.

'Won't be nobody here yet,' Mrs Alexander said. 'Who you come to see anyhow?'

Jack cursed himself.

Too clever by half. No story prepared.

'Oh. Oh, I've got to see the Force doc,' he managed to get out at last. 'Just a check-up. But best be on the safe side.'

'You gonna have to wait till half-past nine, ten o'clock, 'fore old Doc Smith get here. You better come in the canteen with me. I'll fix us up both with a nice cup o' tea.'

'Just the job, Mrs A.'

And just the job it was. If he couldn't get round her while they were companionably sipping their tea, he'd never be able to.

They entered the deserted, echoing building and made their way to the canteen. There Mrs Alexander hung her coat over the back of a chair at the table nearest the kitchen entrance and opened up her umbrella to dry.

'Now you sit there, Mr Stallworth. Take the weight off. I won't be no longer than five minutes 'fore we have that cuppa.'

Jack sat himself down, thinking what a nice old lady Ma Alexander was.

How fair on her was it to trick her into letting him into the Fraud Investigation offices? She'd know it was something she shouldn't do. Still, they were friends, and he ought to be able to blarney her into turning a blind eye for once.

What a curse, when she'd asked him why he needed to be up here so early, he had produced that stupid story about having to see Doc Smith. If he'd told her he'd left something important in Mac MacAllister's office the day before, she'd probably have happily handed him the key.

Or would she have insisted on going up there with him? Perhaps she would. She was a conscientious old duck. He remembered, from her canteen days, how she had once got into a heck of a state because her till was eightpence short at the end of the day and she had no money on her to put it right.

Luckily he had heard her moaning and complaining and had lent her a ten-pence. Ever afterwards he had been well in her good books.

She seemed to be taking her time out there in the kitchen, though. Probably found some washing-up not done, or something.

And then the thought of her coat, folded across the back of the chair opposite, suddenly tapped at his mind. What had he seen the morning before, watching her at the bus-stop? Nothing else than her tugging her fat purse out of her coat pocket while she waited for the bus to arrive.

What was more likely than the purse was in the pocket of that coat now? With in it, besides her money, the bunch of keys she had as head cleaner?

He got up carefully, lifting his tubular chair so that it made no scraping sound on the tiled floor. Noiselessly as he could he crept over to the archway leading into the kitchens.

And, yes, as he had guessed, from inside came the clatter of dishes being washed up.

Should be good for a minute or two more, and, if she found he wasn't there when she came back, she'd think he'd gone to the bog or something.

A dart into the uppermost pocket of the worn beige coat. Nothing. Twist the coat over and wriggle a hand into the other pocket.

Pay dirt. His fingers closed round the heavy weight of an old leather purse. Pull it out. Click it open.

Pay dirt. Pay dirt. Pay dirt. A big, big bunch of keys.

Snitch the keys. Click the purse closed. Shove it into the pocket again. Turn the coat back over. Just as it was? Hard to say. But no time in any case for the niceties.

Bloody pity I got nothing on me, take an impression of whichever key it is. Still there ought to be time, if I'm quickish, get up to that office, use the key itself. Could be all done in five minutes. With luck.

He left the canteen at a trot.

Thunder up the broad stairs to the first floor. And there it was in front of him. The locked door with on it the sign *Fraud Investigation Branch*. Just as soon as he had it open and had nipped through the outer office – no lock on Mac's own door – there would be that old cupboard, all the seized documents from the Fisheries Development Authority crammed into it. With well to the fore, plain to see, easy to snatch, a slim blue-coloured folder.

But first find the key for this door here.

My God, how many are there? All Yales, all the bloody same. And half of 'em without even a label. Plus, most of the others with the labels looking half-rubbed out.

He sorted through fast as he could, peering hard at each rubbed tag as he came to it.

Fuck. No *Fraud Investigation Branch*. Definitely. Only one thing, then – try all the unmarked ones. I suppose old Ma Alexander knows which is which. By the feel. Some little blotch or other. But no way I can tell. Just trial and error.

Ram each one in turn into the lock, try to twist it, yank it out. Lot of trials. As many bloody errors.

Still, only three to go. So in a sec—

'Mr Stallworth! What you doing?'

He jerked round, the big bunch of keys still in his hand.

Must look like a kid in school, caught smoking.

Bloody feel like one, too.

'Oh, it's you. I – er—'

'You took those keys out of my purse, Mr Stallworth. Somehow another, I knew something wasn't right with my coat. An' then I remember. Heard footsteps goin' out, run-running. Thought you mus' be short taken.'

'Yes. Well, you're right that's what—'

Mrs Alexander shook her head underneath her jammed-on old red hat.

'No, you was not,' she said. 'You was taking them keys entrusted to me. En-trusted.'

What could he say? That *En-trusted* showed just how strongly she must feel about her keys. The keys for office after office in Police Headquarters put into her trust.

So what would she do now? She could easily feel she should report me. To, say, bloody Noble Cutts in Admin. And then . . .? Then will it all come out? Emslie Warnaby, and what I agreed to do so's to be given that hotel on Ko Samui?

And who'll get the sticky end of it all, when it comes down to it? Not Emslie Warnaby, friend of the

Chief, and CI Parkinson, staff officer, in his pocket. Cottage down at the bottom of his garden. His grounds. No, it'll be stupid old Jack Stallworthy. No time at all, drawing a helmet from stores and pounding the streets again. If not worse.

'Look,' he said, trying for some sort of a smile. 'Look, I know I didn't ought to have done it. But no harm's done, eh? I mean, I never even got into this office, did I?'

She looked back at him, unbendingly.

'But you come up here to do jus' that. You had it in your head to do it the whole time. If I hadn't of heard you running out like that, if I hadn't notice' that coat of mine all in a mess, then you'd of gone into that office, done whatever it was you want. Something you sure didn't ought. That for certain.'

'No. No, look, I wasn't really going to do anything wrong. Listen, I'll tell you what it was. I left something in there by mistake when I dropped in for a chat with Mac MacAllister yesterday. Something I wanted urgent. That's all it was.'

'Mr Stallworth, it weren't no such thing, an' don't you try to tell me no different. Why you say you was coming here to see Doc Smith, if that was the true reason? When you was saying that, I thought you was choosing a funny time come see the doc. No, no. You was lying, Mr Stallworth. You was lying to Grace Alexander. If you was wanting something you lef' in that office, why, thing to do was up an' ask me let you in. I might of done that, too. Go in with you, see you weren't up to no naughty business. But, yes, I'd of let you in.'

He licked his lips.

'But couldn't you . . . Listen, we've been friends a long time, ain't we? So couldn't you just let me in there now? I—' He felt the tiniest snicker of hope. 'I could just pick up that file I left in there, blue folder sort of thing, and no one need know no more about it.'

'Mr Stallworth.'

It was a blank dismissal.

A sudden memory of his teacher in infants' class came back to him. She had had just such a way of putting a stop to nonsense. Then it had been *John!* not *Mr Stallworth!* but it had been just as definite.

'Yeah, well, sorry I asked. Shouldn't of done, I know.'

Again under her squashed red hat she shook her head sadly.

'But what'm I gonna do? That's the question I'm asking. You know, I did ought to report this, Mr Stallworth. You know that for sure.'

'But – but – Mrs Alexander—'

For a moment he wondered whether it would be any good offering her money. How much would do it? Should it be enough really to stun her? Hundred quid, say? She had a whole string of kids and no husband about, he knew that. She could do with some extra cash. Couple of hundred?

But he knew, too, that not even two hundred quid would influence her. Not the lady who thought the end of the world had come because she was eight pence short in her till.

And then . . . Then a glimmer of a thought came to him. Could it be? Would it . . .?'

'Mrs Alexander,' he said. 'Look, I'm truly sorry for what I did. I know it was wrong. It was just one stupid moment. So can't you forget it? Forget it ever happened? Look, I'd like to do something for you. For you and the kids. Show I'm really sorry. Listen, will you let me bring you round a big, big box of chocs? Bring it round tonight?'

Would she? Wouldn't she?

It hung in the balance. He could see the doubts on her face. The slight frown on the broad forehead under her hat. Big thick lips pursed in thought.

Then . . .

'Okay, Mr Stallworth. You say you're sorry, I forget all about it – soon as me an' the kids have finished them chocs. But mind you make that box one really-really big one.'

Chapter Eight

Ringing the doorbell of Mrs Alexander's flat that evening, really-really big box of chocolates precariously balanced on his other hand, Jack heard from inside two young, angry male voices hard at it in a shouting match plus what sounded like three small girls squealing in shared laughter over whatever was on TV. He wondered whether Ma Alexander would even know he had rung the bell.

But it seemed she was used to the noise because in half a minute the door was opened.

Wordlessly Jack pushed the big, glossy box forward.

Mrs Alexander took it, and shook her head sadly.

'Mr Stallworth,' she said, 'you never did ought to have done that this morning.'

'Yeah. Yeah, I know. But . . .'

'Now, you be a good boy after this, long as you live.'

'Okay. Yes, yes. I'll try.'

But, making his way down the stone steps to the street, he hardly thought of the feeble promise he had made. There was no question of keeping it, of even trying to see how he could keep it. He was committed to being *a bad boy*. By what Emslie Warnaby had pressured him into. By what now after so many tight-for-cash years he could do for Lily. He was committed into being more of a bad boy than he had ever been. Than he had ever thought of himself as being.

And all he could think of, as he tramped across the concrete wasteland outside Mrs Alexander's block, was that he had got away with it. Got away with that terrible bungled attempt on the blue folder.

Got away with it, that was, in so far as he had dealt with the threat of exposure Mrs Alexander held over him. What he had not done, he admitted sourly, was to get away with the blue folder. He had no hope now of ever wheedling his way to his goal through Mrs Alexander and her bunch of keys. No hope of persuading her. No hope of tricking her. She knew he had wanted, for some reason he was not going to tell her, to get inside the Fraud Investigation offices. Nothing now would persuade her to help him. Nothing would stop her, whenever the two of them happened to meet, guarding like a lioness those keys she had been *entrusted* with.

If he was to earn that paradise for Lily, so near and so immovably far away, he would have to think of some other method of doing it altogether. And there was no method he had been able to think of in all the days earlier when he had tussled and tussled with the problem.

Then, plodding wearily in at his own door, he was

greeted by Lily calling out from the sitting-room, 'Phone went for you, love, 'bout ten minutes ago.'

'Not bloody Mr Detch sending me out to some tuppenny-ha'penny break-in again?' he asked, still too heavy with depression to go over and give her his customary peck of a kiss.

'No, it was a lady. Wouldn't give her name. Said she'd ring back shortly.'

She took a chocolate from the box he had bought for her earlier, a box not really-really big, but not exactly small either.

'Funny,' she said, tongue thick with sweet stickiness, 'thought the voice was familiar. Couldn't place it though. Kept thinking. Quite spoilt *Holiday Time* on telly.'

'Sorry about that.'

But he knew now – never mind hard evidence – just whose that voice had been. Familiar to Lily from, of course, the hairdresser's. The nice lady in the next chair. Bloody Anna Foxton. Anna, who looked so like his own little Lily, or, dark and different as she was, somehow so like the way Lily had looked in their first days together.

The phone rang again just as they were opening up the pizzas Lily had bought for their supper in front of the TV. One of her favourite films was on the Movie Channel, *Dangerous Moonlight*. But he was not ready with anything to say in answer to the query he knew Anna Foxton would face him with.

'Mr Stallworthy?'

'Yeah.'

'It's Anna Foxton. I'm calling to ask what progress you're making. He would like a report.'

He. He. Bloody Emslie Warnaby. Wanting whatever he decides he wants now, this minute if not sooner. Well, too bad. Let him wait. Let him bloody wait. For once in his life.

'Well, there ain't been no progress. It's not as easy as kiss-my-arse, you know.'

'All right, I dare say there are certain difficulties. But Em— But he needs to know that you are taking steps. Active steps.'

'I'm doing what I can. Can't do more than that.'

'That's all very well, but we must be sure something's happening. Or we may have to— Is your wife in the room, Mr Stallworthy?'

'Yes, as a matter of fact.'

'Well, perhaps I needn't say any more. I'll ring again shortly and hope you'll have something definite to tell me then. Don't forget, July the sixteenth's the very last day we're willing to wait until.'

'All right.'

He slammed the phone down.

It was not all right. It was far from all right. If svelte little Anna Foxton was going to sit herself down next to Lily in the hairdresser's once again and tell her how Ko Samui and all its fancy pleasures was in his power to give her, he would be done for twice over. Bad enough to have Anna, and bloody Emslie Warnaby, on his back. If that was all, he could still tell himself it was possible to call the whole thing off. Just.

Do what he could to dive from under. But if Lily knew . . . If Lily knew that heart's desire of hers was there, almost in touching distance, then there would be no rest for him till he had done what he had to do to earn it.

And, if he was ever to get hold of that sodding blue folder – if he could ever think of how it could be done – there was only one way to go about it. Carefully.

He'd learnt that in CID if he'd learnt nothing else. Think things out before you go leaping in. Make sure of everything it's possible to make sure of. After that don't hang about. But, beforehand, plan. Think. Work out where the snags are. Otherwise nine times out of ten you go off at half-cock.

It worked over feeling a collar. And, come to that, it worked when what you wanted to do was let someone know their collar was going to be felt, unless . . . But go about things all in a bloody rush and, often as not, you came unstuck. Fast.

He went back to his chair muttering, 'Some nutter of a woman,' in case Lil's attention had been distracted from the TV. His cooling pizza had got leathery as a shoe sole. After one mouthful he pushed the plate aside.

So in the days that followed he was back once more to thinking and thinking. July the sixteenth, July the sixteenth. The date hammered at his mind. Far enough away just now. But all too soon it would be rushing towards him.

July the sixteenth, when, with Warnaby's wife safely installed at her parents' in the south, Emslie and his little mistress could go gallivanting off on holiday. Where to? The Far East? Singapore, just as it was shown on the telly, all dazzling sights, fantastic food, Raffles Hotel and God knows what else? Wherever. South of France. West Indies. That fat cat could go anywhere. Anywhere, as soon as he was safe in the knowledge that those letters Arthur Symes had put into that special blue file were in his hands. The letters that must give away whatever dirty business Symes and he had agreed on when Symes had been taken yachting in the sun, living the high life Singapore way. Ko Samui way.

And, before even the faintest hint of an answer to his problem had come to him, going into work on the next Monday, he realized it was 24 June. He had used up a week, more than a week, of the month Emslie Warnaby had allowed. And had got bloody nowhere.

Slouching despondently to his desk, he was conscious that at the far end of the room the Guv'nor was giving him a look of scowling displeasure.

All right, he pretty well deserved it. The whole of the past week he had done damn all, nothing he hadn't been specifically tasked with. Always, in the ordinary way, if there was no particular crime down to him to detect he'd be out and about himself. Nothing he liked better than sniffing round Abbotsport's criminals, drinking with one lot in some pub or club and getting the dope on what a rival firm was up to. And then going to the second mob and learning about the ill-doings of the first. Either to add to his record of arrests, or, if that was the way it panned out, to add a little something to the nest-egg under the aubrietia. Flowers beginning to be past their best now.

But there should be no need for any more little somethings, he thought, to add dribs and drabs to the Cadbury's Roses tin.

Make up your mind to it. You're going to get what'll make that tin totally useless. More than you ever in your wildest dreams hoped for. Those notes-rustling thank-yous for turning the blind eye, for putting in a cooked-up good word to the magistrates when some-one who's been 'good' to you is hovering on the brink of a tough sentence.

Except I'm not going to be getting that big – no point in ducking the word – that big bribe. Not unless somehow I can get into Mac MacAllister's office.

He sat at his desk staring unseeingly at the notice-board opposite with its pinned-up instructions, yel-lowed with age or white and fresh, plus the odd bright-coloured postcard from someone off on holiday and the cartoons cut from the newspapers, the point of their joke long forgotten. Vaguely in the background he was aware of the Guv'nor's phone ringing, even of his voice barking questions down the line. But now suddenly he realized his own name was being shouted out.

'Stallworthy, you dozy bastard, come 'ere.'

Shaking the gloom out of his head, he went across.

'Sir?'

'You know Marvin Hook, don't you? Well in with all that lot, ain't you?'

'Well, I know Marvin, yeah. What's the mad bugger been up to now?'

'Only holding Aide Jane Lane with a shotgun to her head.'

'Christ. You never sent her to sort out Marvin?'

'I'm not quite as stupid as you like to think, Sergeant. No, seems that silly bitch was passing Marvin's place, out on the St Oswald Estate – she was up there on some inquiry – and Marvin's wife or girl-friend, whatever, comes screaming out into the road saying Marvin wanted to kill her.'

'Dare say he would have done, too. Or damn nearly. Ought to have been locked up long ago, by rights. That mad bugger.'

'I dare say. But, thing is now, bloody Jane Lane just went in there thinking it was some minor domestic, and Marvin seems to have taken exception.'

'So what you want me to do about it?'

'There's a couple of PCs outside the place, called by the neighbours, but they don't know what the hell to do. I'm having the gun team from Palmerston Park get up there, but the last thing we want with any of the Hook lot is a full-scale shoot-out. So how about you get your skates on and have a few quiet words with our Marvin?'

'And get a load of shotgun pellets in my gut? Thanks very much.'

But he wheeled away and left the room at a trot.

Suppose, he thought as he revved away from the parking area behind the station, I do know bloody Marvin better than anybody else. Penalty of drinking with a few of those Hook bastards, time to time. Not that it ever did me much good. Too sodding anti-Law the whole lot of them. And what chance I'll get of talking to Marvin, I don't know. Nobody yet ever talked him out of doing whatever came into his barking mad head.

The St Oswald Estate, street after street of mean little houses put up by Abbotsport City Council in the sixties, was no great distance from the central police station, if well remote from Palmerston Park's big houses and solid Headquarters building. So, before Jack had time to work out how he might go about persuading Marvin Hook to behave like a good little lamb, he had reached the house.

He came to a halt, jumped out and went over to the PC who was dividing his attention between looking nervously at an upper window of the house and trying to keep the small crowd of onlookers on the far pavement out of shotgun range.

'Well,' he asked him, 'what's the sitch?'

'Don't really know, Sarge. I mean, look at the fellow's girl-friend there. My mate's having to hold her back now. Wants to bloody go back in, though whether it's to tell that mad idiot she's sorry and won't do it again or to tear his flipping eyes out, it's hard to tell.'

He looked across in the direction the PC had

indicated. Sure enough, his colleague was holding a thickly made-up blonde girl by her elbows as she bounced and bucked trying to get out of his grasp.

Not much to be done there.

'You know it's an aide to CID in there?' he asked.

'Yeah. Used to be on the beat round here. Jane Lane. Bit of a whizz-kid.'

'I'll say. So, you seen anything of her inside?'

'Yup. He came to that window up there with her. About ten minutes ago. Sawn-off stuck in her neck.'

'And now?'

'Haven't seen either of them since then. Are they sending some fire-power from HQ? Can't see any other way of getting her out.'

'No. Dare say you can't.'

And, turning, he set off at a jolting run across the road.

Only thing to do. If anything was to be done.

But with every step he had felt his wobbly gut turning to water.

Garden gate leaning rottenly back on its hinges. Thank Christ, nothing to have to stop for. Five yards of front path. Six. What if now . . .?

But, no. No, safe. Safe in the lee of the house.

The sweat was thick at his every pore. His breath was coming in long hollow gasps.

In a minute, if I don't pull myself together, I'll spew up all over the front step. Which, no doubt, pissed-out-of-his-mind bloody Marvin's done more times than you could count. And that stupid bitch of a girl-friend of his, too, like as not.

He forced his back straight, and gulped in two or three deep breaths.

So what now?

Got to get in somewhere. No use trying to talk to bloody Marvin unless I can see him eye to eye. Know when to fling meself out of the way of that sawn-off. If I can.

All right, off we go. Sidle round the house. Take a good look in at the windows. See what the back door's like.

It was the back door that in the end provided him with what he wanted. Or, perhaps, did not want.

If I can't get in here, it'll have to be the bloody siege team. Trouble ever after with the Hook firm or not.

Very carefully trying the knob – wondering whether just on the other side of the door Marvin would be standing, Jane Lane with her arm twisted behind her to one side, sawn-off pointing straight ahead – he found it turned perfectly smoothly.

Right. Next, a gentle little push. If Marvin ain't noticed the knob moving – if he's standing there waiting, and not upstairs, after all – then just let's hope he won't see the door opening a fraction. Tell me whether there's a bolt on it or not.

The door moved inwards as he pressed on it. But more easily than he had counted on. A full quarter-inch in a sudden little jerk.

But no shotgun blast came through the thin panels.

He breathed a long sigh of relief. Then swallowed.

So nothing else for it now. Do your duty, Detective Sergeant Stallworthy.

And . . .

Door flung hard back, step away one instant. No reaction from inside. And in.

Kitchen. A filthy mess. Might have expected it. Sink piled with crocks. Three or four empty cups on the little red plastic-topped table. Half a dozen beer cans. Bit of a pong. Probably from the rubbish bin.

And any sound from up above?

He stood still, trying to get his breathing quieter. Feeling the sweat trickling down his back.

But all seemed to be silent. Could Marvin really not have heard that door when I flung it open?

He glanced back at it.

Yeah, it hadn't actually hit that dresser there. Something stopped it? Yes. Some good in the muck the pair of them let lie on the floor. Empty take-away packet. Door never went banging right back. Piece of luck.

And, by God, I needed it. And I'm going to need a lot more before I'm done. Hell of a lot more.

He swallowed, dry-throated.

Well, nothing else for it again. Looking after a fellow officer. Got to be done. Even if it is that stuck-up bitch.

He crept over towards the far door. Ajar, thank God.

Breathing still far from right. Puffing like a fucking grampus, in fact. Hardly make it easy, taking Marvin by surprise.

Narrow hallway. Standard arrangement. Stairs

going up at the side. Any noises from above? No. So weren't they up there, after all? Come down to the front room? Door shut there. Go in? Same old TV trick? Only no gun in my bloody fist. No Hollywood-style crouching. Just wham in and hope.

But, no, if Marvin's there he'll have seen me thundering up that garden path. Certainly heard. And he wouldn't have hesitated to loose off a shot or two then. Not mad Marvin.

Those bloody Hooks. What they call inbred. Years and years of criminals, one after another.

No time for heavy social comment now, though. If Marvin's up there with the girl something's got to be done about him.

Take the stairs at a charge? Or creep? Better make it creep. Doubt if I've the puff to get to the top all in one go. Should have stopped smoking. Cut down on the drink. Been a good boy.

But I didn't. I wasn't. I haven't been.

They could put it on my gravestone. *He was not a good boy*. And this could bloody easily be a gravestone affair, come to that.

Poor old Lil. What'll she do? Needs someone to look after her. Always has. Always knew she did, too. And knew how to get someone to do it. Like me. Still, bloody lucky for me I was the one she picked on in the end. Some good times . . .

Suppose she won't have too much trouble getting somebody new. Even now. A bloody good-looker. And knows how to let a bloke know there's plenty in the way of reward waiting there. If he earns it.

As I—

Oh, come on. Less think. More do. Stairs. Creep, creep, creep. One by one. Don't hurry. Take care. Keep well to the edge.

Yes. Good. Landing. And round we go.

Any doors open up there? Not quite high enough up yet to get a proper look. So, second flight. And—

'Jus' keep fucking quiet.'

Marvin's voice. Talking to bloody Jane. Tell it anywhere.

So, nothing happened up to now that can't be put right. If I manage okay. If I do.

What now? Keep on creeping up? When the least little squeak from one of the boards is going to alert him, me near as this? Do the charge thing? Unless he's standing looking out of the fucking window I'm not even going to get in the room before he looses off.

And then it'll be, *He was not a good boy*, all right. Well, maybe they'll make it, *A good police officer*. After all, killed in the line of duty. They couldn't do much different, not whatever's on my confidential record. What you call ironic, though. Bloody ironic.

Well, try one step more. Maybe two.

Got to see how the land lies, creak or no creak.

One. Heave up on the banister. Okay. But still can't see if that door's open, or ajar, or anything.

One more, then. Hand on the stair-rail, and . . .

Yes. Door just ajar. Think I can hear our Jane Lane breathing heavy. Trace of a sob there? No, don't think so. Good girl.

Right. Well, try the chat. Too old, too fat, too sick inside for anything else.

'Marv. It's me, Jack Stallworthy.'

Silence from inside.

Or may be something like a little squeak from the girl. Well, don't blame her.

'Marv, we should talk.'

'Fuck off.'

'Look, mate, take it easy. You know what's going to happen to you unless you give over now. You'll go inside for life. Life. That'll be it.'

Listen.

Can hear them both breathing now. Marvin thick and heavy. Girl lighter. Managing it.

Good for her. Still got her wits about her.

'Marv? You hearing what I say?'

'Sod you, Jack Stallworthy.'

'All right, sod me, if you like. But you just think of yourself. Let the girl go now, and what're you up for? Nothing too much. Three months, maybe. And you've done more than that in the past, ain't you? And come out laughing?'

'Too right I come out laughing.'

He's talking. I could do it.

From outside, plain to hear, screeching tyres, voices shouting.

The bloody siege team. All guns and loudhailers. Once they start . . .

'Marv, I'm coming in. You be a good lad, eh?'

Don't give him time to think whether he's going to be good or not.

And it's okay.

I'm in. I'm in. And still in one piece.

'Right, Marv. Give us the old gun, and we'll call it a day.'

Reach out. Take it.

Christ, got it. Done it.

Jesus, I feel rotten.

Chapter Nine

Jane Lane took over. Jack felt too bushed to stop her. In an instant she had Marvin Hook, crazy Marvin, in the approved arm-behind-the-back hold. Then, without another word, she was marching him down the stairs and out to the waiting siege team. Through the window Jack heard a scatter of applause from the small crowd of gawping onlookers.

And half of 'em hangers-on of the Hook mob, he said to himself. Marvin's mates, but happy enough to see the mad bugger out of the way. Dare say two or three of 'em already got their eyes on that blonde piece of his.

He wondered if he should go into the bathroom, heave up his guts. Have no trouble doing it. Christ, he felt lousy.

But the thought of what state the bathroom was likely to be in, judging by the mess in the kitchen, decided him against.

He stood, legs apart, in the middle of the room – Yes, bed looked as if the sheets on it had been there since sheets were invented – and took three deep breaths.

Then, with a shake of the head, he went downstairs in his turn. Outside in the fresh air he felt a lot better. Almost back to his old self. The Jack Stallworthy who seldom let a day pass without adding one more collar to his arrests record.

And, he thought wryly, who seldom let a week go by without letting some toe-rag get away without being collared. In exchange for a few notes.

Jane Lane came up to him.

'Well, skipper, he didn't give too much trouble in the end, eh?'

He looked at her.

'No, not too much.'

'Nice the way you came in when you did, though. Made it just that much easier.'

Could this be true? What price *A good police officer* on the old gravestone now?

'Yeah. Well, glad to have been a help.'

'Oh, you were. You really were.'

'That's nice.'

Anna Foxton rang again before Jack had contrived to dream up any other wild possibility of getting at the blue folder. Let alone the foolproof plan he knew he ought to have.

'Mr Stallworthy.'

That voice.

He glanced over to Lily, tucked in her chair with her magazine. Would she recognize who it was? Something in the rhythm some people spoke in told you who they were straight away, even though it was only a sort of squawking you heard from the phone. If the voice was loud enough.

Thank God, at least bloody Anna Foxton's voice was quiet. Quiet, but with a hell of an edge to it sometimes. Like now. In just those two words.

'Yep. It's me.'

'I said I'd call again.'

'Yep. You did.'

'Well, haven't you anything to report?'

'Look, I'm working on it. Christ, it's only been three days since you were on at me last. I told you then, it's bloody difficult.'

Across the room Lily, glancing up from *Hello!* magazine, was looking over at him.

Keep it bit cooler, or she'll think something's up.

'That's hardly good enough, Mr Stallworthy. We expect more than excuses.'

He looked back at Lily again. She seemed well absorbed in *Hello!* But . . .

'Look, this isn't the best of times.'

'Your wife is there?'

'Yes.'

'I enjoyed the chat I had with her at that place. Antonio's, was it called? Some Italian-y name. If not exactly an Italian doing the styling. Still, it might be nice to meet there again.'

'Listen.' He dropped his voice almost to a deep

whisper. 'Listen, you'll get that – You'll get what you want. No need to go rushing off into anything. But you've got to give me time. If something's bloody difficult, it needs time to sort it out.'

'And you're taking time, Mr Stallworthy. Altogether too much, if you ask me. Haven't you thought of anything? Anything at all? I mean, isn't there someone there you could pay to get it for you? Or to let you take it? People will always do what you want if you offer them enough, you know.'

She telling me that. She's got a fucking cheek. Who'd she and her big boss lover offer that bloody Ko Samui hotel to? God, I'd like to . . .

'Listen. You leave my business to me, right? And I'll leave yours to you. I've said you'll get what you want. Just let me get on with it in the way I know best, yes?'

'All right, all right. I'll do that. And you've still got plenty of time. If you make use of it. But, remember, Mr Warn— Remember we can't wait a day beyond the sixteenth. Not a day.'

The phone put down.

Going back to sit down again, his mind blank but boiling with unfocused resentment, he snapped on the TV.

Stop Lil asking stupid questions. God, I'd start yelling at her, she begins.

Slumped in his chair, he could not even see the screen. But only give Lily the idea he was watching something and it would keep her off his back. While he thought. Tried to think. Of something. Some way of getting into sodding Mac MacAllister's sodding office.

Then the voice issuing from the TV impinged on his consciousness. Somebody, a police spokesman – no, a bloody Chief Constable by the smoothie, pumped-up sound of him – talking away about some naughty coppers somewhere . . .

Hey, could be us. Abbotsport City Police. That might be the Big White Chief himself. What if the bloody press has got on to Harry Hook having some-body from HQ on his pay-roll, somebody high up . . . How about CI Parkinson, sodding Emslie's pet boy? Be a right laugh, that.

He swung round to watch the screen.

But, no. Not the Big White Chief. Some other high-up from somewhere, uniform fitting him like he was a bleeding dummy in a tailor's window, silver-wire insig-nia on his shoulders glinting like stuff on a Christmas tree, going on and on about 'determined to root out . . . isolated example . . . the British police officer is still as honest as he ever was . . .'

He leant forward and snapped off the set. You could take only so much of that sort of guff.

Lily looked up from *Hello!*.

'I was listening to that.'

'No, you bloody weren't.'

'I was. I was. It was interesting.'

'What was it about, then?'

She sat back, letting *Hello!* slip on to her lap.

'It was about something. Something to do with the police, wasn't it? Why d'you switch it off?'

'I thought at first it was to do with Abbotsport. Some high-up caught with his hand in Harry Hook's pocket. There's always rumours he's got someone feeding him. How he gets away with all he does. But it wasn't us. Some other bugger.'

'Oh, well, that's all right, then.'

Hello! plunged into again.

And, somehow, an idea in his head.

It must have been half what he'd heard on the telly, the thought that even police high-ups were sometimes on the take. And it had been half – all right, admit it – what that bitch Anna Foxton had said just a few minutes before. *Isn't there someone you could pay to get it for you?*

Because there was someone. Or perhaps, just perhaps, there was.

However far beyond the possibility of bribing Mac MacAllister was, perhaps Horatio Bottomley might not be as much through and through solid, grating iron. Why should he be, after all? He was probably as human as anybody else. Just because he worked under Mac, had done for years, it didn't mean he'd got to be just the same sort of never-a-glance-anywhere-aside fellow as inhuman, impossible Mac.

And! – hey, this was good – once that blue folder had been handed to Emslie Warnaby, the cash in the Cadbury's Roses tin would no longer be something totally necessary. So as much as, say, a thousand quid from it could be used in advance of retirement time. If necessary.

Would an ordinary civilian clerk like Horatio Bottomley be able to resist a thousand nicker? For doing practically nothing? No way.

At five o'clock next evening – no time to waste. He might be wrong about the bloke. Have to think of something else then – he waylaid Horatio just as he was leaving Headquarters. The sky above, never mind June, was ominous with piled-up rain clouds.

Just the ticket. Time he had some luck.

'Hi, there. Day's work done, eh?'

'Oh, hello, Mr Stallworthy. You up here quite a lot just now.'

Think, quick. Yes, same old excuse I used with Ma Alexander.

'Yeah. Yeah, been seeing the doc. Not feeling too fit, you know. Thought I'd better have a check-up.'

Horatio Bottomley gave him a quick glance. Big brown eyes in the creased brown face under its crinkle of greyed hair, offering a cross between sympathy and shy withdrawal.

'Nothing too wrong, I hope, Mr Stallworthy.'

'No, no. I'm hundred per cent really, just been overdoing it a bit.'

'You want to take things easy, you know. Mr MacAllister, he been telling me 'bout you. Says you're one champion thief-taker, only—'

An abrupt halt.

He nearly asked him *Only what?*. But he realized in time what Mac was likely to have said. *Only he's on the take half the time, if I know anything*. Something like

111

that. Mac couldn't know it for certain. But over the years that their paths had crossed he would have developed his suspicions.

So tread carefully. Horatio, for all that trusting look of his, would have been warned against him.

But that was no reason not to push ahead with the plan. Have something to tell pushy little Anna Foxton next time she rang.

'Hey, listen, mate, I could give you a lift. You on your way home? I'm here with the motor. Might as well take advantage. Where d'you live? It looks like it's going to pour.'

'But it might not be the way you've got to go, Mr Stallworthy.'

Yet, giving him a quick look, he could see on his face how tempted he was. Not having to wait and wait for a bus, to face maybe a long walk home from the stop at the far end. Most likely with it pissing down.

'Oh, come on. You go somewhere into the town, don't you? That's where I'm going.'

'Well, if it's near the bus station . . . I can get a 63 from there, goes right past the end of my street. Save me a long walk from the 18 stop.'

'Okay then. Motor's just over there. Get you to the bus station in ten minutes.'

But I won't. I'll find some way of making the journey last longer. Of making it last as long as it takes.

They went over to the car and set off.

And as they did so the rain started. Coming down in buckets.

This should do the trick. Another piece of luck.

If I say I hate driving in these conditions . . . Pull in somewhere. Then we can sit and talk. And if the rain does slacken off, with any luck by then he'll be so hooked he won't even notice.

'Good job you did decide to come with me, mate. You'd have got bloody wet, this lot.'

'That's plenty true, Mr Stallworthy. Fact is, this old mac of mine ain't no use at all if ever more'n just a little shower come down.'

'Yeah. Well, you're in the dry here.'

He drove on in silence for a few moments.

Rain hard enough to justify pulling up? Perhaps. Anyhow, the fellow won't know any different if I say it's too heavy to make driving safe.

'You know, I'm going to have to stop. My wipers are none too good. Don't want to drive you head-on into a traffic island.'

'No, no. You pull up, Mr Stallworthy. I'm gonna get home earlier than I would, even if we have to stay where we are till the rain stop altogether.'

'Right, then.'

And a good place to pull into. Gates at the far end of Palmerston Park itself. Nice clear area in front of them.

He came to a neat halt beside the kerb.

Now, work into the offer good and slowly. Just like with a tricky witness. Getting them to say what they'd promised themselves they never would.

'Tell me something, Horatio. How'd you come by

that name of yours? Horatio Bottomley, wasn't he some sort of dodgy financier, back in the 1920s or something? Read about him somewhere.'

'That's him, Mr Stallworthy. He was a damn famous man, you know. So back in Trinidad when I was born to Mr and Mrs Johnson Bottomley, what more right than they call me Horatio?'

'So that must have been before he was caught out, the financier?'

'Oh, no. My dad didn't take no account of that. That fellow was dead and gone by the time their little boy came on the scene. But, to Dad, Horatio was just one famous man, sharing the name the way he did. So he had me called Horatio too, and he counted on me getting to be famous jus' in the same way.'

Jack produced a laugh.

'But here you are, mate, nothing better than a no-good mac on your back and stuck in my old jalopy with the rain coming down fit to bust.'

'Well, that's sure enough true, Mr Stallworthy. But all the same something good come out of that financier man. You know what happen? When I was at school, back in Trinidad, that old master we had, whenever there was a 'rithmetic class, he always gave me the tough ones to answer. Said, *Let's hear what the famous Horatio Bottomley make of it*. An' he cane me good an' proper when I get it wrong. So there an' then I decided I gonna make sure I get it right, every time. An' that was how, when I come to England, I got the job up there with Fraud Investigation. 'Cos never mind what else, I always gets my sums one hundred per cent correct.'

'Good for you, mate. Good for you.'

'Well, that's okay. I got my job, an' I keep it. But I ain't famous. An' I don't suppose I ain't ever gonna be.'

Oh ho, my chance. I think.

'Well, may be you're not famous, matey. But you could be rich, you know, play your cards right.'

'Rich? Me, Mr Stallworthy? I don't see how I can get to be that, no more than I can get to be famous as that old Horatio. Not working for Abbotsport Police leastways. And I ain't gonna leave now. Pension's just over the horizon.'

'Oh, come on, Horatio. It's because you work for Abbotsport Police you could get rich, or a hell of a lot richer than you are now. If you want.'

Horatio Bottomley gave a deep chuckle.

'Well, 'less they put up pay rates by one great big jump I don't see how I ever gonna do that.'

'Oh, it'd be easy enough. If you truly wanted.'

'You tell me, Mr Stallworthy. I'd sure like to know.'

Aha, beginning to bite. Just like a witness suddenly seeing how they can get out of their fix, tell the truth and still keep it looking as if they never grassed on their mates.

'Well, there's lots of ways, you know. With you there, right inside Fraud Investigation. F'rinstance, there must be documents sometimes right there in your hands that certain people'd be much happier weren't in that office of yours at all.'

'But, Mr Stallworthy, papers like that are there in the office, certain sure. But once Mr Mac get his hands on some document like that, those fellows their goose is right cooked. You know that. Small fraud or big, Mr Mac he just don't let go.'

'Yeah, I know old Mac all right. But, you think about it, there must often be documents, files and such, he hasn't yet got round to seeing. Piled up there waiting for him. All you'd have to do is, maybe, take out just one document, one folder, and slip it to someone outside before Mac sets eyes on it. They'd pay you really good money, you know.'

Now will he ask how much is *really good money*? If he does, I've got him. I'm there.

'But, Mr Stallworthy, I couldn't do nothing like that. When they bring in files from someone's been arrested, like that Councillor Symes the other day, then all those papers have got to go to Mr Mac. That's what they been seized for.'

Christ, how dumb can you get?

'Yeah, yeah, I know that. But I'm telling you, mate, there must be papers from time to time Mac has no idea are in the office at all. Oh, he'll know a whole mass of stuff's been seized from someone or somewhere, but he won't know anything about each individual piece of paper, or file, or folder. So, if the circs are right, you could jump in there, earn yourself as much in one go as you collect in your pay-packet in a month. More.'

'But I couldn't do something like that, Mr Stallworthy.'

Losing him? Or is he just dumb?

'Oh, come on, mate. It's not anything very much. Just picking up an odd piece of paper nobody knows is there and passing it on. Or a bit of a folder, just a few letters in it. Nothing to it.'

Horatio Bottomley shook his grey-polled head sadly.

'What's the difficulty, mate? You know, there could be a nice fat packet of notes in it for you.'

'But, Mr Stallworthy, I jus' couldn't do it.'

'Why not, mate? Why not, for heaven's sake?'

'It's the figures, Mr Stallworthy.'

What the hell is the old fool on about now? Or does he want to know just how much? Bit more on the ball than he looks.

'Figures? You want to know just how much? That it?'

'Mr Stallworthy, I don't understand. There ain't no *how much* to think 'bout. There jus' can't be.'

Jack felt invaded by sheer bewilderment.

'You don't understand, mate? I'm telling you, it's me that doesn't understand. I don't understand a bloody word you're saying.'

'But it's what I told you, Mr Stallworthy. It's the figures.'

'What figures, for Christ's sake?'

'Mr Stallworthy, I was telling 'bout the way I was brought up, back in Trinidad. Where I learnt to add up an' subtract, multiply, divide, take a percentage, highest common factor, lowest common multiple. Mr Stallworthy, that's where I learnt it: figures is sacred.

Sacred, Mr Stallworthy. I couldn't do nothing that would make figures come out wrong. I jus' could not do it.'

With a savage jerk Jack turned the key in the ignition, slammed into gear and shot out into the roadway.

It was raining harder than ever.

Chapter Ten

At home after dropping Horatio Bottomley at the bus station – would the old fool never stop saying thank you? – Jack did not dare go in his usual way and sit with Lily, glancing over the *Argus* and chatting about what she had done with her day. He could not be sure what he would come out with. The sullen rage that had erupted in him when at last it became clear that Horatio, unlike the man he had been named for, was incapable of any form of cheating, was still churning unstoppably in his mind.

And, he had sharply reminded himself as he had pulled the car up outside, feeling the way he did he was all too likely to let it out to Lily that Ko Samui was actually there on the horizon for them both.

It was not Emslie Warnaby's ban on saying anything about the blue folder, even to Lily, that was still keeping him silent about the prospect of owning the Calm Seas Hotel. It was the hope stored in the back of his mind that he could somehow reject that over-whelming bribe.

There was still the possibility – there had to be – of paying the rest of the sum due on April Cottage. After all, the banks were generally good about loans to police officers. The two of them could still, couldn't they, settle down to a quiet life in Devon? Quiet, if not exactly luxurious.

Not that he had as yet brought himself even to tell Lily about April Cottage. About the bet on April Fool, and how he had gone straight round to the estate agent's and paid that deposit.

April Fool on April the first. And, though it was now still June, all too soon it would be July. And then July the sixteenth. With no idea at all, after that infuriating talk with that stupid idiot Horatio, of how he could ever get hold of the blue folder.

So he did no more than give Lily a wave through the window as he trotted – the rain was slackening but still coming down hard enough to give him a wetting – to the sanctuary of the garden shed. Christ, he thought, pulling the lop-sided door closed behind him, what wouldn't I give to be able to say *Up yours Emslie*?

All very well to put out your hand for a few notes from some villain who deserved, one way or another, to be given a hard time. Even to relieve someone like that of more than a few notes. But to let yourself be bought by the huge sum, or its equivalent in hotel deeds, that a man like Emslie Warnaby was flourishing . . .

But how, if word of that offer ever got to Lily, could he tell Warnaby to stuff it? How could he break her heart? And word of the offer would get to Lily all right. Bloody little Anna Foxton had made that clear enough.

He looked at his range of tools, neatly hanging from twin nails set along the shed wall.

Anything needs doing out there? Rain pretty well stopped now. Perhaps I could plant out those lobelias. They're about ready, and the ground'll be lovely after the soaking it's just had.

Carrying the seed-tray with its rows of little lobelia plants in front of him, trowel grasped in one hand underneath it, he let his mind wander through a scenario in which, after all, he had done what Lily would want. If he did bite the bullet, take Warnaby's offer, find himself in the end owning that bloody hotel on bloody Ko Samui . . . Living out there with Lil. No more troubles. Lily with everything she'd ever dreamt of. Sun shining. Life of ease. All that . . .

Me there with my English rose, and her happy.

But how in the hell am I ever going to get hold of that folder? Passport to it all?

In sudden, push-all-aside fury, he turned the tray of sprouting lobelia plants upside down and smashed it on to their place in the bed.

And then, barely a minute later, he began to tease each seedling safely out of the jammed-down upturned layer and put it on the earth where it was to go.

Two days later, on the Friday, he was once again sitting in the car outside Headquarters. With no better idea in his head than to have another chat with Mac MacAllister. See if there was, anywhere at all, some tiny chink in that Scotch armour of his.

For some time he just sat there. Surely to God there must be some approach that'd get behind that sour exterior? Had Mac never in his life 'taken'? Not anything at all? Christ, it wasn't doing much to accept something as a sort of payment for a favour to come, or a favour past. You couldn't be totally rigid about everything, however bloody upright and moral you were. Not in the police, you couldn't.

There'd always be the time you stopped off for a quick bite to eat and the fellow behind the counter, Chinkie, Indian, hot-dog stall owner, whatever, said, 'On me, Officer,' when you offered to pay. Jesus, there was that time years ago in the Chinkie down at the docks when the little old man behind the counter had gone into fits of terror when whoever it was he'd been on patrol with that night had insisted on paying for the sweet-and-sour. Little old fellow thought it meant he was about to be pulled in. For something, for anything. *No, no, please, please, done nothing wrong. No. Never. Never, never, never.* All that.

So you had to accept. And no harm in it either. They gave you something they could easily afford to; you did something for them that was no skin off your nose. Say, made sure you dropped in at the place different times every night, scare away the smash-and-grabbers. Or turned a blind eye, if it was a pub, to a bit of after-hours drinking. Nothing serious. Nothing to get uptight about.

But Mac, bloody Mac MacAllister, just the sort who does get uptight. At the least little hint of not being one hundred per cent strictly honest. And, besides, there are those opinions he's got. About me. Never brings them out to the light of day. But they're there all right. Hidden away. You can't have done hundreds of interrogations without being able to tell what people are thinking, however little they let the words come out. The tiny signs. What they call body language. The not-quite-looking-you-in-the-eye. Or looking you in the eye too long and too hard. The curling fingers. The tic in the cheek they can't stop.

Jesus, how many villains I've put away in the end because of what I've learnt from things like that.

And, from things like that, I damn well know what Mac secretly thinks about me. So how's he going to react now to the suggestion I'm thinking of coming out with? Of coming out with if the signs are by any chance right? How's he going to react to me suggesting he should take money, a good big chunk, not to notice me stooping down and pulling out that blue folder from among the Symes documents? How?

Not any doubt about it.

Yet what else is left?

He pushed open the car door, heaved himself out.

Some days you felt your age all right.

But nothing else for it. Do it. And hope.

Moment of bloody awkwardness going past Horatio Bottomley, sitting there at his desk in the outer office, stubby brown fingers tap-tap-tapping, entering figures on the computer.

Would he up and say, *Mr Stallworthy, I know why you're here. Just don't come in any further?*

He'd be entitled. But, no, damn it, he'd never dare.

So let him have what thoughts he liked under those grey patches of crinkly hair.

Just so long as he makes no attempt to stop me going in and passing the time of day – passing the time of day: what a laugh – with Mac.

But the old clerk did no more than half look up from his computer keys.

Push Mac's door open.

'Hi, Mac. Passing by. Thought I'd see how it's going.'

'Oh, Jack. It's you. How's yourself?'

But back immediately to the page of figures in front of him.

Christ, did the fellow never get tired of looking at rows and rows of figures? Didn't he ever, just sometimes, lean back in his chair, stare up at the ceiling, think about something else? A woman? What he was going to do when he'd finished his day's work? Even what he was going to have for dinner?

Was the bugger totally inhuman?

'Oh, I'm all right, mate. Never fitter.'

'Oh, aye? So what are you doing up in this neck o' the woods?'

Damn it, once again no excuse ready to hand.

'Been seeing the quack, you know.'

And the look of sharp suspicion.

What the hell now . . .? Oh, yes. Christ, he'd just

said he'd never felt fitter. Trust bloody Mac to take both remarks at face value. And to wonder.

'And you?' he jabbed in quickly. 'How are you? How's it all going?'

Mac grunted.

'Getting on,' he said. 'Getting on. Hell of a lot to do.'

'Oh, yes? And have they got hold of that bloke who left the Fisheries Development Authority yet? Forget his name. The one who went for a hippie or something.'

Can I just take a quick look in the direction of that cupboard now? Right behind me. Or will Mac, somehow, guess what I'm after?

'Turner. Fellow by the name of Turner. And, no, they havna seen hair nor hide of the laddie so far.'

'Oh, well, means at least you haven't got to begin on all that Symes stuff yet awhile.'

Now he did take one rapid glance at the battered old cupboard. Doors still bulged a little open. And, just where he had spotted it before, the folder. Just the same half-inch of pale blue card sticking out from between the same two files.

But, damn it, on the top of the cupboard there was now a key. Bright, shiny and new-looking. It hadn't been there before. Could have sworn to that. So had Mac just had it made for him? Was he going to push the cupboard doors closed, straining against that mass of files inside, and lock it up? Then would he put the key in his pocket? Ninety-nine per cent certain he would. Pernickety bloody tight-wad.

Surprisingly, in answer to that casual remark about the Symes documents Mac abandoned his scrutiny of the figures in front of him and actually did lean back in his chair.

'Yes,' he said, 'I canna usefully begin on that stuff in the cupboard till they've found yon Turner. And that's the devil of it. It means DI Cutts'll send me on leave. And, you know, it's no' so very convenient to go just now.'

Jack did his best to conceal a smile. Old Mac and his anti-holiday phobia.

'How's that, then?' he asked mischievously. 'Nice time of year this. Get away before all the families. Kids all over everywhere. I'd have thought you'd jump at the chance. You not having a wife to think of. Anything like that.'

'Weel, no. To tell you the truth, I dinna much like going away. What's there to do, cut off from what really interests you? All I do, when I have to take any leave due, is go down to my wee flat and spend most of the time wishing I could get back to work.'

'Well, it takes all sorts. I must say, nothing I like better than to be away from the job. Off down to Devon or somewhere with my Lily, get a bit of sun, look at a few houses for when it comes to retirement.'

'Retirement,' Mac shot the word out as if it was a gobbet of bad meat. 'Man, that's something I just canna bear to think on.'

'Why not?'

If he couldn't see his way to asking this block of Scotch granite whether he would accept a thousand quid or something not to notice a blue file walking out of here, at least he could tease the bugger.

'Why not, Mac? I'd have thought you'd have had enough of it here. Day after day, stuck in the rank of sergeant, same bloody mingy pay as meself.'

Wait.

Could this actually be a way into it? Into the forbidden subject? Seemingly idle chat about having too little money? And then on to how that could be remedied?

Quick, don't let the talk flag. Bloody Mac'll be face down in his figures in a sec.

'And not much thanks you've had, Mac, for all you've done either. I'd have thought you'd have gone shooting up the ladder by now, in fact. With your head for figures and talent for sorting out the tricky sods. I'd have seen you go way past DI. On to Superintendent, even Detective Chief Superintendent. I can see you as a DCS, easy.'

'Aye. But there's some who can't. Some who never could see me go one step higher than I have.'

'Oh, yes? Who are they, then?'

Was this going in the right direction? Well, not far off it at least. So stick with it, and maybe in a minute or two steer it back on course.

'Well, just the one, if you must know. A certain Detective Chief Superintendent sitting in this very building.' Hey, revelations. Revelations trickling out of the Scottish rock. Never thought I'd see the day.

'What, you don't mean old Detchie? He been blocking your path?'

'Weel, since you're naming a name, yes. Yes, Detective Chief Superintendent Detch has had it in for me ever since I was a beat copper and he was Custody Sergeant at the same nick, the old Mussel Street one.'

'Oh, yes? How did that come about, then?'

Mac did not at once reply.

For a moment Jack thought he had lost him. That his chair would jerk forward and his head go down again to his sheet of figures. If only out of embarrassment at having for once lowered his guard.

But it seemed the silence was no more than a slight hesitation.

'It's a long story, laddie. And one I havna told for many a year.'

'All the same, Mac, I'd like to hear. I've often wondered why you were stuck here when you could have . . .'

'Weel, I called it a long story, and so it is. But its beginning was short and sweet. Or no' so sweet, if you like.'

'Yes?'

Mac gave a grunt of a laugh. A laugh you could still hear the bitterness in.

'Simple enough. One evening on patrol I stopped a man in a car, drunk as could be. I drove him mesel' to the nick to charge him. Drunk driving. His licence like to go, and mebbe a month or two inside. But, when I took him down to the cells to book him in, what should Sergeant Detch, as he was then, say the moment he saw the fellow? What but *Hello, Ginger, what are you doing here*? Did I tell you yon drunk had a fine crop of red hair?'

'No. But go on.'

'Weel, when I told Sergeant Detch the fellow was there because he was dead drunk in charge of a motor vehicle, he just said something like surely there's things friends like us can overlook.'

Jack guessed it then. Mac, however much he and Detchie had been friends in those distant days, was not one to overlook even a minor misdemeanour. Never mind an offence as serious as this Ginger's.

'And, of course,' he said, grabbing the chance to put himself among the law-abiding, 'you said there were some things that could not be overlooked.'

'I did.'

'And you stuck to it? I reckon you would have done. And good luck to you.'

'Aye, I stuck to it. Even when yon Ginger dropped a hint there was a hundred pounds there for me, a hundred pounds at good old pre-inflation value. But it wasna good luck to me, I can tell you. Because Detch was sitting there just above me in rank, then and for ever after. He was the one making out the annual reports, and seeing they looked as black about me as he could make them. In the end, too, he was the one who had me shunted off to this office, little knowing then I was here to stay till I drew my pension.'

Well, well. Fancy old Mac sitting here marooned all these years. And Detective Chief Superintendent Detch, sir, having it in for him like that. And all because of one moment of bloody unrelenting honesty, years and years ago. Makes you think.

Christ, what would I have done in those circs? Back then I was as innocent as Mac was. Innocent? Come on, say it. Honest. I was as honest as Mac then.

Or was I? Hadn't I already once or twice turned a blind eye in payment of a favour, either given or to come? Perhaps I had. Or perhaps that began a bit later. Hard to remember.

The only thing that's clear as day is that I did at some time or other begin. And Mac never did.

He's just sat here, at this desk of his, for years, toiling away at the figures – the figures of how other people have helped themselves from the kitty and lived well out of it – and he's taken it all. The paltry pay. Never having the rank he could easily have got to. The way people have looked down at him.

Yes, the way I look down at him. From a flea's height.

God, yes, and he must be bitter. Bitter as all hell, sitting there quietly adding up, subtracting, whatever it is he does. And knowing he doesn't deserve to be where he is. Thinking it every single day, I dare say. Poor old Mac.

Then, like a purple revealing flash of lightning on the darkest of nights, the thought came to him.

By God, if Mac's so bitter, as he must be, as he is, then surely he won't, despite that Scotch honesty of his, pass up a chance of having his revenge. The chance I could give him. The revenge he'd get by letting Emslie Warnaby get away with a crime Detective Superintendent Detch, sir, would give his ears to be credited with detecting.

And all Mac would have to do is let me walk out of here with that folder under my arm.

He'd be laughing then, old Mac. He'd have done his enemy of old out of the great big triumph of bringing down the almighty boss of Abbotputers plc, and for himself he'd still get credit for nailing Councillor Arthur Symes.

Bloody marvellous.

Mac'll never be able to resist it.

'Listen, mate, how would you like to shaft friend Detch? To shaft him good and proper?'

Mac looked at him.

Suspicion drawing his face into a net of tightness.

'I've got my eye on him,' he said at last, the words dragged slowly out. 'I've had the bugger in my sights for years. He'll no' get away with anything. Not while I'm sitting in this chair.'

He let the chair rock backwards and forwards once or twice. A weighty pendulum.

'Right. And, listen, Mac, I can see a way you could really hurt him now. With no one to know a thing about it. Except you and me.'

Mac said nothing.

Jack took the silence for agreement.

Trust an uptight Scotchman like Mac not to utter an unnecessary word.

'Look, mate, there's something I happen to know. Never mind how. But I can tell you that here in this office, in that pile of stuff from the Fisheries Development Authority, as a matter of fact, there's just one lot of correspondence that could give Detchie the biggest triumph of his career. Probably turn him from head of CID here to Assistant Chief in whatever force was first to grab him. Take him to the bloody top. It's all just in one folder. But when that's whisked away – and here's the cream of the joke – you'll still have a sweet case against Arthur Symes. So you'll be laughing both ways. Laughing. Get it?'

The chair crashed forward.

'Aye, I get it, Jack Stallworthy. What you're proposing, and no doubt there's a good thick handout in it for you, is that I suppress a piece of evidence. Yes? That's it? Yes?'

'Oh, well, yes. Yes, Mac, technically it is. But think of what it'd do to Detective Chief Superintendent Detch. How it would pay him out for everything. Just think of that.'

Mac MacAllister stood up from behind his papers-strewn desk. Shot up.

'Get out,' he said. 'Get out of this office and never show your face in here again. Because if you do, I'll see you're kicked out of the force, kicked so hard you'll never know where you bounced. Now, go. Get out. Get out.'

Chapter Eleven

July the first. Jack saw the date on the wall calendar as he plonked himself down at his desk that new Monday morning.

Jesus, I hadn't realized we've even got to the end of June. End of June already. God, what's happened to the days? I been in a sort of stupor ever since . . . Ever since sodding Mac did that to me.

Come on, admit it. Face it. You got to, sooner or later. Ever since Mac MacAllister kicked me out of his office, and, worse, threatened to have me kicked off the force. And he would, too. Bloody iron from the neck down.

And ever since then I've not really been thinking. Didn't dare really think. Couldn't.

Couldn't even let myself think of how, somehow, I might still get at that fucking blue folder. There, bang in the heart of Mac's office. *Get out . . . and never show your face in here again.*

And now it's three bloody months since April the first and that bet. Weeks since sodding Emslie Warnaby gave me his fucking deadline. July the sixteenth. Just over a fortnight away. And no bloody further forward than I was when I began.

Worse even. Haven't I, one way and another, blocked off every possible avenue to that bloody file? Every possible avenue? Alerted old Ma Alexander. Alerted bloody Horatio Bottomley. Alerted, worst of all, Mac himself.

Only good thing is Warnaby's bit-of-the-other seems to have given up phoning now. Thought she'd drive me wild, yack-yack-yacking on.

He'd like a progress report.

It's been a week since I spoke to you.

Mr Stallworthy, will I have to go to that wretched Italian-y hairdresser again?

I did ask you to keep us fully informed.

Is your wife there, Mr Stallworthy? Can't you speak?

July the first. Christ, and it'll be Lily's birthday in no time at all. The tenth. And haven't even thought what I'm going to get her. Not that she's not been hinting. But she was doing that in May. She was doing it straight after Christmas, come to that. And what the hell it was she wanted I still can't remember.

Can I fake it with a box of chocs? A really-really big . . . Have to be a lot classier than what I had to dish out to old Ma Alexander. More expensive. Lot more expensive. If I can find anything looking as if it cost a bundle. And Lil will know all right. Know to a penny how much. Trust her.

No – the thought struck him like a solid fist in the abdomen – to hell with bloody chocolates, what I'm going to do is: I'm going to tell her. Tell her. Tell her what's there waiting for her. Ko fucking Samui. Calm fucking Seas Hotel.

Never mind if it's next to impossible to get at that folder. I'll do it somehow in the end. I'll bloody do it, and then I'll take my Lil off to her paradise.

Never mind high-and-mighty Emslie Warnaby saying I wasn't to tell anyone. *If I get any hint you've spoken to anyone, even to your wife* . . . Well, fuck Warnaby. I'll tell Lily what's in store for her, for us. And that'll be a better birthday present than anything I could buy for her. Than whatever it was she kept on hinting about.

Because I've got to do it. Get that file. I've still got to do it, however much I've blown every fucking chance I've had so far. I've got to get it. And I'm going to. I'm going to take Lily to live out the rest of our days in bloody luxury. On Ko sodding Samui.

What I'll do is: on the birthday night I'll take her out somewhere posh for dinner. And tell her.

So that evening after a tiring day chasing up the theft of a stone gargoyle from the Abbey church – the Vicar had only just noticed it had gone but was threatening letters to the *Argus* from all his congregation if action was not taken pronto – as soon as he had got in he made his suggestion to Lily.

'Listen, your birthday Wednesday week, ain't it?'

'Jack, you remembered.'

He registered the brightening eyes that were saying, *What am I going to get?* and hastily went on.

'Course I remembered. And, listen, this is what I thought. How about if we go out to dinner that night? Somewhere really nice. And, while we're there, I'll tell you about what it is I've got for you.'

'Oh, Jack, lovely. Lovely. But what is it?'

'Shan't say.'

The look of give-me, give-me redoubled.

'Oh, come on. Let's have just a hint. Is it . . .? Is it something like what I sort of mentioned before?'

'No, my girl, ask away till you're blue in the face, I ain't saying. 'Cept that it's special. About as special as you can get, matter of fact. But we'll go somewhere really-really nice for you to hear about it. Promise.'

'But, Jack, won't you give me the tiniest hint? Not even if, later on, I'm really-really nice to you . . . Or now even, if you like.'

Her eyes went meaningfully to the doorway and the stairs beyond it.

'Jesus, you'd try anything, wouldn't you? See if you can wheedle something out of a bloke. But not this time, my girl. This time what I've got in mind's too good just to tell you between the sheets. No, at dinner. Wednesday week. I thought that place, Romero's. You liked it when we went there before.'

'Oh, come on, Jack. That was months and months ago. There's nicer places than that now. More exciting.'

'Oh, yes?'

What the hell was she going to suggest? Whatever it was it'd cost a bomb. Knowing Lily.

'Well, f'rinstance there's that new place built right out into the sea, out Grinton way.'

'What's that, then?'

But the place did seem to ring a bell. For some reason. Not that he had any idea what it was called or anything.

'Jack, you know. It was in the *Argus*. In "Round and About". Saying it was the new spot all the in-crowd were going to. I'm sure I showed you.'

'Dare say you did, love. But I certainly never took a blind bit of notice.'

'Oh, Jack, you are awful. It's the Costa Loadsa. Everyone's going there. Expensive, but dead classy. Sort of Spanish décor and those flamenco singers an' all.'

But he had heard of the Costa Loadsa. And the name sent a sudden sinking feeling into his gut.

The place might be a mecca for the *in-crowd*, as Lil had said, but the fact was it was owned by Harry Hook. And no detective who'd got his position in CID to think about dare be seen in it. Never mind, however much you made a bloody performance of laying out cash for every penny on the bill, someone was going to hear you'd been there. And decide you were in the pay of Abbotsport's number one criminal outfit.

And, come to that, if there was one detective in the whole of Abbotsport Constabulary who couldn't afford to have the least hint of any more dirt being known about him it was Jack Stallworthy. Detective Sergeant Stallworthy whose evil reputation had produced a nice dinner-party giggle for Mr Emslie Warnaby, head of Abbotputers plc, and his tenant, Chief Inspector Richard Parkinson, Staff Officer to the Chief Constable.

No, the Costa Loadsa was out. Especially just now when one big piece of dirty business still had to be pulled off.

Some of his feelings must have shown in his face. A hell of a lot of them, in fact. Because Lily, who never normally took much notice of what he looked like, was giving him a sharp glance.

'What's up, Jackie? Worried about the prices at the Costa Loadsa? But, cheer up, it's only the once. And it'll be a lovely evening. Just right. For whatever you've got to tell me, leaning across a candlelit table. Oh, I do think it's romantic of you. Really. And, if that's the mood you're in, perhaps we'd better see right away what we can do about it, eh?'

Another meaningful look at the foot of the stairs.

Well, to hell with being linked with Harry Hook's mob. I'll bloody take her to the place. Or perhaps in a day or two she'll have changed her mind . . .

He pushed himself, briskly enough, out of his chair, began heading for the stairs.

And then the phone rang.

He swung round and went over to it.

''lo.'

'Mr Stallworthy?'

That voice. Back again.

'What do you want now? I've told you. Told you it's no use you ringing and ringing. I'm working on it. Working on it. And that's that.'

'Yes, you did tell me. And I stopped calling. But I haven't heard anything from you all the same, have I? We aren't seeing the results of all that working on it you were always talking about, have we? And we're doing our part, you know. The deeds making you sole proprietor of the Calm Seas Hotel, Ko Samui, are all drawn up. But we've heard nothing from you. Not a word. And Mr Warn— And time's getting short. Very short. I hope you remember the date we gave you.'

'Of course I fuck— Yes, yes. I remember. And you'll have it by then. I've got to get it for you, haven't I? Got to. So just stop bloody going on at me.'

He slammed the handset down.

'Whoever was that?' Lily said. 'You sounded really fed up.'

'I bloody was.'

He went back to his chair. Let himself thump down into it.

'Let's have some supper, love. I don't feel . . . Perhaps later on.'

'Just as you like. You men. Never know what you're feeling one moment to another. Still, we can have supper now if you want. It's all cold. A couple of those nice Melton Mowbray pies I bought at the supermarket, and a packet of that salad with the red leaves. And there's some of that nice ice-cream in the fridge, the sort with nuts.'

Anna Foxton did not call again before Jack took Lily to the Costa Loadsa for her birthday treat. But he had felt the pressure on him every bit as much as if she had rung every evening. Perhaps even more so. Because he knew on Lily's birthday he was going to tell her –

all right, at the Costa Loadsa, if that was what she wanted – that her dream of paradise on Ko Samui would come true.

And, unless he could get hold of the blue folder in that old cupboard in Mac MacAllister's room – had Mac locked it? pocketed that new, bright shiny key? – his promise was going to be so much hot air. Drive himself sick worrying away at the problem as he had, the fact still was that he had not come up with any way at all of getting into that room Mac had turned him out of.

Mad ideas had come into his head. And gone. He could go up to Headquarters very early one day, before even Mrs Alexander and her cleaning ladies had arrived, take with him a crowbar or a sledgehammer – 'the big key' as they said when they went to get a real villain out of his bed – and smash his way in.

Only how could I ever get past the night-duty constable carrying a bloody crowbar? Don't be stupid.

He would burgle Headquarters itself. Shin up some drainpipe like poor old Jinkie Morrison, get in at one of the Fraud Investigation Branch windows and force that old cupboard if he had to.

Christ, don't be a fucking idiot. You couldn't climb up anywhere, not in your condition. Think how sodding puffed you got just going up those winding stone stairs in the Abbey church to look at where that bloody ridiculous gargoyle had been yanked off its base. Anything to keep the Vicar half-way happy.

He would steal a heavy vehicle from somewhere

and ram-raid the Headquarters goods entrance, wher-ever it was round the back of the big building.

Don't be a damn fool. You don't even know if there is a goods entrance.

Day after day he had sat at his desk, thinking and thinking. If anyone came up and talked he had scowled them into silence. He had totally ceased going out and looking for collars. He had failed to collect a single penny to put in the Cadbury's Roses tin under the now almost flowerless aubrietia.

What's it matter? he had thought. Either I get fucking Emslie Warnaby's big-big handout, one hotel, island for the living in, or I don't. If I do, then a few quid extra won't make a blind bit of difference. And if I don't, I might as well just forget about the whole thing. Put in my papers and go on living where we are now, scraping by. A pair of sodding old-age pensioners.

'Stallworthy! Get your bloody arse over here.'

Jesus, the Guv'nor. He been yelling at me for hours?

'Yes, sir.'

'Vicar's just been on the blower. Any progress on that gargoyle?'

In fact, he had a damn good notion of who had done that job. His old school friend, or enemy, Herbie Cuddy, fat little twig on the ever-spreading Hook family tree. Herbie had done a lot of pinching lead from church roofs just after he'd left school when there'd been money in that. Most likely someone had told him now there was a market for old statues, and he'd gone back to his former ways. No confining Herbie to one well-loved MO like Jinkie Morrison. His line ought to have been anything to do with the shipping. Pirate blood in the Hook tribe still coming out. But he was willing, too, to climb any risky height to help himself to what he thought worthwhile.

Even back at school, all that long ago, he nearly got away when I had that gang coming to beat him up. Got his paws on to the top of the playground wall before we pulled him down. But why bother chasing old Herbie? There's other things to think of. Like July the sixteenth and what Emslie Warnaby's put on offer.

'Progress? Well, ain't much to make is there, guv?'

'Never mind, *is there*. Get out there and give me something to tell that bloody vicar next time he's on at me. Hasn't Herbie Cuddy got form for something like that? Pinching church-roof lead? Go and chase him up. You never know, that gargoyle may actually be down to him.'

'Yes, sir.'

At least out and about – though he hadn't much intention of actually trying to find Herbie – he'd be out of the way of the Guv'nor. And could think.

Though neither that day nor any other did any of his thinking produce the slightest sign of an answer.

In the evenings it was the same. He gave Lily a hard time. He knew he was doing it, and he hated himself for it. But he lacked the will to do anything else. So he sat staring in silence at whatever she was watching on TV, travel show, nature film – 'if it's not one of those nasties, insects, snakes and all that' – and tried to find some solution to his problem. However fantastic.

Hire a helicopter, drop down on to Headquarters roof . . .

Jesus, I must be going raving bonkers.

But, on the morning of July the tenth itself, table for two booked at the Costa Loadsa, abruptly for no reason at all a plan that seemed totally reasonable came into his head. Why it had come to him all of a sudden after so much fruitless worrying he was unable to guess. But just a few words Horatio Bottomley had said to him, weeks ago as he had barged his way past to go into Mac's office the very day he had first seen the blue folder, had suddenly triggered something off.

When he ever out, Sergeant, 'cept coffee break an' tea break?

At the time he had barely heard what the fellow had said. It had been just an answer to his casually asking if Mac was in. But deep down he must have stored away the words, if only because they had confirmed too bloody well everything he knew about Mac MacAllister, his obsession with his figures, his insistence on security, his damned regular habits.

But no one, he thought now – he was driving lethargically on his way to work – had habits as absolutely regular as Mac's in every particular. Even Mac was human. And humans sometimes had to pee. And even occasionally to be away from their desks yet longer.

So, if he could just contrive to keep watch outside

the Fraud Investigation Branch until he could catch Mac leaving, then there would only be Horatio Bottomley to cope with. And, for all the failure of his attempt in the car in the rain to put into the fellow's head the idea of making a few quid by letting that blue folder walk, he didn't think he'd have much trouble barging past him and into Mac's own room.

Mac with his *Get out of this office and never show your face in here again.*

Then, once in there, with the door swung closed behind him and Mac safely out of the way, if only for a few minutes, it'd just be a matter – if that cupboard was open – of stooping down and whipping out the folder. Stuff it under his jacket, and in less than half a minute come out again to say to old Horatio *Mac not in, then? I'll come back later.*

And if the cupboard was locked, with that shiny new key of Mac's? Well, it was a bloody decrepit piece of furniture, and surely he could force its doors. Grab something from Mac's desk top. Even use one of his own keys as a lever. Front door one. Big enough, when all's said and done.

Then I'd have it. The blue folder. Straight up to Anna Foxton's flat, Seaview Mansions, up above the port. And *I told you you'd get it and here it sodding well is.* Slam it down on the table there and wait for that reward. Jesus, I could actually show those hotel deeds to Lil tonight, over the table at the poncy Costa Loadsa, candle-lit table.

The reward. All right, the bribe.

But, sole proprietor of that hotel at last and with

the air tickets safely in my pocket, fat lot I'd care if I was seen at a Harry Hook restaurant. It'd be wham in my papers, quick as you like. Take what leave's due to me. And away. Ko bloody Sammy here we come. April Cottage goodbye. Never mind the lost deposit. Never mind getting hold of that video *The Lovely World of Lilies*. Lily herself could have all the lilies she wanted out there. Great big blazing tropical ones make whatever I might grow in Devon look like so many little doll's house lilies-of-the-valley.

He almost changed direction and drove straight up to Headquarters to begin that crafty watch on the Fraud Investigation Branch door right away. The door he had once, very early one morning, the whole building deserted except for Mrs Alexander, almost got the right key into. Christ, all that seemed years ago now, somehow.

But caution prevailed.

No, no. Go into the nick as per usual. Sit there a bit. Smoke a fag. Then sign out 'on inquiries' and buzz up to Headquarters. Have to be a bit cunning in working out how to keep watch on that door, of course. Maybe there'd be somewhere between Mac's office and the nearest toilet where it'd be possible to stay nicely out of sight. Or there could be somewhere any officer in the force had a right to be. Just waiting for something, face to the wall, looking at a notice-board. Anything. But keeping a bloody sharp eye out for Mac MacAllister hurrying along to have a pee.

*

Up at Headquarters within an hour of putting himself in position he got his chance. Moseying along towards Fraud Investigation Branch, he had abruptly remembered, as he got near, that precisely opposite there was a door, almost exactly similar to the Branch one, except it had no tight-security lock and the neat perspex plaque beside it said *Waiting Room*.

In a second he was inside.

And – hey, some real luck at last – in the door, precisely opposite the Fraud Investigation office, a nice little glass panel. That reinforced stuff, criss-crossed wire. So I can kick my heels in here for as long as it takes, and, standing well back, have the door opposite under constant obbo.

All right, if they bring some civilian along to wait here till Mac's ready to see him, or for them to see someone else in some other nearby office, I'll maybe have to shove off. But, if I do, there's always this afternoon when I can come back again. Or, worst come to the worst, tomorrow or the next day. Or the next. Pity I won't have the hotel deeds, airline tickets, to show Lily tonight. But I'll be able to make that promise all right, and know it'll come true. I've still got best part of a week before Emslie Warnaby's ruddy deadline. Even passing up the weekend, that's plenty of time.

He leant up against the far wall and settled down to wait. Sooner or later even iron-man Mac'll need a pee. And then . . .

Bloody ridiculous I never properly took in this

place was here. Even when I was stood just outside first thing in the morning when I was mad with hurry sorting through Ma Alexander's big bunch of keys I never looked at the door behind me. Still, no wonder, really, when I was peering like buggery at those tags you could almost but not quite make out. Or trying the blanks one after another . . . And then Ma Alexander creeping up and *Mr Stallworth! What you doing?.*

Christ, the trouble I've had over this fucking folder when you think of it. And it should have been dead simple. Sodding Emslie Warnaby thought it'd be. In some ways he was right, too. Provided it was okay for anyone to go about inside Headquarters – dead easy if you had a warrant card to show at the entrance – then the job should have been a doddle. Just find out where the stuff from the Fisheries Development Authority was, suss out the only blue folder in the whole lot. Tuck it under your coat and away. Piece of cake.

So it seemed, first off, when I spotted the folder there in the cupboard with the doors leaning open like that. And that was when all I'd been hoping for was to get an idea of the lie of the land.

Jesus, I was within a couple of yards of the damn thing at that moment. But Mac sitting there, looking at me like I was going to snitch his precious Petticoat Tail shortbreads. No go. Not the ghost of a chance.

And after that it had all been hell. First that sodding fiasco with Ma Alexander – lost a good friend there, too, really-really big box of chocs or no – then that stupid business with woolly-headed old Horatio, sitting there in the motor pretending it was pissing down too hard to drive and getting totally nowhere trying to get the stupid sod to see sense.

Then, worst of the lot, that idiotic attempt somehow to get at Mac himself. And yet that might have come off. It looked bloody like it would at one moment. Him all of a sudden letting his hair down about Detective Chief Superintendent Detch, sir. If the sodding Scotchman had been any sort of a red-blooded bugger he'd have leapt at the chance of doing Detchie down good and proper. And, instead, it had been that *I'll see you're kicked out of the force, kicked so hard you'll never know where you bounced.*

A great jolt of humiliated rage overcame him again at the thought.

No one should ever have to listen to anything like that. God, how I'd have liked to punch the Scotch sod right in the face. And what I'd had to do was just turn away and walk out. Out of that fucking office, going right past those shelves of documents. I could have put out a hand and jerked the sodding blue folder out. That near. That fucking far.

But at least I never gave Mac an idea of exactly what it was that would have kicked Detchie right up his fat arse. Least he don't know it's just that one blue folder. So when I snitch it at last – and that'll be in a few minutes, hour at the most, well, even two – bloody Mac'll never know anything's gone. And then Mr Emslie Warnaby'll make me the sole proprietor the Calm fucking Seas Hotel, Ko fucking Samui.

And Lily'll have her heart's desire.

Sooner or later, either just now or even on another day before long, Iron Man Mac'll have to break down and go for a pee like a sodding human being. And when he does . . .

Christ, he is. Door opposite opening. It's him already.

He ducked down well out of sight. Began counting up to ten. But before he had got to seven heard the Fraud Investigation door thump back closed. He straightened up again. Hurried across to the glass panel. Peered round.

And, yes, Mac just turning the corner.

Right. Here we go.

Two steps across the corridor. Push open the Fraud Investigation door. Old Horatio sitting there at his desk, looking as if he's been there just like that, stubby brown fingers dipping and darting at the computer keys, since the last time I was in here. *Get out of this office and never show your face in here again.*

Just give him a muttered 'Good morning.'

Mac's own door in front of me. Push.

In, in, in.

The cupboard. And its doors not locked. Still pushed just a little open by the mass of stuff on the shelves. Boxes, files and whatnot. And, yes, just exactly where it's always been, the half-inch strip of pale blue card. The folder. The prize.

It was harder to pull out from between the crammed files than he had expected. He stooped, got a better grip, gave a good hard tug.

Two hands descended on to his shoulders. Stubby-fingered brown hands.

'No, Mr Stallworthy. No, all them papers is evidence. You can't come in here an' take things like that away. Not without Mr Mac says you can.'

He stood up, pushing the fellow off, leaving the shiny pale blue folder where it was, jammed in place.

Turning to face Horatio, he could feel the sweat in a heavy line of drops all across his forehead.

'Look, it's nothing,' he managed to get out.

Christ, his heart was going like a trip-hammer. Thud, thud, thud.

'Listen, mate, there's nothing that matters in that file there. It's just—'

God, what 'just' was it? What could it be?

'Look, it's only something personal. Something a mate of mine asked me to look for. The damn file's got in among that stuff by mistake, and – and it's making life difficult for my mate, not being able to look up what's in it. It's nothing more than that.'

'Then, Mr Stallworthy, you better tell all that to Mr Mac.'

The poor sod. He isn't even daring to look me in the face. Knows I'm bloody lying. He ain't even looking at the cupboard. Eyes fixed on the floor. Expression on his face ashamed as if he'd peed in his pants.

'Oh, hell with it, mate. I – I'll come back sometime and talk to Mac. Why you have to . . .'

He barged his way out. Almost ran across the outer office. Turned sharply the moment he was through the door and into the corridor, and, walking at maximum pace, made his way – sweat now clinging everywhere on his body – round the nearest corner. Out of sight. Into safety.

Chapter Twelve

He felt lousy. Appallingly lousy. He stood where he
was, a few steps round the corner from the corridor
leading to Mac's office just by the head of the stairs,
clutching the red plastic-covered rail of the metal
banister with both hands.

His heart was still thudding away. The sweat all
over his skin had mysteriously turned in an instant
from slobberingly warm to coldly clammy.

Christ, he thought after a while, rising to a sliver of
inward irony, never mind pretending every time I've
come here it's to see the doc. Maybe I should've been
seeing him for real.

The thought helped him to recover a little.

He set off down the stairs, keeping a sweat-damp
hand sliding squeakily along the red plastic.

At last he blundered his way out into the fresh air.
He stood breathing in deeply, and bit by bit felt himself
getting back to his normal state.

Not that that's been anything to write home about
recently, he said to himself.

He set off then to his car.

It was only when he was sitting at the wheel,

before he had even taken out his key, that the full realization of what his situation now was came over him.

I've bloody fucked it up again. I've comprehensively fucked up the last hope I had. The one reasonable last chance. No possible question of doing what perhaps old Horatio Bottomley thinks I will, going to Mac and saying all I was doing in there was trying to help out a mate. No, I've been banned by Mac from his office for ever. And how.

And, truth to tell, however bleeding humiliating that was, it was with good reason.

The only plus, for what it's worth, is I don't think old Horatio cottoned on to which file it was I was trying to get at. My back was to him when he came in like that. He can't have seen exactly what I was doing. So, even if he's told Mac what he found me at, Mac won't be able to go and get that folder out, look it over and find out I was trying to get Emslie Warnaby out of a big hole, and – he'll guess – being paid a hell of a lot to do it.

Because the long and short of it is now that I'm never going to get that blue folder.

It's over. Finished.

Sitting there, in the familiar seat of the car, the wheel in front of him, the windscreen slightly fuzzed with summer dust, he felt a sweep of relief.

After all, he was not going to be the one who in the end had taken a huge backhander. He was not going to have finally shat on everything he'd done since he joined the police.

Since before that even, since that day long ago at school when I detected Herbie Cuddy. No, at least I won't have turned out to be the total opposite of what I should have been all along in the CID. A good detective. At least I'm not going to become a bad detective.

Or not the very baddest sort of detective. A bad detective perhaps I am already. Anyhow some of the time.

But now I'm free of that really-really shitty piece of evil-doing.

Dare say I'll go on in the old way over the little things, right up until I hand in my papers. Hard to stop. And we'll need the cash.

By Christ, we'll need every penny we can get. If I'm to complete the purchase of April Cottage, even with a big, big bank loan.

And April Cottage . . .

That's what I'll have to tell old Lil tonight. It won't be, *Hey, this is my big secret, I'm the proud owner, as from today, of a certain hotel going by the name of the Calm Seas, on a certain island, to wit Ko Samui.* No, she'll never know how near she got to her dream life, old Lil. Not, anyhow, if I can manage to keep my big trap shut. What she'll have to content herself with after all is *Hey, I've done it, my girl, I've bought us one of those houses in Devon we saw last summer. April Cottage. That's where we're going to live when I chuck it in at the nick. April Cottage. What d'you think of that?* Throw in that video *The Lovely World of Lilies*, promise her every kind they've put in it. Once I've found a copy.

And, damn it, it shouldn't be too bad down there. In April Cottage.

Only, fact is, Lil'll take some convincing. Wish to God the bloody telly had broken down that night. The night she saw the programme about bloody Ko bloody Samui.

He yanked the car key from his pocket, thrust it home, jerked it round. The engine rattled into life.

It was only as he parked behind the nick that, vaguely turning over in his mind how he would spend the rest of the day – anybody he could make a few quid out of? – he realized that not only had he got to tell Lily what her future was going to be but he had also got to tell Emslie Warnaby he was not going to get his precious blue folder.

Oh, let the bugger wait. Don't owe him a sodding thing, do I? When that bitch of his rings again – and won't be long till she does, I'll bet – I'll let her know she and her big boss lover will have to find someone else to do their dirty work. Or take the consequences. Why not?

He cut off the engine, climbed out, locked up and headed for the CID Room.

Might, after all, have a word with Herbie Cuddy – if he's at home – about the old Vicar's pet gargoyle. Got to keep the Guv'nor sweet now.

*

The musicians were going at it full blast. Which, as they were mostly strumming away at guitars, was not as noisy as it might have been. But noisy enough. Especially as almost everybody at the tables was adding to it by shouting at the tops of their voices, let alone the girl singing full blast into a mike.

Something Jack supposed was flamenco. Whatever that was. At least a great deal of castanet-clicking was involved. Plus heel-stamping. And fiery glances.

A maitre-d', very Spanishy in looks, ushered them to their table. Little heavily gold-embroidered jacket. Tight black pants, showing all he'd got in the way of tight little bum.

Lots of 'Señor' and 'Señora', too, and "Ave a nice evening.'

'I certainly mean to, it's my birthday,' Lil chirped up at once.

Trust her.

'Ah, many 'appy returns, Señora. It ees twenty-one, yes?' Stupid ponce.

Lily did her sort of bashful look.

'Well, just a teensy bit over, shall we say?'

'But we must finda the special treat for the Señora. Champagne. Tonight you must drinka champagne.'

He waltzed off.

And fuck-all said about, 'On the house-a.'

But, truth to tell, old Lil don't look all that much over twenty-one. Or not over thirty-one. And that's a fact.

Better tell her so. Going to need all the credit I can earn meself. Once it comes to April Cottage time.

Compliment to Lily delivered, more or less – 'my little English rose, still in full bloom' – he looked at the great big menu they had each been handed. Picture of a charging bull on the front.

He skimmed down the list of dishes.

Christ, that bull ain't the only thing that's charging. And to think I'm risking my reputation being here at all. A bloody Harry Hook property. Not that I've got all that much of a reputation, if what that CI Parkinson told Emslie sodding Warnaby's right. But I'm not safely out of the force yet. So the cleaner I seem to look the better.

Still, if this place is what Lil fancies . . . Give her a good time while I can. 'Cos the tough times ain't so very far away. When it's no longer Detective Sergeant Jack Stallworthy, and the odd few quid coming in left-handed – pity I couldn't get hold of Herbie this afternoon, been a treat to squeeze something out of him – but just plain Mr Stallworthy and drawing your pitiful pension from the Post Office every Monday morning.

Meanwhile, here's Lil doing the usual with the menu, choosing and changing her mind and choosing again and changing her mind again. She could have done that at Romero's, where we went before, and half the price.

Well, never mind . . . Last time she gets a night out like this, I dare say.

So when am I going to do it? Bring out the cheery surprise. *We're going to live in Devon, me old duck. So say goodbye to all them dreams of tropical sunshine,*

*brown-skinned servants bobbing and smiling, and nothing
to do all day.*

No, you ain't finished doing the washing-up yet
awhile, my girl. Not never, come to that.

And she won't like hearing that. But she'll just have
to put up with it. Price of having a hubby who's said
no to a big, big bribe. Thank God.

Could I duck out of telling her, though? For tonight,
anyway?

The waiter came up. Another black-trousered bum-
flasher. Bringing the champagne. Making a big performance out of pouring it from a great height. Stupid
prat.

'And the Señora is ready to order? The Señor also?'

'I'll have the same as the wife. Whatever it is.'

'You'll be lucky. I haven't made up my mind yet.'

But in the end, with more than a bit of help from
Bum-flasher, she did decide what it was going to be,
and the waiter lit the candles on the table – there were
candles, there would be – and went prancing off.

At once Lily leaned across towards him.

'Well now, what's this big secret you've been keeping from your Lily? Speak up, me lad. I've waited long
enough.'

So much for ducking out.

He felt a sheen of sweat come up on his face.

But perhaps that's just the white shirt, black tie and
DJ. Truth is, I'm that much thicker round the neck
than I used to be. Anyhow, whichever . . . I've got to
do it now.

Give her the old cocky smile. Used to work. Years

ago. Probably what did it in the end. Got her to say, *Yes.*

'Yeah. Well, it's like this. You know this is the last time you'll be celebrating your birthday with Detective Sergeant Stallworthy, don't you?'

'No? Who else will I celebrate it with, if it ain't you, Jackie boy?'

Well, that's a fucking good start.

'No, no. You know what I mean. I'm going to be off the force sometime in the year ahead, ain't I?'

'Off the—'

Oh, God, she got it arsy-versy again?

But, no.

'Oh, you mean when you retire. About time, too, I say. It's doing you no good, you know. Chasing about after common criminals all the time.'

'Yeah, you're right. I'll be glad to be shot of it, tell the truth. Used to be meat and drink to me, it did. Nothing I liked more, but—'

'Hey, *nothing you liked more*. Ain't there something you liked more than your old police? Something sitting right here in front of you this minute?'

Another boo-boo. Christ, this is going about as badly as it could do.

But she's right, all the same. Was something I liked more than the police. The little darling sitting right opposite. Did from the moment I set eyes on her. Still bloody do.

Arrival of Bum-flasher with first course. And more smarm. 'This ees ver' ver' special. The Señora will love this. The Señor also.'

God knows what the muck is, but if it makes my Lily happy . . .

So put up with all the Spanish bowing and smiling. Even try and look as if I think it's not a lot of fucking cobblers. At least it'll give me a chance to get off on the right foot again, once little Bum-flasher's on his way.

"Ope all ees to your satisfaction, Señora.'

And off he goes. Wiggle, wiggle, wiggle.

Straight away he leant across the candle-lit cloth towards her. If it's got to be done . . .

'Right. Well, when I am retired we won't want to stay in Abbotsport, will we?'

'I should hope not. You know I hate the place. Always have, even when I was just a kid. Nothing ever happening. No life. And the cold. Even in summer. And as for winter . . .'

Quick. Get in. Or she'll be on to bloody Ko Samui in a moment.

'Okay, so what do you think about Devon? Glorious Devon, right? Remember those nice little houses we looked at last summer, just outside Torquay?'

'Not sure I do. You dragged me round so many places.'

Yes, and who's been dragging me off to bloody Ko Samui every five minutes ever since? But, quick, don't let her mind drift off to that bloody tropical paradise.

'No, you must remember those houses. On that little estate. Nice little places, all named after the months of the year.'

'Oh, yeah. Yeah, I remember those, couple of 'em

160

called something else, weren't they? Spring Cottage, Christmas Cottage. Bit small, I thought. Hey, you know what I saw in the *Argus* yesterday?'

What the hell was she on about now? Just like her. Batty-brained, always was.

'I ain't talking about the bloody *Argus*. I'm talking about those cottages in Devon.'

'Yeah, I know. But this is important, Jack. It's to do with us when you retire. I've been meaning to say about it ever since yesterday. You know what it said in the *Argus*? In the business pages, it was.'

'The business pages? You don't read the business pages. You ain't got the least idea what any of that's about. Nor have I, come to that.'

'Oh, yes, I know all that. It was just what I happened to see when I was looking for the stars. See what my future was.'

And I know what you'd have found there, my girl. Always do. A future lolling in the sun on bloody Ko Samui.

But better humour her. Need to keep her sweet just now. If ever I did.

'Well, what was it you saw reading the business pages? My little financial wizard.'

'Oh, go on. You know, I can't make head or tail of all that. But this is what I did see. *Abbotputers Shares Jump*. It was a big headline. Don't know what that was all about, something to do with some big American computer firm. Didn't understand it at all. But what I did think is: Jack, why do we go on putting all the money into that tin in the garden? Why didn't we buy some of those whatsits – shares? Abbotputers shares. We could of made a killing. P'raps we still could.'

Oh, God, how to explain to little bird brain.

He gave a sigh.

'Because, my darling, everything what goes in that tin is naughty money. Maybe not very naughty money, but naughty enough. Anyone come along and want to know if I been bunged the odd wedge, then they only got to look at our bank account, see we've bought a whole packet of shares in Abbotputers. Never mind then how much they'd jumped, we'd be the ones for the high jump, I can tell you.'

'Oh. Oh, yes. I never thought of that.'

'So let me go on with what I was saying, yes?'

'Yeah, what were you saying? Oh, I know. Those bungalows with the funny names. Can't say I much—'

Quick. Stop her. Say something, or it'll be too late.'

'Yeah, you got it. The names of the months, and there weren't no November Cottage neither. Just Autumn. But you said at the time they'd suit us just perfect. Well, this is the news. Your birthday present. Plus a little something more to come.'

Oh, it's okay. I've hooked her again. That give-me light in her little eyes.

Whizz on.

'Well, thing is, the other day – well, it was April, April the first, really – I got lucky with a horse. Called April Fool. One of the lads in CID had said something about me being an April fool, and I thought it was a kind of omen. Anyhow, it worked. I put something on.

Well, a hell of a lot, as a matter of fact. Some spondu-licks I'd just got lucky over. And April Fool came in at sevens. So I had enough to put down the deposit on one of those bunga— on one of those little cottages. And April Cottage was still going. So I've bought it. Bought it, all bar fixing up a loan on the rest of the price. April Cottage, how about that?'

For a moment it seemed to hang in the balance.

But then the enthusiasm he had managed to put into telling her paid off.

'You mean you've bought a house? For me? Oh, Jack, you are good. I mean, even if it . . .'

She was doing her best to make him feel good. He knew it in a deep corner of his mind. It was not all that often she put him totally first. Only really when he was in bed with the flu or something. Then she would do anything for him. The nicest side of her coming out.

Like it was now.

'Yeah, well,' he said, 'I think we could really make something of the place. I mean, I know it's only just been built and it's all pretty rough round there. But that'll improve. When there's grass put down on the verges of that entrance road an' all that. And the garden's great, our garden. Not too big, not too small. I thought I'd put in a lot of lilies. Lilies for my Lily. Right?'

'Oh, Jack . . . Jack, thank you. Thank you. What a birthday.'

'Twenty-one today, eh?'

He lifted his glass, drank to her. To April Cottage. To a life after the police.

And, in secret, to his own life for the rest of his police time. The life of a good detective.

Well, a not-too-bad detective.

Chapter Thirteen

It was only the next evening when Jack's world, seemingly – when he had paid the Costa Loadsa's massive bill – safely set on a secure course, was turned in a moment upside down.

He had had a day of mixed fortunes. In the morning he had gone out on an aggravated burglary case, a woman battered and tied up while a couple of young tearaways ransacked the house. The place was up near Anna Foxton's block of flats, and, for a moment, he had considered stopping there and, if Emslie Warnaby's svelte little mistress was at home, telling her straight out that he was no longer in the business of being bribed. But second thoughts prevailed.

No, let the little bitch wait. She'll be ringing up soon enough. *He would welcome a full report.* Well, he'll get his report then, and it'll be a sight fuller than he'll like.

At the scene of the burglary, going round talking to the neighbours, he had got from a sleepless old lady not a bad description of two youngsters she had seen running past the lamp-post opposite, lugging between them a big brown holdall. Both white, one dark-haired, the other blond. The dark one, she had said, was wearing a black leather jacket with a word in big white letters on it, a word that looked like *Raider*. Nothing wrong with the old lady's eyesight; he'd checked. And one of the skinnier lad's arms, the one nearer her, had looked as if it was withered.

Back at the nick, half an hour going through the files had thrown up a neat description of one Mortimer Brown, known as Morty, with a withered arm and a single conviction under the Football (Offences) Act 1991. Not one of the world's most dangerous criminals. A swift visit to Mortimer Brown's address – in the crime-rich St Oswald Estate, where else? – had given him a sweet collar. Towered over by his irate mum, naughty Morty almost at once identified his tougher friend, Raider – 'I told you to have nothing to do with that boy, but you never listen to a word your mother says, do you?' – and snivellingly claimed it was this mate of his who had kept the loot. Once Morty had been dealt with, slamming the *Raider* on that black leather jacket against a wall a couple of times had produced the brown holdall from – guess where – the attic of the house. Beginning-in-crime Raider with a lot to learn from Jinkie Morrison.

And in the holdall, besides all the goods, there was something over two hundred pounds in cash. Half of which there had been no need to hand over as evidence.

The afternoon had not gone so swimmingly. He had decided to have another go at Herbie Cuddy. Little though he wanted to.

Tramping up the path to the house – garden wall crudely knocked down to let a wreck of an old van in – he felt his dislike of the fellow redoubled by the sight of the straggle of sour and neglected plants fighting for life in what remained of the garden. But at least when he hammered at the door Herbie opened it.

He was no naughty Morty to get hauled over the coals by his mum, however, nor was he a Raider to cave in after being slammed against a wall a couple of times. He stood squarely blocking the doorway. Look of disgusted contempt on his round-as-a-football head. A football beginning to lose its pumped-in air, topped by a frizzle of blondish hair. Two little blue squinting eyes. A tiny mouth pinched up in a permanent wet kiss.

'Bloody Jack Stallworthy. What you want?'

'What I always want, Herbie, my friend. Turn over your drum.'

'Well, you can fuck off for a start.'

'Okay. And I'll come back with a warrant, and plenty of lads in blue.'

'Clever sod, ain't you?'

'Yep. That about sums me up.'

'All right, then, why you want to go poking your snotty nose in my place?'

'I'm looking for an angel, me old mate.'

And at once the quick glance to the side told him his guess had been right. It had definitely been Herbie who one night – but which night? Trust the old Vicar not to have noticed for days or even weeks what he'd lost – had got up on to the roof of the Abbey church

167

and prised that angel gargoyle from its base. Then had got down to the ground with it, weighty as it must be. And now, almost for a cert after the days that must have passed, had it safely flogged to some half-bent dealer somewhere miles away.

Without a precise date for the theft, it would be no use asking Herbie where he had been at such-and-such a time. Not that, when asked, he wouldn't have lied himself black and blue. But, no genius our Herbie, you could always hope to trip him up on the porkies he was telling. Or he might have something in the house that would be evidence, of a sort.

'What angel? What you bleeding talking about? You always was a prat at school, Jack Stallworthy, and you ain't no better now.'

'I'll prat you, Herbie, my friend.'

'Oh, you will, will you? You and who else? And I ain't no friend of yours neither. I'll tell you that for nothing. I never much liked you first day we was in Infants together. And after that time you and your poncy mates done me up in the playground I've hated your bloody guts. An' that's a fac'.'

'Can't say I've exactly loved you, Herbie. But that don't mean I ain't going to come in and turn your place over. Looking for an angel, stone, one for the use of.'

'Dunno what you're on about. But if you want ter look round the place, feel fucking free. No skin off my nose.' The cockiness had told him that, search as he might, he was not going to find any sort of evidence. No scrawled address of some crafty dealer, no traces of scraped stone somewhere, no wrappings with something on them for Forensic to hop up and down about. So he had given Herbie one final glare and told him he'd come back before long.

It had been a defeat, and he knew it. But there had been no way to mark up any sort of a victory.

Parking at home behind Lily's little bright red Mini, still looking almost as good as when years ago he'd succumbed to the bed strike and got it for her – no wonder, since all she did in it was go to the supermarket – he decided to wait till after supper to put his hundred quid in undeclared evidence into the Cadbury's Roses tin. He might do it when he went round with the watering-can, and take the chance too to nip off a few dead heads. This time of year it was light till nearly ten.

So he went straight in to see Lily, ready to give her his customary peck on the cheek and settle down for some chat and a read of the *Argus*. Only for her to bounce out of her big chair the moment he came through the door.

'Hello, love,' he said, a flicker of perplexity going through him.

'Jack Stallworthy, let me tell you right out. I've had a phone call about you.'

Even then he failed completely to grasp the situation.

'Phone call? About me? Who . . .? Hey, what's up?'

'I'll tell you what's up. It's all up with you. It's all up between you and me.'

'Christ, love, what're you saying?'

'I'm saying that a certain lady I've sat next to at the hairdresser's once or twice got on to me on the phone. God knows how she found out who I was or where I lived, but she did. And she told me something about you, Jack. Something you've been taking bloody good care to keep from me for weeks and weeks.'

Then he knew. He saw it all in a moment. The deadline bloody Emslie Warnaby had given him now only a few days away. Emslie furious with impatience. His pint-sized mistress told the time had come to tell Lily what was on offer. And finally the call to the familiar number when he was bound to be out and Lily likely to be at home.

So now she knew all about the Calm Seas Hotel on Ko Samui, and how it could be theirs. Once he'd got hold of a blue folder.

'Listen, love,' he said cautiously. 'Listen, I know all about that woman, and I'm not saying she was telling you a pack of lies. But I am saying you don't want to trust her. What exactly did she say to you? How much did she tell you?'

'She told me everything, and don't you think you can get away with it by trying to blacken Anna. She and I had a good heart-to-heart, and I know a lot of things about you now, Jack Stallworthy, things I didn't know before.'

'Well, all right. So you know there was a chance of us ending up living the life of Riley on your precious Ko Whatsit. But did she tell you what the price of that was? Did she tell you what I had to do? And who I had to do it for?'

'Yes, she did. Just you getting hold of some silly folder belonging to Mr Emslie Warnaby – he's the boss at Abbotputers, isn't he? – a folder that got taken away by mistake. Nothing more than that. Dead simple. And don't you go saying *Your precious Ko Whatsit*. It's Ko Samui. Ko Samui. And it may be precious, but it's not just mine. It's ours. Our precious Ko Samui. And you were doing damn all about seeing we got there. Damn all.'

Then he felt the flame of rage.

It was not often Lily really got under his skin. He knew his English rose had thorns on her – none better – but all during whatever spats they had had, he had always known in the back of his mind that she was his Lily and that he never would willingly hurt her.

But now he had been hit too hard. All his feeling of being on the right side again – despite the hundred quid bulging his inside pocket – the feelings that had flooded through him from the moment he had definitely decided he was not going to take Emslie Warnaby's folder, were now being made to crumble like a landslip on a cliff edge.

'Damn all? Damn all?' he shouted. 'Christ, I only did a right nasty thing and stole the keys to the Fraud Office where that fucking folder is from that nice old Mrs Alexander. I only had to wriggle and squirm to someone I'd always liked to get out of that, when she found me trying to find the right one. I only tried to bribe the clerk there, and made a right prat of myself doing it. I only got myself thrown out of the place by Mac MacAllister, had my nose bloody rubbed right in it. I was only caught red-handed inside later on, and lucky not to find myself on a Form 163. Let alone put in fucking gaol. And you call that damn all.'

But he knew, while every word was spilling out, that none of it was what was really getting to him.

What had in a moment dropped a black bucket of darkness down on to him was that now he would no longer be a not-so-bad detective.

Because now he was going to have to take Emslie Warnaby's bribe. He was going to have to – somehow, somehow – get that blue folder.

He would not be able to resist Lily. In the end.

He never had been able to when it came to it. All right, when she'd gone on bedroom strike about the car, he'd fought her for more than a month. But she had won in the end. And it had not been just the strike that had done it. It had been because, when all was said and done, he could refuse her nothing. There had been other times too. Not so bad as the car strike. But in the end he had always knuckled under.

And it was not because she was the tougher one, either. It was because, sod it all, he loved her. Always had. Always would.

But perhaps if he told her the real truth . . .?

If he said now it wasn't because he'd tried to get Warnaby's bloody folder and had failed that he had told her last night it was Devon and April Cottage for them? Said that it was because at the last he hadn't been able to make himself take Warnaby's fat bribe. Perhaps, if he told her that now, she would relent. See it his way. See he couldn't do what, under pressure, he'd agreed to in that damn little flat up at Seaview Mansions. Perhaps she would.

'Look, love. I don't know if you understand all there is to it. That Anna of yours got me up to her flat, flat Emslie Warnaby's put her into, in fact. And the big boss himself came in and offered me this hotel, exactly where your friend Anna had found out from you was your favourite place in all the world. Right, I said at the time I'd do it. I'd take that fat big bribe he was offering. But I've thought about it since, and I can't do that. Oh, yes, I know, I've taken bribes before. Bribes, right. No messing about with pansy words. But they never were for money that really mattered. Otherwise we wouldn't be keeping it all in a ruddy sweet tin in the garden. No, what I took I only took from criminals who deserved to have something done to them. Or I just snitched some cash that had been snitched by someone else already. None of that was really bad. Because I couldn't do anything that bad. I'm a detective, love. You know that. You know what the job means to me, always has. Christ, you've complained of it often enough. But, you see, I couldn't ever do nothing that would go against the whole of what I've been doing all my life. When it comes down to it I'm on the side of the law. The good side. And taking Emslie Warnaby's fat bribe would put me on the other side. For ever.'

At least she isn't shooting me down straight away.

Maybe all that – Christ, I've never said anything like it before, hardly really thought it – maybe it's getting through to her . . .

'Listen, Lily, love, I know Ko Samui's been on your mind ever since you saw that programme on the telly. But wasn't that idea always– Look, wasn't it always a bit of pie in the sky? I mean, did you ever really believe we'd get there one day?'

'Oh, Jack. Jack, you know I did. You know I did. How can you be so cruel? You don't care the least bit what I feel, what I want. No, the thought of us going there, living there, it was all just too much trouble for you. Sit back and take it easy, that's you. No thought for anyone else. Ever. Specially not for me.'

Unjust though all that was, he kept himself in check. Was she still perhaps thinking at the back of her mind about what he'd said? How there were some things, some offers, some bribes, that in the end he just could not swallow?

'No, come on, love, think,' he said. 'How could we ever have got enough together to get ourselves out there? Let alone be able to live there?'

'But that's it. But that's just it. Anna told me. We're going to get given a whole hotel. The Calm Seas Hotel. The Calm Seas. Given it. We'll live like a – like a duke and duchess. And in the sun. In the sun with, yes, that's it, calm seas for the rest of our lives.'

No, she hadn't understood. But then she never had understood, really. About him and the job. Let alone how he could both want to do the job as well as it could be done, and at the same time was prepared to let a criminal go free every now and again if the money was right and it could be done without come-backs.

But he must go on. Keep on trying to persuade her to settle for Devon. For April Cottage and what was right at the last.

'Look, love, the sun shines here in England too, you know. Sometimes. And in Devon the weather's lovely, lots of the time. Nearly all the time. All right, I know you don't like Abbotsport. Who would? But in Devon, in April Cottage, our very own April Cottage, you'll be happy. We'll both be happy together.'

'Not as happy as we'll be on Ko Samui.'

'Yes, we will. Well, all right, maybe we wouldn't be. Not as happy. I suppose sunshine all the time's fine and dandy, if you can get it. And having servants. Not needing to do a hand's turn. But, all the same, we could be happy down there in Devon. We really could. There's that garden to make something of. And you'd have me being there all the time. You're always complaining you never see me, that I'm always on duty. Think of the fuss you made that night I was called out late when Councillor Symes was up in the air because his place'd been done.'

'But you wouldn't be at home there any more than you are now. You wouldn't. I've been thinking about how it would be, living down there, ever since you told me you'd bought that place. You've only paid the deposit on it, you know. There'd be a bank loan to be paid off. So you'd have to get a job. Security or something. If you could even get that. And then I wouldn't see you no more than what I do now.'

True enough. That was something he'd been dodging. Dodging ever since April. Sort of telling himself that he'd bought April Cottage and all their troubles were over. But, of course, they weren't. And trust Lily to think of that. She must have begun thinking that way from the moment they'd rolled out of the Costa Loadsa.

'You wouldn't, would you, Jack?'

'What? Wouldn't what?'

'There you go. You never listen to me. Oh, all right, you pretend you do. You pretend you're the one who does the looking after round here. But you don't. All you really think of is Jack Stallworthy. Jack Stallworthy and that garden of yours.'

'But – but you like the garden. You like the flowers I bring in from it.'

'What I'd like a sight more is flowers you'd bring in from the flower shop. As if you ever do, and—'

'That's not true. Not true.'

'Oh, yes, it is. Or, if it isn't hundred per cent true, it's true enough. And what would happen in Devon? Same blinking thing. You'd come in with a pathetic bunch of something-or-other you'd grown all on your own and expect me to say, *Thank you, thank you, come to bed, my darling, come to bed*. Well, I won't. I won't, unless I see you coming in from the hotel garden in Ko Samui with a bloody great bunch of tropical orchids. And then I might think about saying come to bed. But, unless that's what does happen, you can forget about your nice times under the duvet. Once and for all.'

'But, listen. If we were going to be given that hotel,

what I'd still have to do is get hold of that folder of documents that bloody Emslie *I-own-half-of-Abbotsport* Warnaby doesn't want anybody to know about. But that's past hoping for now. Past hoping for. I've tried everything I could, and all I've done is put myself in a series of bloody hairy situations.'

'Well, you'll have to think of something else, won't you? It can't be so difficult. Anna told me it's only one slim file they want. You could tuck that under your coat easy, and walk right out of that place.'

'Well, I can't. What the hell does Anna fucking Foxton know about how things are up at Headquarters? I tell you I've tried everything, and there's nothing more left. I can't get at that folder.'

'So you think, Jack Stallworthy. And, if you ask me, that's the real reason why you got on your holy high horse and said you didn't want to take a bribe. As if you haven't taken bribes for years. As if you haven't filled that tin out there under that clump of what-you-call-it with all the bribes you've taken.'

'But I told you, love. I explained. That was different. Different.'

'Oh, don't kid yourself, Jack, my lad. You've been on the take for years, and on the take is on the take. There's nothing so different about what you're being asked to do now.'

'But there is. There's one hell of a difference between the hundred quid that – all right – that I've got in my pocket this minute, or between the thousand quid I took off a nasty piece of work with a video shop down by the docks and put on a horse called April

Fool . . . There's a hell of a difference between things like that and what millionaire Emslie Warnaby's offering me.'

'Oh, don't be so soppy. Mr Warnaby says the file's only something somebody took away from the Fisheries place by mistake. It's not important really.'

'If you believe that you'd believe anything. You don't think a man like Warnaby's going to pay out all he's offering us just to get back some papers he'd find a bit useful? No. Whatever's in that folder is dynamite for him, and he knows it. He knows it so bloody well he's willing to give me a whole fucking hotel, and first-class air tickets thrown in. And that's not for nothing. It's to get back a folder that'd tell Fraud Investigation they've got a major bloody criminal in their hands. Someone who'll make poncy Councillor Symes look like chicken-shit. That's what your Mr Emslie Warnaby wants. That's why I'm being offered one hell of a bribe: because there's one hell of a crime, whatever in the end it turns out to be, to be kept from the light of day.'

'Well, what if there is? What if there is? Emslie Warnaby wouldn't be the first big-time crook who's been allowed to get away with it. And it's just our piece of luck that you're the one who happens to be able to do what he wants. Just our luck that at the end of it, even if Emslie Warnaby and Anna are laughing, we'll be living a lovely life on the island of Ko Samui.'

And then he knew he was really and truly done for. Nothing he had said had changed Lily's mind. It had been no use telling her all he'd done and all he'd risked to get at that folder. It had been no use trying to persuade her that a life down in Devon would be well enough in its way, that they would even be happy together there. It had been so much wasted breath trying to make her see that there was a difference between the thousand quid he had screwed out of that nasty villain Norman Teggs and the cost of a whole hotel on a far-off paradise island that Emslie Warnaby was dangling in front of him.

No use at all.

It would have to be getting the blue folder. And just hope getting it wouldn't result in it getting him.

Chapter Fourteen

Jack stumbled across to his chair, dropped down into it.

'That bitch Anna leave you a phone number?' he asked.

'Yes, she did, matter of fact. Why d'you want to know?'

Rage simmered in him. Words urgent to burst out.

Because, as you could've damn well worked out, I've got to tell her I'm still going to try to get Mr Emslie Warnaby his precious folder. Because what I've got to do is beg, bloody bloody beg, to have that deadline extended so that somehow – and God knows how, even now – in the end I get you to Ko Samui.

'I'm going to ring her up. That's why. Why else would I want her fucking telephone number?'

'Language.'

'What's the number?'

'It's there inside the lid of that box of chocs, where I wrote it down.'

He pushed himself up, feeling his own weight like a heavy punching-bag dragging at his heart, and made his way over to the phone.

'Anna Foxton?'

'Ah, it's Sergeant Stallworthy. I thought you'd be calling.'

Oh, yes, you bitch. You knew I would. God, how I'd like to take you by your two shoulders and shake you till the last bit of cockiness comes rattling out.

'Yes. I am calling. You know where to put the pressure on, don't you?'

'Well, I certainly enjoyed talking to your wife, Sergeant. Most enlightening.'

'Never mind my wife. Look, if I'm to get that sodding folder for you I've got to have a bit more time.'

'Yes. We thought you might want that. Well, Mr War – or – or, shall we say, my principal is over in America on business at present. But we've discussed things, and, though it's not exactly convenient, we think we can change the dates for our little holiday. So we can give you another two weeks. Not a day more.'

'All right.'

'That's till the thirtieth. A fortnight next Tuesday. Don't make any mistake about it. Up till midnight that day. Till midnight. By then we've got to have that folder. All right?'

'All right.'

He had wanted to add *Damn you*, but he checked himself. He might need yet another extension, and the little bitch had better be kept as sweet as possible. Not that he was likely to get any more time. Not from the way she had spoken.

So bloody Warnaby must be beginning to sweat then. Serve the bugger right.

In the meanwhile, how the heck to get at the folder?

He went back to his chair, sat and huddled himself up in a cocoon of misery.

'Well, how are you going to get Mr Warnaby his folder?'

Lily's voice sliced into his wrapped-up gloom like a buzz saw.

He looked across at her.

'How the hell do I know?' he said. 'I told you, didn't I? I've tried every sodding thing I could think of. And all I've done is make it harder for myself.'

'But there must be some way you can do it.'

Oh, yes, there must be some way. Just because you want it, Lily Stallworthy, there must be a way. Just because you want to spend the rest of your life lazing in the sun on Ko bloody Samui there must be a way of getting there.

'Well, there ain't no way. Or not any way I can think of.'

He shifted round till he was facing the wall and could no longer see her, tucked into the corner of that big chair of hers like a contented little squirrel.

Or not so contented.

'Well, if you haven't managed to trick your way into that office, wherever it is up at Palmerston Park, why can't you just go up there and break into it?'

There had been a distinct whining note of complaint in that.

'Oh, yes? Just go and break in there? Easy, wouldn't it be? A break-in inside fucking Abbotsport Constabulary Headquarters.'

'All right, if that's too difficult for you, think up some new dodge. You ought to be able to think of something, tricks you're always playing at. Holding on to half of what you find when you arrest someone, pretending you haven't got a case against someone if they've paid you to keep mum, turning a blind eye when some crime's staring you in the face.'

'Okay, so I do all of that. No need to throw it in my face.'

'I'm not throwing anything in your face. I'm just telling you that you could find a way of getting that folder for Anna if you really tried. You could. By trickery. Or burglary. Never mind which.'

'Oh yes? Easy enough to say. But what you seem to forget is you married a police officer. I may have learnt a few dirty tricks in my time. I don't say I ain't. But, by God, I've never taught myself to go housebreaking.'

'Well, if you haven't, you'd better find someone who can to teach you, hadn't you? You've got enough mates in among the villains. You're always saying so. Get on to one of them. Learn whatever it is they know and you don't.'

'If I've got villains for mates, my girl, it's only because it's part of my job. How d'you think I've got myself the best arrest record in the whole of Abbots-port CID? It's by going drinking with the villains and keeping my bloody ears open. That's how.'

'All right, then, go drinking with them some more. And when you find the right one, ask him what you've got to do to get in there. Or, better still, get him to go along with you. Show you on the spot. Get him

183

to do the hard work for you, if you ain't up to it yourself.'

He nearly upped then and gave her a slap.

Only he never had yet, and knew he never would.

And also because he had come to realize, as she had hammered away at him, just who it was he would have to go to and ask to be given an on-the-spot break-in demonstration.

Herbie Cuddy. Roof climber. Hook family member. Old enemy from faraway schooldays.

But he still had sense enough to go cautiously. Herbie would never, he saw at once, consent to try breaking into Abbotsport Constabulary Headquarters just for the asking. Even if he told him there would be plenty of good pickings there.

So, a bribe of some sort? For a little he totted up the total in the Cadbury's Roses tin and wondered how much of it would be needed to get Herbie to take the risk. Let alone to rush him into helping his old enemy.

If only Herbie was skint. But just now he was almost certainly in funds. Hadn't he, not so long ago, stolen from the Abbey church an angel gargoyle, God knows how old? Been there for centuries. Valuable beyond words, the Vicar had said. Said time and again.

So Herbie, almost for a cert, would just laugh at whatever he was offered. In a month or two things might be different. Herbie, the gargoyle cash boozed away, might well jump at a bribe then. Only there was not a month or two before Emslie Warnaby had to be handed that folder. There was only a little over three weeks, even with that extension he'd just got.

And then, trying to bring himself to think of how a meeting with Herbie might go, seeing himself making his way up the path to that house on the St Oswald Estate, he suddenly remembered the van in the front garden there.

A wreck of a van in the wreck of the garden.

And a wreck of a van would not be easy to drive at speed for a good long distance. When he had first thought of Herbie as the one who most probably had stolen the angel he had said to himself that, in the time between him prising it off its perch on the church roof and the Vicar noticing it was gone, he would have had weeks to have taken it to a dealer *miles away*. But with that van of his in the state it was, in all likelihood he would not have gone miles away. Could not have done. He would have to have sold the gargoyle to the nearest dodgy dealer he could call to mind.

Any thief who knew his stuff – and Herbie had been brought up in the Hook family – would hang on to a stolen object only for the shortest possible time. But with a dealer it would be quite a different matter. However much they knew or suspected something they had been sold was hot, they would have to keep it till they had found some more or less legit buyer.

So that angel gargoyle – he had a good description, thanks to photos that had been taken for a historical pamphlet they sold in the church – might well be hidden away somewhere not too far from Abbotsport itself. Somewhere that could be fairly easily located.

And when it was, there might well be something there that linked it nicely to Herbie Cuddy.

Which would give him as good a hold over Herbie as he could possibly ask for.

He called up the files as soon as he got in next morning, on time for once. 'Look who's here,' cheeky bugger Pete Hoskins called out. 'Fire broke out at your place, Jack?'

He had hardly bothered to answer. Five minutes head down in the files and he had come up with a perfect answer. *Grinton Metals, Prop. Jeremiah Mickleton*. And a list as long as your arm of inquiries made at the place. But no prosecutions for three or four years past. Old Jeremiah – he remembered him from when he had been out there himself long ago – must be somebody's snout, then. Allowed to do a bit of fencing, or more than a bit, in exchange for information received. And someone's promotion prospects improving.

Almost for a cert, Jeremiah was the one. Grinton only some ten miles along the coast, the place where Harry Hook had built his smarty-pants Costa Loadsa, a twenty-five-minute run, even in Herbie Cuddy's rotten old van. Herbie probably had got rid of the angel inside an hour from when he had lowered it down from the Abbey church roof. And, if Grinton Metals did turn out to be a no-no, there were still two or three other possibles on the file. But, let them wait, get out to Grinton straight away.

A picture came into his mind of some fly antiques dealer from London or somewhere even at that moment negotiating with scrawny old Jeremiah over buying the gargoyle. *Can't tell you where I got it, mister. Just don't ask, right?*

But at least when he arrived at Jeremiah's pigsty of a yard – yes, there were a few stone garden urns about, plus a statue of some old god or other wearing a flat hat with little wings sprouting out of it, and half a running leg missing – there was no one in a vehicle with London number plates there haggling.

'Sergeant Stallworthy. I remember you,' unshaven, peering-eyed Jeremiah snarled as he stepped out of the car.

'That's right, my son. We have met before, long time ago though. Load of stolen scaffolding, wasn't it? Couldn't quite pin it on you.'

'Weren't for want o' trying.'

'Well, we have to do our job, you know. And that's why I'm here now, matter of fact. Anything on your conscience, by any chance?'

'Last time you was here you said I hadn't got no conscience.'

'Did I? I wonder what made me make a remark like that. Fancy you remembering. Can it have been because I knew you were lying in your teeth every minute we talked?'

'I don't know what it was. And I don't care neither. What you want now?'

'Oh, I just want you to be your usual self, Jeremiah. Just the angel you always are.'

And, bingo, a flicker of alarm at the word *angel* as he had put just that little extra emphasis on it.

'What you give Herbie Cuddy for it then, Jeremiah?'

'Herbie been – I never gave Herbie Cuddy nothing. I don't even know him. Who is he?'

'Oh, Jeremiah, really. You ought to be a bit cleverer. If you're going to end your days out of prison.'

Look of alarm yet plainer now.

Jack let his body sag into a more relaxed state.

'Not to worry, old son. Not to worry. It ain't you I'm after this time. It's just that Herbie gave me a nod in your direction, and I thought I ought to chase it up.'

And now a look of vicious fury came on to the old man's dirt-seamed face.

'He'd no call to go talking about me, that Herbie. What's he said? I ain't done nothing wrong. If I bought something from him, and I ain't saying I did, I bought it in good faith.'

'Oh, yes? He tell you how he happened to come by a sodding great stone angel then?'

'It wasn't that. That wasn't what I got off him.'

'No? Mind if I have a look round?'

The old man's eyes went like two lasers straight towards a tumbledown shed at the corner of the yard. It was laughable.

'Okay, Jeremiah. Now, if I take a look in that shed there and say nothing about what I find, will you tell me exactly when Herbie Cuddy came to you and flogged off that stone gargoyle from Abbotsport Abbey church? You do that, and it'll be the last you hear about it. Scout's honour.'

'But can I believe you, Mr Stallworthy?'

'Well, you ain't got much option, have you?'

So then Jeremiah had gone with him over to the shed, hauled the key for its padlock from somewhere in his ancient sagging trousers, and opened up.

For a moment or two, coming out of the bright July sunlight beating down on Jeremiah's dusty shambles of a yard, Jack could make nothing out. But soon his eyes became accustomed to the darkness. And he picked out in a mote-thick ray coming in through a gap in the boards something wrapped in an untidy shroud of sacking.

'Let's see then,' he said to Jeremiah.

The old man pulled the filthy sacking aside. And it was the angel. Jack hardly needed to take out the photo to check.

'Right,' he said. 'Herbie Cuddy sold you this? When was it?'

'Fortnight ago. Three weeks.'

'No, come on. I want the date exactly. Don't tell me you haven't got it stored away in your head, even if you're damn careful never to put anything in the books.'

The old man gave him a glare. Hardly softened by the gloom inside the shed.

'Three weeks ago today, if you must know. June the twenty-first. Friday.'

'You're sure of that? It was that night Herbie came out here with it?'

'You're the one who says I keeps it all in me head. Well, I do. It was the twenty-first. By about ten minutes. Ten minutes to midnight he came.'

'All right, keep your hair on. So, what you give Herbie for it then?'

'Five hundred. And he was lucky to get that.'

'And how much will you be lucky to get when you can find a dealer who likes it, eh? No, don't answer. Far as I'm concerned you can get what you can. I've found out all I want.'

'But you won't tell Herbie, Sergeant? Promise me you'll keep my name out of it.'

'Oh, I don't think you need worry. Any business between Herbie and me is private. Strictly private.'

Chapter Fifteen

Jack was tempted to drive back straight away into Abbotsport and out to the St Oswald Estate to transact his strictly private business with Herbie Cuddy. But a little reflection decided him otherwise. However much ammunition he now had to pressure Herbie into doing what he wanted, having a car parked outside his house that plenty of people on the crime-infested estate would recognize would not please him. And now more was needed than just Herbie's agreement to breaking into Headquarters. His full co-operation.

So he went back to the police station, caught up with a bit of paperwork – his Incident Report Book was way behind: catching villains higher priority than writing down their names – and eventually made his way home.

Then, as it began to get dark, he went round the garden with the watering-can. The night before in the end he had been too exhausted by his row with Lily to go out. And at last, when the pubs would have safely called last orders and fewer people be about, he set off.

At the estate he left the car, well locked up, at

some distance from Herbie's house and walked through the soft summer darkness. With ever-slowing steps.

Now that the moment for winning over Herbie had come, he found it hard to make up his mind as to the best way to go about it. He had still come to no decision when he reached the house and saw, as he had begun to hope he would not, lights in the downstairs windows.

But he had to talk to his old enemy. No getting past it. There was precious little time left. You couldn't arrange a break-in at Abbotsport Constabulary Head-quarters all in five minutes. You couldn't even count on coming out of Herbie's house after this evening's bargaining with his agreement in your pocket. Or, rather, in your head.

Then, could you trust Herbie?

He went up to the door, past the battered old van that must have conveyed an angel gargoyle from the Abbey church to its eventual hiding place in Jeremiah Mickleton's shed. Inside, the TV was blaring out. A video by the sound of it. Something with plenty of female screaming. Perhaps one of Norman Teggs's specials. He pressed the doorbell, long and hard. But it was plain it was not working, probably been broken for months, even years. He lifted instead the tinny chrome door-knocker, in the shape of a naked woman – what else? – and banged it sharply down three, four, five times.

Almost a minute passed without any reaction from inside – Herbie got something to hide away? – then he saw the flimsy curtain on the window nearest him pulled back. Gritting his teeth, he stepped away from the door to where he could be seen in the light.

A moment later there came the sound of heavy steps and the door was jerked open.

'Fucking Jack Stallworthy. So it is you. What you doing here?'

'Want a word with you, Herbie, old mate.'

'Well, you can fuck off.'

'Be to your advantage, mate. God's truth.'

'Fuck off I said.'

'No, Herbie, I mean it. This isn't police business. Or not exactly.'

Something in the tone of what he had said must have penetrated. Herbie stepped back.

'Come in quick, then. D'you think I want everyone to know I'm talking to the filth?'

He stepped in.

Herbie thrust a fat, brawny arm past him and slammed the door closed.

Uninvited, he walked into the front room.

Yes, by the look of it it was a video nasty on the box. Not that the girl screaming away on it seemed to be upsetting Herbie's woman. She was crouching there on the sagging sofa staring fixedly at the screen, her out-of-the-bottle harshly golden hair falling in two heavy swags in front of her.

He turned to Herbie.

'Can we talk in private?'

'What the hell . . .? Nah, I should think she could hear anything you got to say.'

'Just as you like, mate. Only if she does hear, you're going to regret it.'

Herbie shot him a look. His two little blue pig-eyes bright with suspicion.

But he went over to the TV and flicked it into silence.

'I was watching that.'

'Then you can bloody watch it another time. Out.'

With a look of mutinous dislike the woman got up and slouched out. Herbie banged the door closed behind her.

'What's all this, then? Not like you to keep mum about anything you think I wouldn't like people knowing.'

And still he had not made up his mind how he was going to broach the subject. It was a subject that should not be broached. But had to be.

He took a sudden plunging decision.

'I want you to break into Police Headquarters up at Palmerston Park.'

'You gone raving bloody mad?'

'No, Herbie, I ain't. I'm putting a plain proposition to you. There's something I want to get hold of, in one of the offices up there. I've tried to do it the crafty way, and I've come unstuck. That's the truth of it. So now I want to do it the other way. And for that I need your help.'

Herbie suddenly sat down, squatting like a toad on the sofa where his woman had been watching the video. He looked up.

'Christ, this is good,' he said. 'This is the bloody best yet. Nose-in-the-air Jack Stallworthy coming to

194

me and saying he wants to rob his own fucking Police Headquarters.'

'Good or bad, that's what I want.'

'And you think I'm going to help you? You stupid sod. You've just given me what I've waited forty fucking years to get. My revenge on you, poxy Jack Stallworthy. Boy fucking detective.'

Jack sighed.

'Oh, yes. You can't say anything to me I haven't thought of already. But, all the same, I still want you to do it. It could be well worth your while, you know.'

'Oh, yes? And how's that, then? You're not going to try telling me, while you're getting whatever it is you want up there, I get my pick of anything going?'

'Well, I am.'

Herbie wagged his football head from side to side.

'Let me tell you something, mate. If I was able to go up there to that place and come away with enough stuff to keep me in dinners till the end of my bleeding days and then some, I wouldn't go one step into it with you. Not one sodding step.'

'Yeah, that's what I thought you'd say. More or less. But I gave you your chance. And now you've got to listen to me.'

Herbie looked at him, a grin of pleasure still on his face.

'Got to, have I?'

'Yes, you bleeding have. And I'll tell you why. I spent this morning out at old Jeremiah Mickleton's place, and what d'you think I found there?'

'How the hell should I know? Nosey fucking copper.'

But there had been a split second when it was plain that Herbie well knew what there was to be found at Jeremiah's.

'Yes, you're right. The gargoyle you climbed up to the roof of the Abbey church to nick. And, what's more, I can link you to it. Right down to the night you did it. And the time. A Friday, right? June the twenty-first. Just before midnight.'

'You can't pin it on me from that.'

'Oh, but I could. If I wanted. Might have to pretty up the evidence a bit, but I could get you bang to rights, mate.'

'Coppers.'

'Yes, coppers. Nasty lot, aren't we? Almost as nasty as your lot, Harry Hook and his numerous bloody family, in and out of wedlock.'

'Don't you try tangling with Harry. He'd eat you for dinner.'

'I've no intention of tangling with Harry. Just as soon as I've got what I want up at Headquarters, I'm away out of Abbotsport. I'll tell you that for nothing.'

'Away off, are you? End of great crime-busting career, is it?'

'That's about the size of it, yes.'

'So you wouldn't be around after to try and pin that gargoyle business on me?'

'That's right.'

A shifty look in the little blue eyes.

'But, if I don't come with you on this break-in lark you're on about, you'll drop me right in the shit before you go? That it?'

'That's it.'

'So I s'pose I ain't got no alternative.'

'That's it.'

But before Jack set out with Herbie to break into Abbotsport Constabulary Headquarters – the job had to be done at a weekend when the place was closed up, with all phone calls transferred to the Central Police Station – he found that his dealings with Herbie had brought him, if only indirectly, more trouble.

The two of them had already done a recce, armed with a pair of binoculars, police issue, lying in the grass on the hill at the back of the big Headquarters building. It was then Herbie had announced it looked as if the job was going to be easier than he'd thought.

'Christ, mate, that window you said, it's only one floor up. You ought to have gone nipping up there on your tod. Wouldn't have had to come begging to me then, would you?'

'And you'd have likely found yourself doing a three-stretch for nicking that gargoyle. At the least. The old Vicar's hopping mad, you know. Bloody *Argus* flooded with letters from all the bigwigs in the town.'

'Fat lot I care.'

'And, in any case, how would I have got up to the window? That wall there's like a cliff. It's the sodding gymnasium on the ground floor at the back, you know. All bloody wallbars inside and no windows looking out.'

'Don't you know nothing, you dozy copper? Ain't

you never heard of a grapnel? Easy to see you ain't never been out to sea.'

'Grapnel? You mean something you throw and it hooks on something?'

'What the fuck else would I mean? And take a bleeding look up there. Nice little stone ridge just above that toilets window with the reeded glass. Easy as pie, get up there, smash a pane, have the window open.'

So for a couple of days after that Jack had felt he might in the end, despite the ridiculous riskiness of what he planned, bring the whole business off. The blue folder. The Calm Seas Hotel, Ko Samui. Then, from a quite unexpected quarter, came the trouble.

Before he could see if Herbie's way into Head-quarters was as easy as he had claimed, he was summoned up there himself. To see Detective Chief Superintendent Detch.

When the Guv'nor told him he was wanted he thought, in immediate panic, that somehow someone had got wind of the whole plan. Herbie double-crossing him? No. No, it couldn't be. Herbie had too much to lose. Or was convinced he had.

So eventually it was with only the smallest niggling of worry that he presented himself in front of DCS Detch's wide, polished desk.

'I've heard something about you, Stallworthy.'

'Yes, sir?'

Keep it respectful. Think of what this sod did to old Mac MacAllister. Dangerous bugger, if ever there was.

'Yes. Name Teggs mean anything to you? Norman Teggs?'

For a moment it did not. That productive quarter of an hour at the Video Magic shop back in April had faded almost to nothing in his memory.

But then he remembered.

Christ, has that shitbag Teggs found a way of saying I took that thousand quid off him, all without laying himself open to trouble?

'Yes, sir,' he answered. 'Teggs runs a video place down by the docks. I had occasion to give him a going-over some months back. Thought he was selling porn.'

He hesitated then. But there seemed nothing else for it but to stick to the story he had entered in the files at the time.

'Didn't find anything though, sir. Could be he took warning when I first went in the shop. I was just looking for a gardening video I wanted, matter of fact, and I happened to see something I thought was a bit dodgy.'

'So you took it on yourself to harass this chap, Sergeant?'

Harass?

Well, of course I did. But didn't the fucker deserve to be harassed? At the very least. Christ, that tape he tried to get me to look at. But go carefully. Detchie could be leading up to something.

'Well, sir, I wouldn't say harass. But, as I'd seen some tapes on his counter that looked iffy, least I could do was follow up.'

'Was it, sergeant? Well, let me put it to you that the least you could do is a bit of hard detecting.'

Hey, nobody could say I'm not . . . What is this? But keep it down.

'Yes, sir?'

'Hard detecting of whoever it was who stole a very valuable gargoyle right off the roof of the Abbey church, and seemingly got clean away with it, yes? Bloody paper full of letters talking about police incompetence. The Chief on to me two or three times a day.'

Bloody Herbie. Fucking Vicar. Sodding Chief.

Stupid me, too. I could've had that business nicely sewn up, 'cept for Herbie. Could have had him charged and in the cells. Had the bloody gargoyle waiting to go back to the bloody church. Had a nice one on my record, what's more. Vicar writing to the Chief, and, I dare say, another of those smarmy letters signed R. J. Parkinson, Chief Inspector.

If it hadn't been I had to have Herbie showing me how to get up into that fucking Fraud Investigation office. That fucking old cupboard. That fucking, fucking blue folder.

But keep on playing it cool. Lick arse. Nothing else to do.

'Sir, yes, I was put on to that gargoyle case. And I've done a hell of a lot of work on it, Sir. Tried every angle I can think of. I was out last Friday interviewing a certain Jeremiah Mickleton, Grinton Metals. List of inquiries against him long as my arm. But he's too fly to be caught with anything dodgy on his premises, Sir, and that's all there is to it.'

'Is it, Sergeant? Well, I suggest there's a hell of a lot more to it than that. So just you keep your nose to that particular grindstone from now on, and leave petty villains like Norman Teggs to peddle whatever it is they're peddling without wasting a hell of a lot of costly police time. Yes?'

'Yes, Sir.'

Thoughtfully he made his way down from Detective Chief Superintendent Detch's lofty office. But at the first floor he could not help coming to a halt.

Should he take one more look at the Fraud Investigation door? If it should be open by any chance . . . Then it could be *Sod off Herbie Cuddy, don't need you any more. Got what I wanted now.* I could even have Herbie for the gargoyle job, after all. Wouldn't half please bloody Detch, that.

But, no. No point. The Fraud door'll never be left gaping wide. Pigs never do fly.

But all the same, he thought as he resumed his downward march, a nasty piece of work like Norman Teggs, copying that kiddy porn filth. He wasn't any petty villain to be left to get on with it, never mind what Detective Chief Superintendent Detch, Sir, said. The shitbag had probably not even done anything about disposing of those tapes he'd told him to burn. Was probably still selling them at a fat profit to whatever creeps he had coming to that place, and making yet more copies.

Getting into the car and savagely revving his engine, he decided he would damn well go straight down to the docks and pay a call on Master Teggs. Detch or no Detch.

Video Magic looked from the outside just as unmagical in the hazy sunshine of July as it had looked in the clear sunlight of April.

He went in.

The place was doing no business. Norman Teggs, wearing the identical shiny brown suit with the barely visible white stripes he had on in April, was sitting idly behind the counter on what looked like a seat from some disused cinema. Cigarette dangling from thin-lipped mouth. Only the plastic of the counter seemed a bit more buckled than he remembered it.

'A very good morning to you, my friend,' he said. 'Remember who I am by any chance?'

The only answer he got was a look of animal malice.

'I asked if you remembered me. And I've got something else to ask, too. I told you to get rid of that filth you made copies of. You done it?'

But now Norman Teggs was not as easily cowed as he had been before.

'Yes, I remember you now, copper,' he said. 'And I've got news for you. I ain't the owner of this place any more. Sold out, I have. Just the manager now. Manager for a certain Mr Hook. Heard of him, have you? Harry Hook?'

'Harry Hook own this shitheap now?'

'Yes, he does. And, if you want my advice, you'll keep that in mind. Mr Hook ain't exactly anybody I'd like to come up against if I was giving him any aggro.'

Jesus, no, nor would I, certainly not at this bloody moment when I'm counting on Herbie Cuddy, cousin of some sort to the whole bleeding Hook family.

'Well, then, let's hope this place is going to be run a bit better from now on,' he said, knowing it was feeble though the best he could rise to. 'If I come in here again, looking for a video of *The Lovely World of Lilies*, perhaps that's what I'll get, and not a load of blinking nasties.'

'P'raps it's what you'll get, and p'raps it ain't. I just wouldn't come in here again ever, I was you. I'm surprised you poked your nose in now.'

Game, set and match to Mr Teggs. And Harry Hook behind him.

He turned and walked out.

Nothing else to be done. And, come to think, not all that surprising Harry Hook's got his paws on the place. Must be a sweet little racket.

There was a time when I wouldn't have rested till I'd put an end to it. But those days are gone. It's do what you're told to do by the big money now. The Emslie Warnaby money.

Sod it.

Chapter Sixteen

Jack's only contribution to the equipment for the break-in at Police Headquarters was his trusty old garden trowel. Bringing it with him was a last-minute thought. All right, it looked as if Herbie could be relied on to get them both into the building. And, of course, Herbie would have a jemmy for forcing locked doors there, including the one into the Fraud Investigation office. But when that was open Herbie might well say he needed the jemmy himself, for desk drawers or whatever. Be his idea of a big joke. Get his playground enemy to give him the freedom of all the goodies in Police Headquarters, and then stop him getting whatever it was he'd come there to get. It was almost certain now that the cupboard with the Symes material would have to be forced open. If Horatio Bottomley had said anything at all to Mac MacAllister about finding him trying to take something from it, Mac would have pushed in those bulging files, turned his new key in the lock and put it firmly in his pocket.

The idea that Herbie might play such a trick had come to him only on Sunday a few hours before they were due to make the break-in. No chance of shopping for a lever or a heavy chisel. So, going to the shed, well knowing there was nothing neatly hung up among his gardening tools that would really be right, he had at last taken the trowel. For all its well-worn wooden handle, its blade was still good and strong.

They took Jack's own car. He had wanted to use Herbie's van, but met with a sharp objection.

'Jesus, don't you know nothing? Thought you was meant to be a number one detective. You got any idea how many times I get a pull driving about in the van?'

He reconsidered. Needed a big jump to see things villain's way up. Of course, every traffic patrolman in the force would have the number of Herbie's van in his head. Every time they spotted it they would pull him up. He'd been bloody lucky not to have been stopped going out with the angel to Jeremiah Mickleton. Probably too skint before he got Jeremiah's five hundred quid to be able to hire something else, and not inclined to add to the risks by nicking anything.

Herbie was right. This end of the stick, he did know nothing.

So, putting himself firmly in Herbie's hands – much though it hurt – he drove under his instructions to a place Herbie had spotted when they had been looking out the lie of the land.

He tucked the car in under the shadow of the tall hedge and cut the lights.

'You'll have to lug the gear,' Herbie said, a tang of spite in his voice. 'Nice little job for you. But this is as near as it'll be safe to go. Just you hope we don't have to run for it, anything go wrong.'

In silence Jack let himself be loaded up with two heavy sacks of climbing ropes and a large, empty holdall for whatever goodies Herbie found. Then they set off through the muggily warm darkness.

Herbie, who was carrying no more than his small leather bag of tools, looked up at a full golden moon.

'Could have done without that,' he murmured.

'Too bad, mate. Moon or no moon, it's got to be tonight. Any later it'd be not at all.'

'Don't you get ratty with me. Got its good side, that old moon. Least I can see what I'm doing when it comes to throwing the rope up.'

They walked on without speaking and climbed a gate into the field directly behind the building.

At the high brick wall running the whole way round Headquarters Herbie came to a halt.

'Tree somewhere about here,' he said. 'Saw it with them binocs. Should be near enough to the wall to get us over.' Leaving Jack standing in the shadow of the wall, the two heavy sacks lowered gratefully to the ground, he set off to look.

Christ, Jack thought, I'm glad I chose my side of the law when it came to it. Couldn't take too much waiting about like this.

A car went swishing along the road behind him, its lights climbing into the night as it took a rise.

Jesus, what'll happen if some bloody courting couple take it into their heads to stop off somewhere up there and don't cut their lights straight away. Bloody great twin beams show me up, standing here looking like fucking Bill Sykes.

Suddenly Herbie was beside him again.

He gave a nervous start.

Herbie laughed.

'Got the wind up already, mate? Be a lot worse 'fore we're done.'

'All very well for you, you're used to this sort of bloody lark.'

'And lucky for you I am. You'd be in the shit otherwise, Jack Stallworthy.'

And am I going to be dropped in it still? No love lost with you, Herbie Cuddy. I've never wished before I hadn't sussed you out at school pinching from the coats. But I'm not sure now I was as clever as I've always thought.

'Come on then, sod you.'

Herbie set off into the darkness underneath the high wall, leaving Jack to hoist up his two weighty sacks and the empty holdall and follow as best he might.

But at the spot Herbie had chosen for getting over the wall he did give Jack some help. Using the tree on one side and the rough surface of the wall on the other, he had scrambled himself up on to the top in half a minute. But then, straddling the wall's width, he had at least leant down, heaved up the two sacks one after another as Jack had held them up to him and finally had given Jack a hand to haul himself up, scraping and scratching at the rough brick surface, in his turn.

Dropping to the ground like a sack of ropes himself, Jack thought with dread about the yet harder task that confronted him.

God, am I ever going to get all the way up to that toilets window we picked on? Jesus, I ought to have kept myself fitter. Gone up to the gym just inside here, done me press-ups, whatever.

Herbie had sat himself on the ground now.

'Come on, mate,' Jack said. 'I don't want to be here any longer than I have to, thank you very much.'

Herbie looked up.

'Got to put me socks on, ain't I?' From the pocket of his dark-coloured windcheater he pulled out a pair of thick seaman's socks and began tugging them on over his boots.

'What you—' Jack began.

And then he realized.

Christ, yes, how many times had he watched the Forensics lads lifting shoeprints with the electro-static detection apparatus – *You need a bit of the old ESDA here, skipper* – when there had been a break-in big enough to justify it? And now, out here in the middle of the bleeding night, on the wrong side himself, he had damn nearly had to ask Herbie what he was doing. Like a sodding schoolkid.

And should he have thought of taking the same precaution himself? Okay, he had surgical gloves for fingerprints, but he had never thought about the marks of his shoes being traced. And nor had Herbie, when they were discussing what would be needed, suggested socks. Happy if his old enemy did get detected? Quite likely. The bastard.

But, in fact, he was almost certainly safe enough. Lifted shoeprints were only any use when you had some reasonable expectation of finding the person who wore the shoe. And was it likely anyone would suspect Detective Sergeant Stallworthy, best arrest record in CID? Especially when Herbie was going to break into half a dozen other offices besides Fraud Investigation.

He waited till Herbie had got the big pair of socks well over his battered old boots, picked up his burdens and plodded off after him.

Like a bleeding Arab servant or something.

Then they were standing at the foot of the building, right underneath the toilets window they were aiming for. The toilets where Mac MacAllister – *Get out of this office and never show your face in here again* – had gone for a pee, leaving behind, guarding his files and figures, trustworthy Horatio Bottomley. *No, Mr Stallworthy. All them papers is evidence.*

'Right, let's have that sack, then.'

Herbie pulled the sack he wanted roughly out of Jack's grasp – he had held out the wrong one, bound to have done – opened it up and took from it a long double coil of thin rope with a three-pronged grapnel and a small pulley on the end. He stepped away from the blank wall of the building for some five or six yards. Stood twirling the end of the ropes in the air. Leant backwards and with an extraordinarily graceful movement for anyone as squat and well padded, sent grapnel and pulley flying high up into the air.

In the strong pinkish moonlight Jack could follow the flight of the grapnel as clearly as if it was day. With a clunk that sounded much too loud in the pre-dawn stillness it struck the wall a few feet above the reeded glass of the toilets window.

It struck the wall. It slithered down. It caught on the ornamental white stone course running all along the building just above the tops of the windows.

Even Herbie, giving one of his ropes a cautious tug, looked pleased with himself.

'Piece of cake, I told yer,' he said, as it became clear the grapnel had bitten firmly in.

'Good on you, mate,' Jack said.

Keep the bastard happy. Butter him up, every inch of the way. I need the sod. Need him. All I got between me and that fucking blue folder. Between me and taking Lil to Ko Samui, as promised.

Working with practised rapidity, Herbie had now hauled a narrow rope-ladder up to where his pulley dangled just beneath the grapnel.

''Ere, 'old this.'

Obediently Jack took hold of the rope running down from the pulley Herbie had thrust at him, and stood there feeling like a lemon.

From his second sack Herbie took a thick hooked iron spike and a heavy mallet. Choosing a spot just clear of the building's foundations he began banging the spike deep into the ground.

To Jack's nerve-stretched ears the noise this operation made seemed to ring out like a clanging alarm far and wide into the night.

He turned and looked up the hill to where they had left the car.

'Hold that fucking rope, you cunt,' Herbie spat out.

Jack turned back to face the building, took an extra turn of the rope round his wrist.

And waited.

All the events that had brought him to his present ridiculous, absurd, dangerous predicament went processing through his mind.

The first ever call from that little bitch Anna Foxton. The visit to her flat, Seaview Mansions. God, and how nearly he had not gone up there. Curiosity killed the cat.

Glancing up at the thin, dangling rope-ladder he was holding in place by hanging on to his rope, he thought, *And that may have been one curiosity that'll kill this poor sod of a cat here.*

Then Emslie Warnaby, dark suit, heavy cloth, tailor-made to the last stitch, steam-rollering him into doing precisely what he wanted. And all the attempts he had had to make to do what it was bloody Warnaby had wanted. Pathetic. Ma Alexander at the bus-stop. In the canteen, digging and diving into her coat pockets. And being caught red-fucking-handed. Really-really big box of chocs all that saved him.

And, worse if anything, sucking up to old Horatio there in the car, rain pissing down. And getting nowhere. Taking him off afterwards to the bus station. Had he given him a cheery wave? Christ knows.

Then Mac MacAllister. Listening to his sad story. And having the stupidity to think he'd want to avenge himself on bloody Detective Chief Superintendent Detch, sir, by letting him pick up that blue folder almost at his feet. The folder he had actually got between finger and thumb later when old Horatio had come poking his silly grey head in, see what was the matter.

And he had believed, just for a little, just for twenty-four marvellous hours or so, he had got himself off the hook. Lily seeming to be ready to settle for Devon and April Cottage. Not overjoyed, but for once being a bit realistic. Until fucking Anna Foxton had got on the phone.

And then Herbie—

'Come on, mate. Give us the bloody rope. What you doing? Having a fantasy wank?'

He handed him the rope, saw that the spike had been driven into the ground right down to its hook, watched while Herbie made the rope fast to it.

The seamanlike little sod.

'All right, give me the holdall, stupid. You're the one in a hurry to get out of here.'

Suppressing any retort, he stooped, picked up the holdall, handed it over. Herbie dropped into it such tools as he would need in the building.

Then, feeling with every moment a terrible sense of about-to-come vertigo, he watched Herbie climb up his well-secured rope-ladder. Like a fat little monkey, he thought.

My God, and I've got to do that in a minute.

If I'm going to get that folder. And I must. I must. Rest of my buggering life depends on it.

Oh, Christ, how did I ever get into this?

But I know. I know. I got into it the first time I ever

took a real backhander. From then on I was done. If I'd only known it.

But I had to do it. Would never have kept my Lil with me otherwise. Little English rose.

Come to that, I'm not so sure I wouldn't have gone that way, Lil or no Lil. Time would've come when I felt short of a few quid, and the chance would've been there. All too easy to grab.

There came from above a tinkle of breaking glass. Looking up, he saw Herbie haul open the toilets window and heave himself inside.

And after that, before he had had time to think, it was Herbie's head re-emerging from the window and a hissed command to him to climb up in his turn.

Now for it.

He slipped his surgical gloves from his pocket and pushed his hands into them. Never do to leave his dabs on the wood of the window sill – if he ever got up there – he'd seen too many lifted from just that place himself not to know it was the most dangerous spot of all. To a bloody criminal. Setting his teeth, he grasped the highest point he could reach on the twisting wooden rungs, kicked a foot on to one of the lower ones, heaved.

Well, I've begun.

Another reach up. More floundering with a foot underneath him. Another heave. And on up and up again. And again.

Must be nearly there now. Don't feel too bad. This is easier than I thought.

He looked up to the window.

He was not nearly there. He was hardly a third of the way there.

With a gulp and a big indrawn breath, he set off again. But, before he had hauled himself up as many rungs as at his first effort, he felt a trembling weakness in his arms and a lurch of sickness in his belly.

He halted. Clung there in the bright moonlight. Felt sweat starting up all over him.

'Christ, Jack, hurry up.'

Herbie's voice, raised above hissing point now, floated down to him.

The shitty bugger.

He attacked the rungs above him again in a frenzy of rage.

And had to stop once more before he had got three feet higher.

He looked up. Herbie's head was no longer jutting out of the window.

What if he closes it on me? The sod. He would. He'd do something like that. Wanting his revenge. Always has. Bugger it. Bugger it. Bugger it.

He clung there again. Hands in his thin plastic gloves swimming in sweat.

Don't look down. Don't, whatever you do, look down.

What if somebody shone some car headlights up to where he was now? It would be the end of everything. But, Christ, he'd welcome that. He really would.

Only, as the breath came back into his lungs and

his heart stopped thudding, did the reason he was there where he was begin to make sense to him again.

Jesus, yes. The blue folder, this time, really there for the fucking taking.

He felt a surge of energy.

Almost sobbing, with relief, with pain, he set himself to go on climbing, managing this time to take it more slowly. Or not being able to do anything else.

And then, at last, he was there. Reaching up for one more rung he found he had taken hold of the sill. Another leg-up. Another. And he was high enough to thrust the top half of his body in.

The room he was able to see, taking one swift look, was empty. Herbie, despising such a wally, must have set about making hay inside while the sun shone for him. Oh well, fine, so long as what he was doing stopped any investigation deciding that the Fraud Investigation office had been the real target.

He lay for a few moments where he was, half in and half out of the window. Then with a painful wriggle and a heave he got the rest of his body in, if at the cost of finding himself eventually with his nose pressed against the tiled floor.

He scrambled to his feet, made his way, unsteadily, to the door Herbie had left open behind him.

Rounding the corner into the corridor, he saw that Herbie had done what had been agreed. Gone along the whole corridor breaking open every locked door. When he got to the second door along he saw him inside, already busy breaking open the drawers of a desk.

Yeah, he won't be in any hurry to lend me his jemmy. That's for a cert. Still . . .

He dug in his pocket. Trowel still there okay.

He hurried on past.

Then there it was. His door. His door broken wide open.

The door he had so nearly got the key into before Ma Alexander had pounced on him. The door he had watched from the waiting room opposite until Mac had come out on his way to the toilets when, even after the way had been clear, he had still failed to get to that cupboard. That folder.

Never mind, he had the trowel now. And for a cert it'd be strong enough to bust open a rotten old cupboard like that. Thank God, for the decent steel of its blade, and that he'd kept it cleaned in all the years he'd had it.

He went inside at a run, through the outer office – Horatio Bottomley's desk meticulously tidy – and into Mac's room. There was the cupboard. Doors tight locked. As he had expected. But he had the trowel.

He knelt and thrust the tip of its blade into the gap between the two doors. They were, he saw now, thicker than he had thought. In the days when a cupboard like this had been a standard item of office furnishing they made things to last.

But lever at the gap. Lever carefully. Decent steel or no decent steel, too much pressure and some part of the trowel could give.

A deep breath. Hold steady. And, now, gentle continuous force.

'Jack! Jack!'

He looked up, a startled thud jabbing pain through his heart.

Herbie was there at Mac's door.

What the—

'Can't you fucking hear?'

'Hear what?'

'Fucking police siren, you stupid berk. Someone must have seen us climbing in, phoned up. Come on, we got to scarper. They'll be here in no time.'

And, now that he was not concentrating on the cupboard, he could hear it perfectly well. The familiar wail of a police car in hot pursuit.

'Come on, you berk.'

'No.'

He turned back to the cupboard.

'You go on, Herbie. I'll just . . .'

He seized the trowel again, dug the blade in, just conscious behind him of Herbie's steps running through the outer office, along down the corridor.

Not now. Not now. I'm not going to be stopped now.

Chapter Seventeen

The trowel broke.

Jack's head, his eyes intently fixed between the cupboard doors, thumped hard forward on to the scarred surface, as the tool's wooden handle, gripped in his hurry instead of the metal blade itself, came away from its holder.

Rocking backwards on his knees, his mind shrill with despair, for a moment he stared on at the doors, transfixed. Then, scarcely conscious of what he was doing, he dug the fingers of both hands into the tantalizingly wide gap and tried scrabblingly to prise the doors apart. They did not budge by as much as a millimetre.

At last, impinging again on his ears, came the sound of the police car's siren. Yet nearer.

For a moment more he knelt there where he was, stricken. Then he forced his mind grimly to admit the truth. He was not going to get to the folder.

And, unless he was bloody quick, he was going to find himself arrested by a member of his own force, caught bang to rights.

He scrambled up to his feet, headed for the outer

office. Stopped, remembering the trowel. Evidence. His prints from all the days and years of work in the garden still on it somewhere. Despite all the rubbing it had got from the surgical gloves on his hands.

He darted back, scooped up the two pieces of his once trusty companion, shoved them into his pocket, went haring along the corridor towards the toilets and escape.

Would Herbie have gone swinging hand over hand down the ladder to the ground, have jerked the grapnel free, gone off into the moonlit night with ropes, rope-ladder, everything?

But, no.

No, thank God, the ladder was still there, hanging down from the wide open window, reaching almost to the ground.

Thrusting his head further out, he saw, below, Herbie hurriedly stuffing things into his leather bag. His tools. The tools of his trade. Which had not let him down. Which he was saving. For another day.

Quickly he knelt up on the window sill, managed to swing himself round – Christ, but it was a tight fit – and putting his legs over the side he felt and felt for the first of the ladder rungs.

Would Herbie flick at the grapnel rope now? Bring the whole lot down to the ground, himself with it? Or leave him grabbing at the window sill above and hanging there? Could he?

With his foot more or less on the rung he had felt, he let his whole body drop and then clutched hard with one hand at the ladder's side-rope.

The ladder was holding.

Safe. Safe so far.

But what if that car, siren still shrieking, was heading directly for the back of the building?

For a brief instant he imagined its occupants leaping out, sprinting towards Herbie across the twenty yards or so of well-kept lawn between the building and the tall surrounding wall. Sprinting as, in the past, he had done himself more times than he could count in pursuit of some suspect. And in the end, with a bite of savage joy, had collared his target. Would the car's crew now, in a minute's time or more, go sprinting towards Herbie, collar him? And then turn to the pathetic figure dangling up above.

No. Not in sight yet.

He let himself fall again. Grabbed for an arm-tearing moment at the ladder once more. Let himself fall again.

And at last, every nerve screaming, every muscle shooting with pain, he found he was on the ground. He forced himself to look round.

Herbie at the boundary wall was just throwing his bag of tools over. A squat distorted moonlit dwarf.

Putting his head down, propelled as much by the prospect of falling flat on his face as by anything he was able to force his legs to do, he set off towards him.

Herbie, he realized as he came panting and gasping up, had failed to climb the wall. Without any convenient tree growing close by as on the far side, he had not succeeded in jumping up high enough to get a grip on the coping.

For one past-looking flash of time he saw fat little ten-year-old Herbie trying in just the same way to scale the dingier brick wall of the school playground, his own gang running towards him yelling, *Thief! Get him! Thief!*

Then Herbie, landing at the foot of the wall again after another unsuccessful jump, must have heard him coming up. He turned, round face glistening with sweat in the cool moonlight.

'Christ, give me a back, quick.'

For a moment he did not understand.

'Make a back. Make a back. Christ, you dumb fucker.' He saw then what he had to do. And never mind if, scrambling up on him, Herbie got over, dropped down on the other side, left him to the mercy of that car crew.

He bent down, pressed one shoulder hard against the wall, braced his legs.

Herbie was on top of his back in an instant. He felt the boots inside the protecting socks dig hard into his flesh. Then they were there no longer.

He pushed himself straight, looked upwards.

Herbie was sitting astride the wall, and, yes, lowering an arm for him to take.

Good for Herbie. When it came to it . . .

He reached up. Grasped Herbie's hand.

'Sod it, don't pull me off, you fucker.'

He put his other hand on the harsh brick as high as he could reach, hoped for some tiny bit of purchase, flung himself upwards, scrabbling with his feet at the wall's surface. He felt Herbie, their hands entwined, heave his weight on to the far side as a counterbalance. He was off the ground. He reached up with his free arm.

And grasped the edge of the top of the wall. Herbie changed his grip, held him under the armpits.

A few seconds of confused struggling, and, the next thing he knew, he was on the ground at the far side. Shocked and winded. But safe.

'Come on then, come on,' Herbie yelled. 'They'll take it into their heads to drive round this way in a minute.'

Feeling totally devoid of any energy at all, he made himself set off behind Herbie across the field towards the gate they had climbed over on their way in.

Above, the big moon shone implacably down.

Lily, coming sleepily into the room when the row he made stumbling in had woken her, was at her best the moment she saw him.

'Oh, Jack, what a mess you're in. Look at your face. That's a terrible bruise. They try to give you a pasting?'

For an instant he could not think what she was talking about. Then his brain began to work. He had told her the evening before he had to go out with a team dawn-raiding a crack house.

'Certainly feel I've had a pasting. Pasting and a half.'

Let her believe the places where he had bruised himself getting down that bloody rope-ladder, scrambling over that wall, the bang he had given himself on

Mac's old cupboard when the trowel broke, were the result of a ruck with some criminals. The last thing to tell her now was how the crazy attempt to get at the blue folder had gone so horribly wrong. Christ, if she started asking questions . . .

But she seemed to be satisfied with what he had said.

'Here, let me get those clothes off you. What you want is a nice hot bath. I'll run it, soon as I've got you undressed. And then it'll be out with the old bottle of witch hazel. Been a long time since you needed that.'

'Thanks, love. You're right. That's what I do need. Bath, bit of tender loving care with that bottle of stuff, and then sleep.'

'And that's what you're going to get, you poor old thing.'

Lying in the hot water, feeling his bruises and scratches becoming minute by minute less painful, he thought that it was at times like this, and not the times under the duvet however well they went, when he felt closest to his English rose.

But in the morning – another bloody Monday – he was still feeling the bruises and his hands were still rawly tender. His mental state was, if anything, even worse.

Much though he had longed to stay wrapped up in bed thinking of nothing, he had forced himself to get up, get into work on time. Turning up late would only draw attention to himself. The Guv'nor might start to wonder why he had given himself a lie-in. Head filled with the news about the break-in at Headquarters he might, just, just possibly, put two and two together . . . Especially if he happened to notice the bruises and sore hands.

In the CID Room the gossip, naturally, was all about the daring raid.

'Ransacked the place, the cheeky fucking sods. Thousands of quids' worth just bloody disappeared.'

'Yeah, but they had to scarper. Left a lot of their gear behind. Some sort of ladder, I heard. Something like a firemen's one. Great big affair.'

'Well, it'll be covered in dabs any road. Happy hunting ground for Fingerprints. The lads'll be there for a week.' Christ, he thought, the idea entering his head for the first time, Herbie's prints on that grapnel they'd had to leave behind, or the pulley. Jesus, if they find anything, who's most likely to be sent out to bring Herbie in? Fellow who knows most about him. Fucking Jack Stallworthy. And who won't dare bring in someone who'd blow the gaff soon as he'd put one foot inside the Custody Area? Jack Stallworthy, that's who.

Jesus, it could all blow up in my face any second.

He sat at his desk, pretending to be doing his expenses – the one sacrosanct activity that almost guaranteed him no interruptions – and let the misery soak into every corner of his mind. He had totally banjaxed everything now. He was never going to get the folder. He was never going to be able to get near that cupboard again. He was never ever going to have the satisfaction of handing that little bitch Anna Foxton the papers sodding Warnaby had been ready to give him so much to get hold of.

Warnaby, when that second deadline had come and gone, would find someone else to get him out of his trouble, whatever it was. You were rich enough, and ruthless enough, you could always find someone to do the dirty work for you. If you were ready to give them something like a whole sodding hotel on some poncy tourist isle. Something he would never get now. Something Lil had set her heart on. Something she thought was going to come her way at last. A jackpot. A lifetime's secret hope suddenly in sight.

Well, it was in sight no more.

'Stallworthy! What you sitting there for like a pile of damp shit?'

The Guv'nor. Christ. Was this it?

No, he'd been noticed sitting slumped where he was, and was going to be found some tuppenny-ha'penny task. Cyclist reported riding without lights, tobacconist selling ten fags to a kid, offence of operating a loudspeaker contrary to Section something-or-other of the Control of Pollution Act 1974.

He pushed himself to his feet.

'Just going out on inquiries, guv. Was sorting meself out.'

So long as the bugger doesn't want to know what inquiries.

But his record came to his rescue. Detective Sergeant Stallworthy had gone out on inquiries so many times and brought back the bacon. No one was going to want precise details. Especially as the details were often the sort people with noses to keep clean preferred not to hear about.

He shambled from the room.

What to do? Where to keep his head down till he felt more able to cope? If ever he would.

He went to his car. Sat in a huddle in front of the wheel, not even able to think about his predicament. Lily. What would she say? Warnaby. What might he do? If he wanted to, there'd be ways of making life hell for him. Spend a few quid, get a few lies told and he could end up off the force. No bloody pension. Nothing. What about April Cottage, then? Never mind the Calm Seas Hotel, Ko Samui.

And, God, if he sat here much longer some inquisitive sod would come up and ask if he was all right.

All right? He was fucking all wrong. That was what.

He started the engine, drove out into the street.

A van he had nearly put his bonnet in front of hooted angrily.

Fuck you.

But it did come over him that he ought to pay a little attention to what he was doing. Even if he was paying no attention to where he was going.

Which is how, he thought fifteen minutes later, I come to be sitting here in the car park up at fucking Headquarters. The last place on earth I want to be. The last place I ought to be. The murderer revisits the scene of the crime.

What if some nosey sod here – they're all over the

place, count on it – comes up and asks once more if I'm all right?

Could say I've come to see the doc. As per usual.

And, truth to tell, it'd probably be no bad thing if I did go and see him. I feel totally rotten.

Worse even than last night's caper entitles me to feel.

But, likely as not, that's just because I'm in such deep shit. Enough to make anybody feel bloody ill.

Should I start up again, drive away somewhere? God, but I haven't even got the energy for that. Still, p'raps I ought to get out of the motor. Make a show of going somewhere. Suppose, in fact, this is the best place I could be, up here. *Murderer revisits the scene of the crime*. Nobody believes that in real life. So being here's going to be an alibi for me, if anything.

So . . . Well, could I actually go and have a look at the Fraud office? That door broken open . . . What if I find I can just stroll in there, and that cupboard's been unlocked, and . . .

Christ, don't be more of a silly bugger than you can help, Jack Stallworthy. Do you really think old Mac MacAllister's going to leave all his precious confidential files unguarded? God, he'll have a couple of wooden-tops sitting there twenty-four hours a day till the lock on his door is hundred percent back in place.

No, just head for the canteen here – fuck the doc – and be grateful you're well out of the way. No chance of the Guv'nor finding me stupid things to do. Or, worse, seeing that bruise on my forehead and taking it into his head to start asking fucking awkward questions.

Jesus, what I wouldn't give to be shot of the whole bleeding lot. Retired. With the sodding pension, however little it is. Feet up for ever. Unless every now and again I go for a trot out into the garden. Spread a bit of mulch under the lilies.

Not that I'm ever going to have a garden with lilies now. Can even see myself not having my Lil any more. When she hears the full tale.

He heaved himself out of the car, made his way into the building, flicking open his warrant card for the benefit of the constable on security duty.

God, and the trouble I had last night getting inside here.

But the canteen. Can I really show my face there? Will I run straight into old Ma Alexander? *Mr Stallworth, what you doing here? You ain't come to steal my keys again?* No, she'll be gone long ago now, early start she has. But Mac? What about Mac? His time for his Petticoat Tail shortbreads?

He looked up at the big clock with the golden hands at the far end of the marble-pillared entrance hall.

No, okay again there. Mac'll never enter the canteen till the stroke of eleven, however much his sacred office was broken into in the middle of last night.

If just one day Mac'd let himself go, order chocolate digestives instead of shortbreads.

But if Mac was capable of that, he'd have been the sort to take the bait of fouling up Detective Chief

Superintendent Detch's onwards and upwards career. And have let me slip that blue folder under my coat and walk out with it.

In the canteen he ordered a tea, grabbed two packets of sugar and half a dozen little plastic stirrers with it. Never mind he hadn't put sugar in his tea for years. He'd take the buggers here for every penny they'd got.

Or, anyhow, every sodding plastic stirrer.

He slumped down at the nearest table.

Oh, God, who had he plonked himself next to but bloody Horatio Bottomley.

That talk in the rain in the motor. Those two stubby-fingered brown hands coming down on to his shoulders as he had knelt in front of that cupboard that time when its doors had still been tantalizingly open, the crammed files and boxes bulging on its shelves.

Get up? Run out?

He hadn't the energy to run a single step. Not even enough to hoist himself to his feet.

And it was in that way that his troubles, all within ten minutes, came to an end.

Chapter Eighteen

'Mr Stallworthy. Funny you should sit here. I was jus' thinking 'bout you this very minute.'

Oh, yes, and I know what you were thinking, you old idiot. How there are detectives in the force with tiptop reputations as thief-takers who yet aren't to be trusted one inch. Or how there's one like that in particular.

Only, if you are thinking along those lines, old chap, why is it you're looking at me as if I was the answer to all your prayers?

'Oh, yes, mate? And what was it you were busy thinking?'

'Mr Stallworthy, you tell me please: is it right there are times when what you got to do is put your own feelings before your duty?'

What is this? Doesn't quite sound like Horatio in the motor, not even understanding how he could make a decent few quid by turning a blind eye when asked.

Play for time. See what the hell he's on about. If he even knows himself.

'Now you're asking, old son. Now you're asking.'

'Yes, Mr Stallworthy, I am asking. I am asking you.'

'Me, matey? You're asking me? Why me?'

Horatio shifted round in his chair and gave him a long searching look, big brown eyes sombre beneath his scanty fuzz of grey hair.

'I'm asking you 'cos I got to thinking you was one who did put hisself before what they call duty. Or you done that sometimes, 'cordin' to what Mr Mac tol' me. An', Mr Stallworthy, I'm wondering if this is one time I gotta do jus' that.'

More bloody puzzling remarks. What the hell is he on about?

'Oh, yes? How's that, then?'

'Mr Stallworthy, it's like this. You know Mr Mac just gone on holiday? Went Saturday, 'cept he came in for an hour just now when they told him 'bout the break-in.'

He was so astonished to hear Mac had gone on leave that he hardly gave a thought to him standing there by the wrecked door of his office, and perhaps connecting that splintered jamb with what Horatio must have told him about his own attempt to take something from the Symes case papers.

'On holiday?' he spluttered with laughter. 'Mac? Gone on holiday?'

He had thought he would never laugh again. But the idea that Mac MacAllister, who not so long ago had said that going on holiday was the last thing he wanted to do, had now suddenly agreed to go was such a surprise that laughter had burst out of him.

'Oh, yes, Mr Mac's gone all right. It was the big joke all over Headquarters. The big, big joke. Only for old Horatio it ain't no joke at all.'

'Oh, go on, matey, it is funny. It's dead funny. Mac off to sunny Spain or somewhere. It's unbelievable.'

'Oh, he ain't gone to no Spain or nowhere. He told me he'd go an' sit in his flat and count the days till he could get back. But Mr Cutts said he mus' go. Mr Cutts said he couldn't run the admin here if people would never take no leave they was entitled to.'

'And so poor old Mac had to obey orders, eh?'

Well, serve the starchy bloody Scotchman right.

'Yes, sir. But it's poor old Horatio I'm thinking of, Mr Stallworthy. 'Cos I'm in big, big trouble.'

'And you think, somehow, there's something I can do about it? Well, what's it all to do with anyhow?'

For a little Horatio seemed unable to answer. He sat on his tubular canteen chair, rocking to and fro as if he had a pain in his belly. At last he spoke.

'You got any children, Mr Stallworthy? No, I think somehow you ain't. Well, I got jus' one. My daughter, Julie May. And she going to be married. An' that's jus' fine by me. He a nice chap. A good man. Young fellow she met at university. 'Cos she's a very clever little girl, my Julie May. Met her Ian right up in Scotland. Aberdeen University. An' that's where the wedding's going to be. Aberdeen, Scotland. But now there's one deep, deep problem.'

Silence. And more bellyache rocking.

'Well, mate, what is it?'

'Oh, Mr Stallworthy. It's Mr Mac's holiday.'

'Mac's holiday? I don't get this at all, Horatio. How's that give you any sort of a problem?'

'It's the cleaner, Mr Stallworthy.'

'The cleaner? What cleaner? I dunno, mate, you're making this more and more confusing every minute.'

'I confused myself, Mr Stallworthy. Right confused, start to finish. An' that's why I'm wanting your advice. The best advice you got.'

'Come to Doctor Stallworthy, mate. Consultations free. But try and make it clear to the poor old fellow. He's not feeling too good this morning, matter of fact.'

'Yes. Yes, sir. I will. You see the wedding's Saturday. Up in Aberdeen. Long, long way away. And Mr Mac . . .'

'Back to Mac and his holiday, are we?'

'That's it, Mr Stallworthy. You put your finger right on the problem. When Mr Mac went off, he say to me I got one duty I must do. An' that's to come in Saturday morning early when the cleaner goes through the office. She a new lady, and Mr Mac he don't know he can trust her. Mrs Alexander, she gone on holiday too.'

'I'm there, old son, I'm there now. Mac's told you you've got to be in the office early on Saturday morning, make sure the new cleaner doesn't pinch his secret packet of shortbread—'

'No, no, Mr Stallworthy. Mr Mac don't keep no shortbreads—'

'Okay, okay. Keep your hair on. Only joking. Let's put it this way, Mac wants you in that office to make sure the new cleaner don't go poking about seeing something she shouldn't.'

'That it, Mr Stallworthy.'

'But you, you want to be up in Aberdeen, your daughter's wedding, on the same day. Got to go by the night train, eh? Yep, see you've got a problem. But I was you, I'd forget about looking after that cleaner. Whizz off to bonny Scotland. Have a good time.'

'Oh, Mr Stallworthy, I jus' couldn't do no such thing.'

'Well then, mate, you'll have to miss your daughter's wedding, won't you? I suppose it can't be put off or anything?'

'All the guests is coming. Function room booked an' all. My missus been up there whole week.'

'It's what they call a dilemma then, matey. One way or another you've got to let somebody down. Still, I know which one I'd give the go-by to.'

Once more Horatio lapsed into silence. Looking at him, Jack could almost see his mind uselessly working. Churning and churning, and getting nowhere.

If it was figures, he thought, old H would have had the answer in two seconds flat. But this . . . Well, there wasn't any answer really, not if you felt about things the way Horatio did.

And suddenly it came to him that it was altogether in his own interests to give old Horatio a push. More of a push than, totally without realizing what all this might mean to himself, he had done already. Tell Horatio one hundred per cent firmly it was okay for him to waltz off to Scotland and he would go without another thought. Then, once again, the Fraud Investigation offices would be there to be entered. Mac away on holiday. Some new cleaner going round the place with her vacuum cleaner, not knowing anything. And nothing easier then – couldn't be – than to bluff his way in, right up to that cupboard. Deal with that somehow or another, and he'd be neatly in time to give bloody Emslie Warnaby his precious blue folder before the second deadline ran out.

Perfect.

Only it wasn't. Somehow it wasn't like that. Somehow it'd be altogether too iffy to take advantage of someone like old Horatio. Figures apart, he was too easy a touch. Innocent as a new-born babe.

So what to do?

For God's sake, I've already told the old fool if I was in his shoes I'd bugger off without a second thought. I keep stumm now, he'll probably do what I just said's okay after all.

But . . .

'Listen, mate, I don't think you—'

Then Horatio, with a rush of words that showed how twisted up inside he was, stopped him. Totally ignored the fact that he had begun to speak.

'Mr Stallworthy,' he broke out, 'what I'm needing bad, Mr Stallworthy, is someone who won't think I is a – who won't go thinking I is a damn no-good if – if, just this once, I'm not doing my duty.'

And I can guess who that is. See, in fact, what the old fool means. Not exactly a compliment. Jack Stallworthy, the only man in Abbotsport Police villain enough to be let in on the secret that old Horatio Bottomley for once in his life's going to be a bit naughty. Thank you very much.

'Well, you're right, me old mate. I ain't exactly in any position to yack at someone not being hundred per cent kosher. So, if that's all you want, you got my vote. All the way.'

'Mr Stallworthy, it more than that. Mr Stallworthy, if that someone who didn't think I is wrong was there Saturday morning to look after that new cleaning lady, then I could go to Aberdeen and be happy. Mr Stallworthy, will you be that person?'

Horatio lunged towards him now, big brown eyes moist with feeling.

'And don't you worry, Mr Stallworthy, I know it safe to let you in there. Mr Mac, when he went for his holiday, he took the key to that cupboard. You know the cupboard I is talking about, Mr Stallworthy? Jus' lucky when those fellows broke in here last night, they didn't touch it, nor nothing else in the whole Fraud office.'

'Yes, Horatio, I know the cupboard you mean.'

Don't I just. Christ, was it only eight hours ago, more or less, I was digging that trowel of mine in between its two tight shut doors? And now here's Horatio thinking, because that time when I had my hands in there he came in and caught me, he's got a right to ask me to help him cheat old Mac. He's got a bloody cheek. Still, I'm in no position to complain. I was out of order when he caught me then, right out of order. And we both know it.

And, by God – the blood began suddenly to race in Jack's veins – by God, I'm going to be out of order again. I've been licensed. I've been given the bloody freedom of the Fraud Office. Next Saturday I'm going to get that new cleaning lady out of the way somehow and bust that cupboard wide open. Poor old Horatio, I'll be letting him down. Dropping him right in it. But I can't pass up this chance. A godsend. A ruddy godsend.

'Yes, Horatio, old mate, I'll do that for you. Why not? You go off to your old Aberdeen, get that daughter of yours well married. And I'll hold the fort Saturday morning. Stand by me.'

Before Saturday came, however, Jack had seen how, with a little bit of luck, he could leave Horatio's conscience clear. And his own as well, more or less.

All he had to do, he realized, was to get hold of another key that would open the cupboard. Hardly difficult. The key Mac had found or had had made, when he had seen it lying there on the top of the cupboard before those crammed contents had been squeezed in, had looked a simple enough affair. The cupboard was no state-of-the-art security safe, after all. With most of a week to go he could easily get hold of a dozen or more keys like Mac's. Bound to find one that fitted. And if there wasn't one when it came to it, well then, he'd have to betray Horatio's trust after all and break the damn cupboard open for all to see afterwards.

Because this time there were going to be no mistakes. This time he was going to walk out of the building with the blue folder.

So, very early on the Saturday he presented himself to Mrs Alexander's deputy as head cleaner, a sour-looking old biddy he had never met before, and, as Horatio had instructed him, told her that for security reasons he had to be present when the Fraud Investigation offices were cleaned.

He met with no objection.

Three minutes later together with the new cleaning lady, or girl rather – she seemed to be only about seventeen and had a trick of sniffing regularly once every five seconds – he was watching old Sour-face putting one of Mrs Alexander's big bunch of Yale keys into the newly mended door Herbie Cuddy had jemmied open almost a week earlier.

The door he had watched so hungrily through the thick glass window in the waiting-room door opposite. The door he had once almost got open with one of that very bunch of keys before Ma Alexander had pounced on him.

What trick Sour-face had learnt he did not know, but she had had no difficulty selecting from the unmarked keys of that big, jingling bunch the one that straight away turned in the lock.

'There you are, then,' she said. 'And don't you linger over the job, my girl. There's plenty more to be done this morning.'

All the answer she got to that was a sniff coming just two seconds after the one before.

Jack walked in, followed by the little sniffer dragging her heavy-duty vacuum cleaner.

So here I am, he said to himself. Inside. With fifteen or sixteen keys, any one of which could get that cupboard open, and a good strong screwdriver tucked in my pocket to use if none of them work. I can't believe it.

Little Sniffer had plugged in her machine and begun at once to use it on the outer office. It made a deep whiny roaring, enough noise to make any sound elsewhere totally inaudible. Jack, without a word of explanation, simply left her and walked through into Mac's room.

The only precaution he did take was, with apparent idleness, to push the door almost closed behind him.

Then, in an instant, he was once more down in front of the cupboard. His ring of likely keys was out of his pocket. He pushed the first one that came to hand into the brass-edged keyhole. It slid sweetly home.

He took in a huge gulp of air. Gave the key a turn.

And click.

It was open. The cupboard was open.

He swung the doors wide. And there, there, was that strip of pale blue card he had once had within reach, and infuriatingly not within reach. And now, easily as easily, the folder slipped out from its place and was at last firmly in his grasp.

Yes, on it, in neat black-ink handwriting the single word *Maximex*. Just as Emslie Warnaby had said it would be so long ago.

Would something catastrophic happen now at the last moment? Little Sniffer come in? Old Sour-puss? Bloody Detective Chief Superintendent Detch?

Nothing happened.

He straightened up, shoved the folder under his jacket, well up to his armpit. Then he stooped again, and, with a word of heartfelt thanks to Horatio Bottomley, pushed the cupboard doors closed and turned his key in the lock.

Click.

Job done. No clues left. No one to be any the wiser. First-class bit of work.

Outside in the marvellously fresh air – it was a perfect summer's morning: he hadn't noticed it at all on his way in – he took a long, deep breath. Then he strode over to his car, opened the door, pulled the blue folder from inside his jacket, tossed it on to the seat at the back, got in and drove off.

He could hardly believe it had all happened. As he drove along the still empty road from Palmerston Park he had to twist round more than once to see with his own eyes that clean pale blue folder lying on the scuffed grey of the back seat.

He had done it. Done it. He had done what he had been asked to do by Emslie Warnaby. He had taken from the very heart of Abbotsport Constabulary Headquarters a sheaf of documents that, for some reason he could not even guess at, the all-powerful boss of Abbotputers plc was willing to pay him for. To pay him – yes, yes, yes – with a hotel, the Calm Seas Hotel, on the island called Ko Samui. The one place in all the world where Lil, his English rose, wanted to live till the end of her days. He had done it. Done it, done it.

He drove straight across to the other side of the town to the hill overlooking the port.

If it was too early for Anna Foxton, to hell with her. He'd just have to get her out of bed. And to hell with big man Emslie Warnaby if he happened to be sharing that bed.

His old car went chugging up the hill. The big dark brick block of Seaview Mansions came into sight. He put his foot down and drove up to it in a final burst of shuddering speed. He braked. He reached back and picked up the folder. Without bothering to hide it under his jacket now he ran up the entrance steps to the block, jabbed long and hard at the bellpush for Flat 15 – the number was lodged unbudgeably in his mind – and waited for an answer from the entryphone.

It came quickly enough, though Anna Foxton's voice was sharp with irritation and unfinished sleep.

'Who is that?'

He allowed himself a slow smile.

'It's Jack Stallworthy. You want me to come up? Or not?'

'You – you've got it?'

'Wouldn't be here unless, would I?'

The mechanism of the door-bolt buzzed at once.

He pushed the big door back, and, scorning the lift, marched up to Flat 15.

Little Anna Foxton, dressed only in a sweeping

dark orange housecoat, had opened her door as she heard him coming. He saw her eyes dart first to the folder in his hand. When she had satisfied herself it was really there she pulled the door wide back.

'Well, well, Sergeant. So you've managed it at last.'

'I've had my troubles, but I told you you'd get it, and here it is.'

She held out her hand. He put the folder into it. She turned it over till she could see the word *Maximex* – yes, that was the new big computer system Abbotputers was going into manufacturing, he suddenly remembered – and took a quick checking glance at the papers inside.

Not going to let me get as much as a peep at whatever old Emslie needs so badly. Well, who cares, so long as I get what I've come here for?

Satisfied, she gave him a sharp glance.

'So now you'll be wanting your reward, yes?'

Being paid off. Like a bloody crim taking his cut from a big blag.

Well, fuck her.

'Yep. What I'm here for.'

She went to the sideboard, still with its clutch of expensive drinks on their tray, and pulled open one of its two drawers. From it she took another folder, a red one, and from that she pulled a long, stiff-paper, legal-looking document.

'The deeds of the Calm Seas Hotel, Ko Samui,' she said. 'You'd better look them over carefully. We don't want you coming back saying there's something wrong.'

'Dare say you don't ever want to see me again. Now I've done your dirty work for you.'

'Well, you're right there, Sergeant, as a matter of fact.'

Once again he was tempted to take the little bitch by the shoulders and shake her silly.

But instead he began reading the neatly typed pages of legal jargon, almost every paragraph meaningless to him. On and on until at last he came to the final flourished signature, *Emslie R. Warnaby, Chairman Abbotputers plc*, with next to it *Anna Foxton* as witness. And then he was swept through by a feeling of letdown.

So this was it. It was over. He had got Lily what she wanted. He had got Emslie Warnaby what he wanted. The bugger could go off on holiday with this little bit of his now without a care in the world. And that was all there was to it.

He tried to imagine what Lily's reaction would be when he showed her this thin sheaf of stiff paper with its endless typed paragraphs. He'd have to explain to her what it was, what it meant. That it was the deeds of the Calm Seas Hotel, made out in his name – he had understood that much – and that, once he had got the air tickets and had gone through the official formalities of handing in his papers, they could be off there. To Ko Samui. That in less than a month they could be there. In the sun. Looked after for life.

But, somehow, he was unable to bring into his mind a picture of Lil's ecstatic face.

He shrugged.

When it's happened for real it'll all be all right. Unless old Lil's gone off with the postman.

The joke fell flat in his head.

'They seem okay,' he said, folding the deeds and stuffing them into his inside pocket. 'So what about the plane tickets?'

'You can collect them from the travel agency. They'll be ready first thing on Monday. It's a place called Iris Travels in Albert Street. I expect you know it.'

'Think I may have gone past it, yes. Anyhow, I can find it.'

'Yes, I imagine your detective skills will stretch to that.'

The bitch.

He looked at her. Yes, she did have a similarity to Lily, despite the difference in hair colour, the different complexions, ivory smoothness instead of Lil's English rose pink-and-white, changing-every-passing-second skin. Still fresh as ever. Or almost.

'Right,' he said. 'I'll be off, then.'

'Yes.'

Just that.

Well, if she wanted no more to do with him now he had done what her lover wanted from him, then he wanted no more to do with her. To do with either of them. Nothing that would remind him he had at last taken the great fat bribe that had been dangled and dangled in front of him.

Chapter Nineteen

He decided – he didn't quite know why – he would not, after all, tell Lily straight away. He'd wait till he'd collected the plane tickets from that place, Iris Travels. Then she could see everything all at once.

The tickets would mean something to her. More than incomprehensible legal deeds. Perhaps that was why it had suddenly seemed better to keep it all secret for a little.

Till Monday.

He would go to Iris Travels soon as they opened. Nine o'clock? Well, he'd be there waiting then. And, once he had got the tickets, checked them over, made sure they were all right, then he'd drive back home – to hell with getting in to work on time this Monday of all Mondays – and break the big news to his darling English rose.

He had vaguely thought there would be things to do in the garden on Sunday. Things that would separate him from Lily and stop him blurting out the secret. He knew he ought to have dug up his tulip bulbs to store in their place in the shed till they were due to be replanted. Their leaves had been lying there, dead, pale brown, floppy and unsightly, for much longer than they should have done. But, worrying and worrying about how to get at the blue folder, he hadn't had the heart to tackle the job. There was lots of dead-heading to be done, too. And work over the Dorothy Perkins rose he had climbing all up the back wall, snip-snipping, and you could get blooms on it for a month or more yet.

But, going out to the shed to collect his trowel to hoick up the bulbs, it came to him like a sudden cold wind that the trowel was no more. Its two pieces were hidden from sight in a clump of tall nettles sprouting near where he had dropped Herbie Cuddy that night.

And then he thought with a thump of something like disappointment that there was no point anyhow in doing anything to the garden. In a month or so they would have left the house, paid the final bit of rent, sold the furniture for what it would fetch, be on their way to a new life in a different, sun-drenched country.

He went and sat on the little bench outside the sitting-room window. Go in and fetch the Sunday paper? Not worth the bother. None of what was in it would mean a thing to him out there.

Several times during the evening he was on the point of telling Lily. Saying to her suddenly that all was set for them to go off to her beloved Ko Samui. But he knew he would be unable to give her the news with the right enthusiasm. And at last it was late enough to say he was off to bed.

*

But at five to nine on Monday morning he was pacing up and down outside Iris Travels in Albert Street. And – a bounce of excitement jumped in him at last – at nine exactly a young woman in a bright cotton summer dress came up the street towards the shop, her walk slowing as she ceased to look where she was going in trying to pull a bunch of keys out of the tote bag from her shoulder.

He stood aside when, at last, she got to the shop's door and opened up. He followed her in.

'You're bright and early,' she said as she made her way to her side of the counter. 'What can I do for you?'

For a moment then it occurred to him that there might not have been time for his tickets to have been got ready. What if Anna Foxton had delayed telling Warnaby they were needed now? Or, say, Warnaby in his office at Abbotputers hadn't done anything about putting the order through.

But no, Anna, little bitch that she was, certainly seemed efficient. Had she begun as Emslie's secretary? Quite likely. And she had said the tickets would be ready for him to collect first thing on Monday. And this was Monday, first thing.

'I think you've got some air tickets for me,' he said. 'Name of Stallworthy.'

'Oh, yes, Mr Stallworthy. They rang from Abbotputers on Saturday, confirming they could be handed over today. So I'll just unlock the safe, and you can have them right away.' He waited patiently while she went into an inner office and, after three or four minutes, emerged again with a long white envelope with a bright-coloured rainbow all across its front and the words *Iris Travels*. She handed it over.

'Two first-class tickets for Ko Samui,' she said. 'Just check everything's all right, and then if you could sign for them . . .'

They were all right. Right as rain.

Bloody Ko Samui, he thought. Lil and me flying off first bloody class to Ko Samui.

He signed the receipt, left the shop in a daze, headed for the car.

Now it was going to be the moment. The moment when he would tell Lily that, despite all the difficulties and even the danger he had been in, her wish was going to come true. Had come true. Had come true.

He patted the Iris Travels envelope in his pocket.

That's what I'll do. Just drop this on the table beside her, say *Look, at that, my girl*, and then wait to see the expression on her face when she sees the tickets inside. Then, when she's taken that in, I can show her the deeds, tell her how in the end I managed to get hold of that bloody blue folder, tell her where I really was that night last week when I said I had to go out dawn-raiding a crack house. Tell her everything.

He ran into the house, pulling the long, brightly coloured envelope from his pocket.

What if she's gone off with the postman? This time the joke seemed hilariously funny.

He was still smiling, only just keeping down the laughter, as he came into the sitting-room. Lily was not, as he had imagined she would be, tucked there into her favourite chair. She was standing by the telephone, and he realized now that, as he had come up the path to the door, he had heard it ringing.

'It's for you, Jack. They were asking if you were here.' The bloody Guv'nor. Can't he give a bloke twenty minutes' grace on a Monday morning? Well, before the day's out he'll learn I'm just about out of range of his bossiness.

'It's from Mr Detch's office,' Lily said.

'Detch? Detch? What's he want for Christ sake?'

'I'm sure I don't know. You'd better ask.'

She passed him the handset.

'DS Stallworthy here.'

'Oh, right, Sergeant.' Detch's secretary, poncy tart. 'There you are. You're to come up here at once. Mr Detch wants to see you without delay.'

'Okay, okay. But what is this?'

'I'm afraid I can't say, Sergeant. All I know is Mr Detch wants to see you.'

'All right, then. I'll be there in twenty minutes, half an hour.'

'I'd make it sooner if I were you.'

'I can't go any faster than the traffic lets me, can I?'

He slammed the handset back.

'What's that, then?' Lily asked.

'How the heck should I know? Bloody Detch wants me. You know that much: you know as much as I do.'

He stormed out.

Bugger, bugger, bugger. Come running in, all set to break the good news. Should be smiles all round. Big hug, kisses. Few tears of joy, if you like. And what happens? Sodding phone rings, and I chew Lil's head off. No reason at all.

But, driving up towards Palmerston Park, he felt somehow that there must have been a reason to have had that sudden fit of anxiety. That had made him snap at Lily like that. He seemed heavy with the notion that he ought to be worrying.

There was nothing at all to worry about, as far as he knew. Yet he could not rid himself of a running niggle of unease.

Had they found out somehow about the blue folder? But that was impossible. Yet what if that girl, Little Sniffy, had been spying on him while her vacuum cleaner roared away. But she wouldn't have. Why should she? Or . . . Or could Herbie have been marked for the Headquarters job? It was his MO, more or less. And if he'd been brought in he'd squeal quick enough. But, no. He wouldn't. He'd try everything to wriggle out of it before he came to that. So could he have left his own dabs somewhere on the gear Herbie had abandoned, hanging there from the toilets' window? No. No, definitely. He'd hardly touched anything, bar the ropes, except when he was wearing gloves. And in any case his prints weren't on file. Why should they be? He wasn't on that side of the fence.

Or anyhow he'd only really been seriously on the wrong side once. The time that had, just now, brought him the airline tickets and the hotel deeds nestling in his pocket.

Better hide those somewhere in the motor, though, stick them under the carpet, before I go in and see bloody Detch.

'Right, Sergeant Stallworthy.'

He had never seen Detchie look in such a rage. Leaning forward across his desk, eyes concentrated into two piercing rays. Mouth taut as a stretched rubber-band.

It must be the break-in. Herbie must have coughed, after all. Nothing but that would put Detchie in such a fury.

Oh, God, how am I going to get out of this? And for it to come at this moment. Those tickets there in the motor, just waiting to be used. Lily's Ko Samui there for the reaching out.

'Sir?'

'The last time you were in this office, Stallworthy, I gave you an order. I suppose you don't bloody remember what.'

The last time . . .? Oh, my God, yes. Teggs. Norman bloody Teggs. Was told to lay off him, and what did I do? Only go straight off to give the shitbag a good going-over.

Still, it's not the break-in. And what do I care now if Detchie is in a rage about Teggs? I could tell him straight off I'm putting in my papers. And then see what he can do. But play along. See if it really is Teggs he's on about.

'Yes, sir, I do remember. You told me to concentrate on the gargoyle theft case and leave other things alone.'

'Yes, I did. And what other things were those, Sergeant?'

Right. Yes, it is Teggs. Wonder why that toe-rag means so much to him . . .

'You wanted me specifically not to pursue inquiries into one Norman Teggs, sir.'

'Yes, exactly. So what do I find now? Only that you took a backhander from that man. The sum of one thousand pounds. In exchange for forgetting you'd seen a pile of porno tapes in his place.'

My God, he's somehow got on to that. All that way back. And, Christ, I'm really in trouble now. I could get done for that. Jesus, why did I let myself take from a slimy bastard like Teggs? I could find myself going up the steps for this one. And getting sent down, too. Jesus, a cop's life inside. Torture from day one on.

But – oh, my Christ, my Christ – for this to come out now. Now when I'm on the very point of leaving the force. Of being shot of all that business of making a few extra quid when I could, of filling up that stupid Cadbury's Roses box under the aubrietia. When I'm just about to leave Abbotsport, to leave bloody England. For good and all. To leave behind taking and fiddling. To start a new, golden life. With my Lil. Far away.

What to say to Detch now? How to get out of it? But it can't be got out of. It happened. I did it.

And now, for some reason, out of the blue, it's come back to smack me in the face.

No answer to the accusation, no answer at all, came into his mind.

He was finished. Done for. This was the end. It had all caught up with him. At the last moment. The very last moment.

Blankly he stared at the wide surface of Detch's desk in front of him. Smooth, polished, clear of any scrap of paper. Except for one shiny piece, evidently pushed aside as he had knocked and entered.

And then ... Then something about that glossy sheet struck him. It was headed with a brightly coloured rainbow. And, small and upside down though the writing beneath was, he could, now he tried, make it out easily enough. *IRES TRAVELS*. And that *E* that should have been an *I* had been corrected in red pen.

All at once things began falling into place. What that glossy sheet must be was a printer's proof. A proof Detective Chief Superintendent Detch himself had been correcting. So Iris Travels was Detective Chief Superintendent Detch's pigeon. His. And, yes, surely his wife's name was Iris. He'd heard her called that somewhere. Some official get-together, party, presentation, whatever.

So, what was Iris Travels but just the sort of enterprise he had wished in the past his own Lily had been capable of running? A neat little business into which you could put money you didn't want to be seen in the light of day. So who, then, was on the take besides himself? None other than Detective Chief Superintendent Detch, sir.

And if Detchie was on the take, he wouldn't be just getting a thousand nicker, top whack, from a sleaze-bag like Norman Teggs. He would be being paid by a really big-time criminal. Nothing else would be worth his while. And who had Teggs told him now owned that crappy Video Magic place but Abbotsport's number one criminal, Harry Hook. So how had Detchie learnt he had taken a thousand quid months ago off Teggs? From his pal Harry Hook, of course.

How to play this, then?

Easy.

'Yes, sir, I did take a sum of money off that shitbag Teggs.'

He saw the look of surprise slowly growing on the furious face opposite.

'I admit it, sir,' he went on. 'But what I took's a mere nothing compared to what a big-time criminal like, f'rinstance, Harry Hook must be paying out to someone on the force. And that's the buzz going round, so I hear.'

There was a moment when he experienced a tiny doubt. What if he had put two and two together and made just three?

But, no.

The look of sharp thoughtfulness that had replaced every other expression on Detch's face was enough to tell him he had struck gold.

'Well, Sergeant,' Detch said after a long pause, 'I

take your point. Of course, I don't want to hear that anyone under my command is on the take. Even from a cheap porno shit like Teggs. But I do see that your offence is a comparatively minor one.'

He pushed out his lips – no longer taut rubber-bands – in a pensive way.

'I tell you what I suggest,' he went on. 'A course of action that will perhaps satisfy all parties involved.' A querying look across the wide desk.

'What would you say, Jack,' – *Jack*, so it was Jack now all of a sudden – 'what would you say to letting yourself take a medical? And ... and should old Smithie, Dr Smith that is, should he find you unfit, you could retire on medical grounds. Get your full pension, of course. And be – shall we say? – well out of the way, if any further accusations come up.'

The old sod. *Satisfy all parties involved.* He means bloody Harry Hook, who's ordered him to have me sent up the steps to show he looks after his own on the one hand. And on the other hand yours truly, who seems to know more about his own dirty tricks than he'd reckoned. Well, sod—

Hey, no. Why not take Detchie's way out? I just hand in my papers all of a sudden: bound to be talk. Just possibly could lead back to Emslie Warnaby and what I did for him. Which might mean bad, bad trouble for me. Worse, far, than the Teggs cock-up. So bad p'raps they'd come after me all the way to old Ko Samui. But if I take a nicely fixed medical discharge – wouldn't be the first one to do that – anybody gets to thinking why, they'll guess I did something just a bit naughty, and Detchie has taken this course to preserve the good name of the force.

Yes, that's the word. *Preserve the good name of the force.*

'Yes, sir. I can see my way to that. It'll preserve the good name of the force, if you like. Thank you very much, sir.'

You shit.

'Right, then, Jack. I'll arrange for Dr Smith to see you. I dare say he'll be able to do it right away. I'll have a word with him myself.'

Oh, yes. I bet you will. And I bet I know exactly what you'll say to him on the QT, too.

Driving away after his medical check, he made up his mind he would go straight home and tell Lily the good news at last. A narrow escape like the one he'd just had – God, that moment when Detchie had brought out that about the thousand nicker – made you think twice about keeping anything good a secret till just the right moment.

No, hell with it, right moment or wrong, he'd give Lil her great big present of a life-time just as soon as he could get back home.

And, damn it, he'd been kept away long enough.

You'd have thought the doc, when he'd been tipped the wink by Detchie, would just content himself with running the old stethoscope over the chest and then tut-tut and say, *I'm afraid I'll have to recommend you for an immediate medical discharge, DS Stallworthy.* But, no, he'd poked here and probed there and then asked a lot of damn-fool questions about how much I smoked and how much I drank – surely to God, a police quack ought to know detectives needed to drink, had to smoke if ever they were to relax – listened again endlessly to whatever it was he could hear through that stethoscope of his, taken my blood pressure, made me pee into one of his little test tubes, even had a drop or two of blood off of me. Given me the works, first to last.

Silly old fool. Bloody hypocrite, in fact. Going through all that rigmarole just to cover himself from signing a duff discharge chit.

And he hadn't even done that in the end. Gone into a bleeding pantomime looking all grave-faced instead, and ending up saying he'd let me know *in due course.*

What due fucking course for God's sake?

He came to a halt outside the house, once more smiling at a joke. Not as funny as *Gone off with the postman,* but funny enough. What was it they called the oath doctors took? Hippocratic, yes. Ought to be Hypocritic. Hypo-blinking-critic. Certainly in old Doc Smith's case. Number one fat little hypocrite there.

And then, all of a sudden, he was in the midst of telling Lil with the TV she'd been watching going on and on blaring away on top of it all. Forgot about his idea of planking down the Iris Travels rainbow-arched envelope. Messed up leading into it all bit by bit, with first the tickets, then the deeds, then the final getting hold of the blue folder, then the recounting of all his troubles on the way there.

Instead it was 'Lil, Lil, my darling, we're off. Off to your blinking Ko Samui. It's all fixed. I done it. I got that fucking folder. Old Warnaby's coughed up. I've got the tickets. Here, look – oh, Christ, no, left 'em in the motor.'

But Lily – bless her – had somehow cottoned on at once.

'Oh, Jack, Jack, you've done it. I knew you would. I knew if I asked often enough my old Jackie would do it. Ko Samui, Jack. Ko Samui. Imagine it. Imagine. Feet up for ever,' as if she don't spend most of the time just like that, my little laze-about, 'blue sea, coconut trees, sandy beaches, *the most perfect retreat from the rest of the world*. That's what they called it on that TV programme. The most perfect retreat.'

But – perhaps it was Lily saying *that TV programme* – suddenly he became aware of what was coming out of the set she had had on at her usual high volume. The midday news, the local stuff coming after the calamities and complications of the rest of the world.

'*The giant American computer firm, Californeutics, has been successful in a take-over bid for the Abbotsport concern, Abbotputers plc. It is understood that Abbotsport businessman Emslie Warnaby, who was today unavailable for comment, has resigned the chairmanship and is to leave with a golden handshake believed to be in the region of five million pounds. The president of Californeutics, in London to conclude the negotiations, said this morning that his company had the highest expectations for the new Maximex system that—'*

'. . . and what I'd like to be sure is: has our hotel got air-conditioning? Did I tell you I went to the travel agent's the other day, got a lovely Ko Samui brochure, and I saw that all the big hotels—'

'Lil. Lil, for Christ's sake, shut up. Didn't you hear that? On the TV?'

'Oh, come on, Jack. What could be on TV that's more important than this? Forget your racing results and your blinking bets. We're off to Ko Samui. The island that time forgot. Just think—'

'You just think, damn it. Emslie Warnaby's sold Abbotputers. He's sold the whole bloody firm. He's picked up five million quid and gone skedaddling off. And – and the deeds of our little hotel out there. They were signed by fucking Emslie. *Chairman Abbotputers plc*. We were given the place by Abbotputers. Do you think we're going to still get it now?'

Chapter Twenty

Jack left Lily standing where she was and ran out to the car. Almost a madman in his wildness, he flung aside the floor covering at the back where he had tucked away the deeds and tickets before going to his nearly fatal interview with Detective Superintendent Detch, sir. He opened out the stiff paper of the deeds. With the hungry fury of a ditch-digging machine eating into the earth, standing where he was beside the still open door of the car, he went one by one through the interminable legal paragraphs.

And, as he had thought – as in fact he had known in an instant the moment he had heard those words *in the region of five million pounds* belching out of the TV – it was plain the sale of the Calm Seas Hotel, Ko Samui, was by Abbotputers plc itself, and that to take effect it would have had to be signed by Abbotputers' chairman. But there opposite Emslie Warnaby's flourish of a signature was not even today's date but tomorrow's. When from yesterday, or even a day or two before, Emslie Warnaby had no longer been chairman of Abbotputers plc.

Taking no bloody chances were Emslie and that sly bitch Anna Foxton.

The deeds of the Calm Seas Hotel, Ko Samui. You'd better look them over carefully. We don't want you coming back saying there's something wrong.

God, how she led me by the nose. Something wrong. Only the whole bloody transaction wrong as could be. Only the deeds deliberately post-dated to a time when it was certain Emslie Warnaby of that great big flourish of a signature would no longer be the Abbotputers boss.

All right, I didn't notice the date. Glad to get to the end of all the rigmarole. Dare say that's why they dated the whole sodding document at the end instead of the beginning. Counted on stupid, gullible Detective Sergeant Stallworthy being too fucking impatient at the last to notice a tiny thing like that. And that bitch ready, I bet, with some bloody plausible explanation even if I had.

And where would Emslie Warnaby and his precious little Anna be now? Nowhere in bloody Britain. That's for sure. Winging their way to some Pacific island paradise of their own, if not snugly there already.

Because – Christ, yes, there's more to it yet – fucking Warnaby must have wanted very, very badly that blue folder slimy Symes left among all the documents seized. Jesus, hadn't it been by a team led by Detective Chief Superintendent Detch himself? The documents in that folder, letters from Warnaby himself most likely, if signed by no more than, another bloody flourish, *Emslie*, would be what Symes had been keeping to show there was something dodgy about the sale of the Maximex system. His insurance in case Emslie renegued on his promise of giving him a Ko Samui hotel.

He could see, clear in his mind's eye, that single word in Symes's black-ink writing on the pale blue folder at this very minute.

Yes, this is what it'd be. The whole sodding Maximex system must be no good. Some bad miscalculation somewhere while they were designing it. And when Emslie had realized that, what he'd done was get hold of Arthur Symes, Chief Purchasing Officer of the Fisheries Development Authority, and take him and his luscious Raymonde on a no-holds-barred luxury cruise to the Far East and, as they sailed on, persuaded him into not having the Maximex system properly evaluated. So, once a major contract had been finalized with a reputable concern, the Americans would see Abbotputers plc as something worth taking over. With a golden handshake to Emslie Warnaby of five bloody million quid.

No wonder he'd been ready to pay out such a fat bribe to the man in Abbotsport police force most likely to get hold of that damning folder for him. A folder that would reveal too early the almighty scam that, when the truth at last came to light, would lose hundreds of innocent Abbotsport people their jobs and their livelihoods. And a bribe, when what it had been offered for was safely obtained, that could be neatly made so much rubbish.

And who was going to be blamed if it ever came

out there had been, actually in police hands, a document proving Warnaby's guilt? Good old Jack Stallworthy. That's who. Jack Stallworthy, very nearly the owner of the Calm Seas Hotel.

The Calm Seas Hotel. There were going to be no calm seas for Jack Stallworthy from now on. That was certain.

Go back and explain all this to Lil?

Not now. Not now. Jesus, I couldn't face it. Her, most likely, not even cottoning on. And then, when I'd got through to her at last, God knows what sort of a storm we'd have. Can hardly blame her, though. Talk about snatching the cup from the lip, or whatever it was they said. Christ, worse for her than for me. I've been thinking I was home and dry for all of two days. She only just this moment heard we'd got it made, or so we thought, and then that newsreader's voice had come blaring out of the TV.

So should I, after all, go back in, put the old arm round her shoulders? offer a bit of comfort?

But what comfort could I offer? There ain't no comfort. Anywhere.

He had at last simply driven into the town, put the car into its slot behind the Central Police Station, and gone wearily treading up to the CID Room, feeling sicker and sicker with every step of the stairs.

Without much trying to work anything out, one thing was clear. He still needed his job. For a while at least. Till that medical discharge was properly fixed.

So, get into work any later than he was already –
had he been missed all morning?' – and he could find
the Guv'nor putting him on a disciplinary. And, whatever happened in the days ahead, he needed to keep
his nose maximum clean.

Take my nice, neat little medical discharge when
it comes along and quietly fade from the scene.
That'd be the thing. When the big Emslie Warnaby
scam comes to light – Mrs Emslie, down there on her
holiday in the south, creating an almighty row when
she finds hubby's gone off with little ex-secretary and
all that loot – just hope and bloody pray nothing of it
comes back to me. Herbie Cuddy, caught for some
other blag, tryin to earn Brownie points by owning
up to what had happened at Headquarters that night?
Old Horatio having an attack of conscience? Mac,
the suspicious bastard, smelling a rat somehow? Anything.

'There you are, Stallworthy.'

Jesus, the Guv'nor, and sounding like he's in a
right paddy. Don't let him go on at me. The state I'm
in, I'll punch his nose or something.

'You're to go up to Headquarters. Right away.'

Oh, God. Detchie again. About a much bigger bribe
than Norman Teggs's thousand quid this time? Offer
of a hotel, the Calm fucking Seas, on the island of Ko
Samui?

But, no, it couldn't be, not yet. Surely not yet.
Unless bloody Warnaby had left a nice little note for
his tenant and dinner pal, Chief Inspector Parkinson?

'You've got to see Dr Smith. Right? And it's urgent.

Or so he says. Caught a dose, have you? I wouldn't be surprised.'

But that was the extent of it.

He even wondered, chugging up in the car to Palmerston Park again, whether he actually had caught a dose. But, no, no, no. Hadn't been over the side for years. Well, for a year or so at least. No, couldn't possibly be that. Probably old Doc Smith making even more of a meal of getting him his duff discharge.

Or . . . The old doc ain't going to jib at it, is he? He can't. He mustn't. Not now. Not when all the plans for everything have gone down the pan. No, after Detchie made that call to him, there can have only been one way he could've played it. Definitely.

Unless Detchie didn't do what he'd promised. Unless the old bugger said nothing about a nice, neat discharge when he fixed the appointment and gave the doc the hint he'd need. Could I have just hung around there to hear what was said on the blower? No. Devious old sod like Detch would never have begun that sort of conversation with a witness there to hear.

He found somewhere to park outside Headquarters. Sat for a moment pulling himself together. Got out. Went in and up the stairs.

Dr Smith's secretary waved him in as soon as he put his head round the door. Sitting behind his desk, Old Smithie was looking like nothing so much as a contented little Buddha.

'Ah, Sergeant Stallworthy. Yes. Yes. Take a chair. Sit yourself down. Yes. Well, I asked you to come and see me again today because, quite frankly . . .'

Dried to a halt.

Was it, after all, going to be no dice on the discharge? Bugger looks solemn enough.

A long, rattly cough.

God, by the sound of it he needs medicine more'n I do. And I dare say I could do with a good dose of something or other, way I'm feeling this moment.

'Because, as I was saying, I'm afraid I am going to have to be absolutely frank with you. The fact of the matter is that you're in very poor shape. I was astonished when I listened to your heart this morning. I could hardly believe my ears. So I had tests done urgently on those specimens I took from you, and I'm afraid they absolutely confirm my diagnosis.'

For an instant he'd looked mightily pleased with himself. With his sodding diagnosis. Then back had come the ultra-solemn face.

'I won't beat about the bush, old fellow. There's no point. No point at all, I'm afraid' – get on with it, get on with it, you old fool – 'the fact is you have been abusing your body for far too long. You're in a terrible state all round, not just the heart. So now – well, now you've not got very much longer to live. Two years, I'm afraid. Two years at the outside.'

He sat there.

He had taken it in. It had been clear enough, despite Doc Smith's bumbling and fart-arsing about. But he had not taken it in, either. He knew what the words had meant, but they meant nothing to him.

Two years to live. But that couldn't be so. A few minutes ago he had had years and years in front of him. It had never occurred to him there was anything else. He had had years to live. All right, it had turned out that they weren't going to be years spent in the sun on Ko Samui, looking at the blue sea, watching the wind waving the stupid coconut palms about. And, no, he hadn't really thought how all those years were going to be spent instead. April Cottage, probably, the garden, growing lilies. But there were going to be a good many years. Christ, he was only just past fifty. You didn't die when you were in your fifties.

Dr Smith was yakking on.

'You know, old fellow, you could have dropped down dead at any time in the past year or so. At least now you're getting some warning. I like to think, when it comes to my turn, I'll get as much. It gives you time to – to repent – that is, to make, as it were, your dispositions.'

Peering now at the papers in front of him.

'I see you've got a wife. Yes, a wife. Fairer to her really for her to have time to . . .'

My God. Popped off at any time. That's what he said I could have done. At any time. Jesus, could have happened when I was hanging there from Herbie's fucking rope-ladder. Put the cat among the pigeons all right, that would've done. Jesus, yes. Or, say, when I was being a sodding hero dealing with mad Marvin Hook. Drop dead then, and bloody Jane Lane wouldn't have found it so easy to hog all the credit. Could've really got that *A good detective* on the old gravestone then.

And what was that the old blitherer was saying?

Repent? He say that? What've I got to – oh, well, yes. Yes, that bloody blue folder. Doing what I did there's something to repent about. Doing it for that big, big bribe. Calm sodding Seas Hotel. Letting big-deal criminal Emslie Warnaby get away, laughing.

Yeah, shouldn't have done that. Shouldn't have done that at all. Right.

Dazedly making his way out, going down the broad stairs like some sort of mechanical doll, a voice – distinctly ringing with cheerfulness – forced itself to his attention.

'Jack! Hello there. How's it all going?'

It was Mac MacAllister.

And cheerful. Brimming over with totally uncharacteristic cheerfulness. Mac, the dour Scot. Mac, the ever suspicious.

'Oh, hello, Mac. Er – how's yourself?'

He had had difficulty finding the words. Words for the ordinary world. The world, it seemed, he had now left for ever.

'I'm just fine, Jack. Fine as could be.'

And, so bubbling over with well-being Mac was, he found despite the distant universe he felt he was now inhabiting that he was actually communicating.

'You're very bright this afternoon, Mac. Have a good holiday, did you?'

'No holiday's any good. You ought to know that. But, no, it's what I've just this moment heard that's making me feel all of a sudden on top of the world.'

'Oh? And what's that then?'

It wasn't as if he really wanted to know. But he felt, faintly, deep down, that perhaps he could somehow attach himself to this spilling-out good cheer. Perhaps, in the depths he had been plunged into, the as-yet-not-fully-tasted depths, Mac with this totally out-of-character sunniness might somehow be what he needed.

'Team from London up here.'

'London? Team? What is . . . ?'

'From the CIB, laddie. The great old Complaints Investigation Bureau.'

'Oh, yes?,

He could hardly bring himself to take the least bit of interest.

'What's the CIB here for then?

Mac's eyes shone with delight.

'For my auld friend Sergeant Detch, Detective Chief Superintendent Detch, as the bugger now is. That's who they're here for, laddie. For Detch. Corruption. Receiving undue reward to induce him to act contrary to his duty. Conspiracy so to do. As many charges as there are in the book.'

The vigour of it penetrated a little way to him.

'You mean . . . You mean, they've caught on to Detchie's links with Harry Hook? That it? You know, I just had an inkling that was on the cards. When was it? Few days ago? Yesterday? I don't know. Can't even remember what it was all about.'

A sudden sharp look came on to Mac's face.

'You all right, Jack? You look pretty terrible, laddie. Now I come to see.'

'Yeah, I'm all right. Well, no. No, I'm not really. Just had a bit of bad news.'

'You look as if you had. What's the trouble then?'

'Oh, it's – it's – well, I've just been seeing Doc Smith, and . . .'

'And he's spotted something gone agley? That it? What is it? Nothing too bad, I hope.'

What to say?

Hell, with it. Why shouldn't other people know about this? Jesus, I've got to tell Lily in a few minutes. Got to. Might as well sort of rehearse.

'Truth is, Mac, the old doc told me I ain't long for this world. Couple of years max, he said. Seems I've been treating the old heart something rotten, and now I've got to pay for it.'

'Oh, man, that's terrible. Terrible. You poor devil. I— I had no idea. And there's mesel' coming out wi' all my good news about that wicked bugger Detch, and you all the time nursing this to yourself. Listen, I was just on my way home. Going for a wee celebration. But – but, well, why don't you come with me for a bit? No celebration. But a drop of the right stuff comes in just as well for trouble as joy.'

And, again, something from the world as it had been until a few minutes ago came through to him.

Mac leaving the building at this hour. Less than half-way through the afternoon. And going home for a *wee celebration*. Human, after all. Mac. Even Mac.

So why not take him up on the offer? Okay, the doc's parting words had been all about stopping smoking, giving up drink, sick leave as from today's date, taking things easily, fresh air and good food. But after getting news like that a fellow was entitled to a little of Mac's right stuff.

And generous of the Scotch sod to offer it.

Besides, it would put off for a little the moment when he had to face Lil and tell her the whole of it.

'Right. Yes, Mac. Nice of you. Very nice. And I'll take you up on it.'

'That's the style, laddie. And have you got that car of yours here? If so, I'll take a wee ride with you. Always glad to save a bus fare.'

Good old Mac.

Chapter Twenty-One

Two stiff whiskies at Mac's had done him a lot of good. If telling Lily still seemed a task that would need all his strength, it no longer appeared impossible. And, another extraordinarily unexpected thing in a day of the totally unexpected, he had there beside him on the car's passenger seat as he drove towards home something he could use somehow to soften the breaking of the news.

The Lovely World of Lilies video, no less.

Fancy, old Mac turning out to be a gardener, too. Whenever he had happened to think about him, he had always imagined that flat where he spent his holiday times, counting the days till he could get back to his files and figures, as being that and no more. A bachelor bolt-hole. But not at all. Mac, whatever impression he had liked to give, must have actually spent much of the time of his holidays, and all the time-off he ever allowed himself to take, in keeping in trim the short strip of garden that went with his ground-floor flat.

'Aye, I like to grow things, you know. They're coming along fine just the noo. D'you see yon round bed at the far end? The dahlias, a right treat. Ballego's Glory for the red, and Colonel W. M. Ogg for a contrast in cream. Plenty of water every evening, and gamma-HCH powder against the earwigs. That's the secret.'

'They make a great show, Mac. A great show.'

'Aye. But this is the trick. You perhaps canna quite make out from the window here, but I've wee lettuces interplanted among 'em. Avon Defiance, the variety I always grow. Three or four weeks and they'll be ready to eat. Too many for mysel', of course. But I sell to my neighbours.'

'That's my boy.'

'Aye, pays for the new plantings. I've just put in my autumn crocus corms, and, man, the price they charge these days. Are you a gardener at all, Jack?'

No one had ever asked him that at work. He felt another tiny rush of warmth for old Mac.

'Well, yes. Yes, I am, matter of fact. The wife likes flowers, you know. Don't go in for any veg. Garden's too small. But I like getting this and that into bloom. Yeah.'

And something impelled him to go on.

'Hoping to have more room to grow things when I retire. Got a new-built place down in—'

He stopped.

When I retire. But I ain't going to retire. I'm going to bleeding die, that's what. Won't be any time for digging that big plot goes with April Cottage. Won't be no great big display of lilies. For my Lily.

Mac looked at him, reached over and patted him on the shoulder.

He felt tears forcing their way forwards.

God, must take hold of meself. If I start, I'll sit here and blub for ever.

'Yeah,' he managed to make himself say. 'Lilies. That's what I fancied. Wife's name's Lily, you know. Thought it'd be nice. But . . .'

'Ah, don't despair, man. Doctors always look on the worst side. I dare say you'll have time and time enough to grow every variety of lily there is. And, wait a minute. Wait a minute. I've got just the thing for you. A video on lilies. Canna abide getting my information that way mesel'. But an old aunt I have sent it to me at Christmas. You can have it, if you like. I'd be glad for you to take it off my hands.'

And there it had been, *The Lovely World of Lilies*.

'Mac, that's wonderful. It's what I've been looking for for months and months. *The Lovely World of Lilies*. Wonderful, wonderful. Thanks a million. You know, you've done me the world of good. This. And the whisky. Really a world of good. But – but I think I'd better be on my way now. Can't put off having a word with my Lil for ever, you know.'

'Right, laddie. Right. You be on your way. And good luck with the telling her.'

'Thanks. Thanks, mate. Oh, and Mac?'

'Aye?'

'What's-his-name. Turner. Yes, Turner, that's it. Don't know why I suddenly thought. They ever find that bugger, went off from the Fisheries Development outfit to be a New Age traveller or whatever they call it?'

'Aye, man. They did. They did. Stonehenge. The summer solstice. All those wee nutters trying to get there to say their prayers, trample the ground, play pop music, smoke cannabis. Half of them got arrested. And, there among 'em all, was our Mr Turner, ex-technical manager, Fisheries Development Authority. So soon I'll start work on the Symes papers, and in a couple of months or so I'll have a fine wee case to take to court.'

Then that shit Emslie got away just in time.

'Well, good for you, Mac. Good for you. And listen, can I pay you something for the video? These things are worth a penny or two.'

'Ach, no. No, not at all. Weel, mebbe you could give me just a fiver. Put in my garden fund, ye ken.'

Good old Mac.

He was not exactly laughing as he went up the path to the house – nothing like the *Gone off with the postman* joke – but he did feel more nearly light-hearted than he thought he ever would again.

And then there she was. Lily. Tucked into her big chair, same as ever.

Only not the same. There were tear-marks on her cheeks. Little channels in the powder.

So, before he knew what he was doing, he lost at once his chance of saying the fearful thing he had come to say.

'Oh, Lil, Lil, it's Ko Samui, you're still upset,' he burst out instead. 'Lil, my darling, you shouldn't fret.

You mustn't. It'll all come out right in the end. It will. It will.'

But then the tears came again. In floods.

'What's the use?' she gulped out. 'What's the use? I've thought and I've thought, and I see it all now. We ain't never going to get to Ko Samui. That Emslie, he's done a flit, ain't he? You got him what he wanted, and he's just gone and buggered off. Leaving us here. Here. In bloody Abbotsport, I've been trying all my life to get away from.'

'But we will get away, my darling. We will, I promise you.'

'To Ko Samui, Jack? You'll do it? Manage it some-how? Oh, I know you will.'

'No, darling. No, you got to forget about Ko Samui. But – but we'll leave Abbotsport. We can do that. I'll do it somehow. I won't have you left here when I'm gone. I promise you that much.'

'Oh, Jack. Jack, I knew you'd do it. I was wrong to sit here and think we were stuck in this place for ever. I knew my old Jack'd find a way out of it all. How you going to manage, love? How – hey, what you mean about *when I'm gone*? You ain't going to be going nowhere, my lad. Not if I have any say in it.'

Oh, God, she's gone and got it arsy-versy once again. And how the hell can I tell her now? When she just thinks I'm planning to skedaddle somehow. As if I would. As if I could.

'Listen. Listen, my darling. I've got something to tell you.'

In an instant her face was transformed. Expectation shining brightly from every feature.

'What is it, Jackie? What is it? Don't keep a girl in suspense.'

Oh, God. Again.

'No. No, Lil. No, it's not something good. Jesus, it's not good at all. It's the worst. The worst you can think of.'

'Oh, no, Jack. No, I've thought of that already. Not getting to Ko Samui. To the sun, the sea, the palm trees, the tropical moon at night. That's the worst.'

'Darling. My darling, it's not that. It's – Jesus God, Lil, I'm going to die. To die. I've just been up to the quack. Up at Headquarters. And he's told me. I've done in my heart. Pretty well most of the rest of me, too, far as I can gather. Lil, he gave me two years. Two years at the outside. Two.'

'Two years for what? You ain't going to be sent down for a two-stretch . . . No. No. No, it's not that, is it? But you can't mean dead. You can't. He can't of told you you're going to be dead in two years. No, Jack. No.'

And all he could say in answer was 'Yes.'

But it was enough. Somehow that one word penetrated where all his explanations and hesitations had failed to.

She went white. Dead white for a moment. All the come-and-go colour in her cheeks that had been for so many years what had made her beautiful in his eyes vanished in an instant.

And then she flung herself on to him.

'Jack, Jack. My poor darling. Jack, I'll help you. I'll look after you. Oh, Jack, you're not to worry about it. Never. Jackie, my Jackie, I'll be here for you. All the time. Till the last. The very last. Oh, my poor old Jack.'

Now it was his turn for tears. The tears he had stopped himself shedding when suspicious old Mac had been so suddenly kind. The tears he had all along held back.

He slumped down in his chair, put his head in his hands and cried. Cried as he hadn't done since he was a kid of three or four.

And Lily was with him in a moment.

'Jack. Jack, my poor darling, I feel so sorry for you. So sorry.'

At last he was able to lift up his head.

'No, don't feel sorry for me. You shouldn't. Jesus, I was the one who got it all wrong. I should've done better all along. I dare say that's what put me on to the drink, kept me smoking when I knew I shouldn't. Made me go after the scrotes, way beyond what I needed to do. To try and level up the scores. Oh, I don't know.'

'Never mind, my darling. Never mind. Forget it all. We'll manage between us. Stay here if we have to, in Abbotsport. It'll be all right.'

He shook his head, wearily.

'No, love, maybe it's none of it been worthwhile. Taking that big bribe, going through all that to earn it. But at least we won't have to stay here. I was thinking on the way over. We can still get that place in Devon.

April Cottage. We've got those air tickets. First class. Should be able to cash them in, part of the price anyhow. And that'll make a difference, raising the money to complete that purchase. And then I'm bound to be able to get a bank loan, if I put in for it right away before my medical discharge comes through. And—'

He broke off. Looked up at her.

'Well, my darling, it might be better, anyhow, if I was not around Abbotsport. I think maybe there's trouble coming. Old Mac MacAllister's beginning work soon on the papers they seized when they got on to that fellow Symes, out at the Fisheries Development place. And— and, after all, it might sort of come out then about Emslie Warnaby. What he's done. And, if it does, they could begin to think about me. It'll probably be okay. If I'm not around to point a finger at. But we'd be a lot cleverer to be well out of sight.'

'Jack, wouldn't Ko – no. No, I've got to give all that nonsense up. No, Jack, we'll go down to Devon. To April Cottage. We'll be happy there, Jack. My Jackie.'

'Well, my darling, I hope so. I hope it'll all be all right. Till the end. I hope so.'